# GHOST STORY

## ELISA LODATO

**Elisa Lodato** grew up in London and read English at Cambridge. Her debut novel, *An Unremarkable Body*, was longlisted for the 2016 Bath Novel Award and shortlisted for the 2018 Costa First Novel Award. Her second book was *The Necessary Marriage* and *Ghost Story* is her latest novel. Elisa lives in Gloucestershire with her husband and two children.

# GHOST STORY

## ELISA LODATO

MANILLA
PRESS

First published in the UK in 2024 by
MANILLA PRESS
An imprint of Zaffre Publishing Group
A Bonnier Books UK Company
4th Floor, Victoria House, Bloomsbury Square, London WC1B 4DA
Owned by Bonnier Books
Sveavägen 56, Stockholm, Sweden

A CIP catalogue record for this book is
available from the British Library.

Hardback ISBN: 978-1-78658-336-9
Trade Paperback ISBN: 978-1-78658-337-6

*Also available as an ebook and an audiobook*

1 3 5 7 9 10 8 6 4 2

Typeset by IDSUK (Data Connection) Ltd
Printed and bound in Great Britain by Clays Ltd, Elcograf S.p.A.

Manilla Press is an imprint of Zaffre Publishing Group
A Bonnier Books UK company
www.bonnierbooks.co.uk

*For my mum*

From: Tess Gallagher
To: Jamie Doughty
Cc: Charlotte Kinsella
Date: 20 November 2023 at 10:48
Subject: ghost story

Dear Jamie,

Please allow me to express how sorry we are for your loss. Seren was a bright light whose books were enjoyed by countless readers. It will always be a source of huge regret to us that she died so young, at the height of her powers.

I would like to take this opportunity to reiterate our intentions. At this stage, Charlotte and I are asking only to read the manuscript you have in your possession.

We are happy to meet and discuss in person, if easier. Edinburgh is no problem.

Best wishes,
Tess

From: Jamie Doughty
To: Tess Gallagher
Cc: Charlotte Kinsella
Date: 20 November 2023 at 13:12
Subject: ghost story

Tess,

At the risk of sounding bitter, it doesn't surprise me that you've wasted no time before reaching out for a book that, with all the publicity surrounding her death, promises commercial success.

The answer is no. The manuscript you're so desperate for is not what you think. Admittedly, I've only glanced through it but it's not a work of fiction. I'm quite sure of that.

Jamie

From: Tess Gallagher
To: Jamie Doughty
Cc: Charlotte Kinsella
Date: 21 November 2023 at 09:08
Subject: ghost story

Dear Jamie,

I think there's been a misunderstanding. Seren signed a contract undertaking to write a ghost story. It is entirely possible that what you regard as non-fiction is, in fact, her ghost story.

In cases like this, where an author predeceases publication of her work, it is normal for the commissioning editor to work with the next of kin to establish if there is a salvageable manuscript.

Please let me know your thoughts.

Best wishes,
Tess

From: Jamie Doughty
To: Tess Gallagher
Cc: Charlotte Kinsella
Date: 21 November 2023 at 09:13
Subject: Seren

My thoughts? My thoughts are that Seren would never have been on that island were it not for you and your bloody ghost story. She would not have suffered as she did.

Now please leave me alone.

From: Tess Gallagher
To: Jamie Doughty
Cc:
Date: 21 November 2023 at 23:13
Subject: Seren

It's late and I'll probably regret sending this in the morning, but don't you think you should actually read Seren's book before making your decision?

Tess

# Part I

# One

I WAS ASKED TO APPEAR before a select committee. That's as good a place as any to begin. It was a cool afternoon in late March. I was seated beside the MSP who had tabled the amendment, a woman in her late fifties who smelled of something musky and iconic like Opium or Poison or one of those big labels from the nineties. On my left was a small Asian man. He was hunched over, his fingers knitted in some quiet act of prayer. He had just finished telling the panel how his daughter had been stabbed seventeen times by an ex-boyfriend he knew nothing about. Imagine that. He didn't even know his daughter was seeing someone and then learns that this person had been rejected, grown angry and then murderous, all in the space of a few weeks. In the time it took for a cold to come and go, a leaky tap identified and fixed, new, more supportive, shoes broken in – all that time someone you've never met has been nursing an injury, feeding a grudge and gathering themselves to inflict unthinkable harm on the very person who makes your blameless, placid life possible.

'Ms Doughty?'

'Yes?'

'Your sister had been living at the property for two years. Is that correct?'

'Twenty-two months. Not quite two years.'

'Were you aware of any attempts by her former husband to ascertain her whereabouts?'

'Yes. He followed her, waited for her outside work, called on members of her family. He was relentless.'

'Your sister,' he looked down at his notes, 'Alana Teuling. She contacted the police on numerous occasions?'

'She did. Though we only discovered the extent of it, after.'

'I know this is a very difficult topic to speak on – especially given the level of your own personal loss – but in your view, how would this amendment help prevent deaths like that of your sister?'

'And daughter.'

He looked down at his notes again. 'Of course, my apologies. Your daughter.'

'When a victim of stalking or domestic violence, a known victim – someone who has been to the police and reported offending behaviour – when they call for help; be it police, fire, ambulance, that call should be prioritised and immediately placed in the highest category. Irrespective of any other contextual information.'

'Do you have any reason to believe your sister's calls for help went unheeded?'

'In the end the facts speak for themselves.' He lowered his head, as if to look at his notes but his eyes never left mine. 'She was burnt alive in her own home,' I said, interlacing my fingers in symmetry with the defeated man beside me. 'It's hard to conclude, in such circumstances, that her calls went anything other than unheeded.'

It was just beginning to rain as I left the parliament building. A young woman was waiting outside, twenty-two, maybe twenty-three years old with long, very blonde hair. She was holding her smartphone flat and horizontal to her rapidly moving lips. I heard it clatter to the concrete as I walked past. 'Shit.'

I stopped. 'Is it OK?'

She crouched down and picking it up gingerly, examined the edges of it between her outstretched finger-tips. At the crown of her head were new, dark brown strands of hair.

'Yeah, it's fine.' She had a London accent. 'It's really old, I use it for work.' She stood up and shook the locks of hair from her face. 'It's Seren Doughty, isn't it?'

'It is.'

'You're the author.'

'You say it like I'm famous.'

'You are famous. I've read all your books.'

'All? There are only two.'

She looked embarrassed. 'Yeah, well. I love them.'

'Thank you. It's always nice to meet a fan. I knew there had to be one out there.'

'Are you working on something new at the moment?'

'Nope.'

'Do you plan to?'

'I've got to go. I hope your phone is OK.'

'Can I get a quote from you, please?'

'A quote? On what?'

'I'm writing a piece on domestic violence for the *Edinburgh Shout*.'

'OK.'

'My editor's asked me to come down to the parliament and cover the select committee hearings. So – can I?'

'Can you what?'

'Get a quote from you.'

'I think I said it all in there. You can probably get hold of the transcript easily enough.' I turned to walk away.

On Canongate I heard footsteps and heavy breathing. 'Your daughter,' she shouted. 'She also died. In the fire.'

I stopped.

'It must have been hard today. Talking about your sister when – you know – you lost so much more than that.'

She was clearly more perceptive than I gave her credit for. To my mind, Johan murdered Matilda. That's it. Alana, much as I loved her – and I did, I do – Alana is a full stop way down at the bottom of the page. But of course, that is the ugly, raw, viscous stuff that no panel on a select committee wants to hear. It is the stuff of the id. We only ever really love our children. And when their death is mixed up with the death of others, even if that other person is your own little sister, then you see it. Then you know.

'You want a quote from me? Something conclusive and poignant, I'm guessing. The kind of *real loss* angle?'

She shifted her weight and smiled at me encouragingly.

'The problem is, and one I hope you never have to discover, any attempt to comment on the pain is futile. There are no words.'

She nodded.

'No, there really aren't. Even if you're good with words, as I am, you end up discarding them one after another because you realise there's just no point. There's really nothing to say.'

I left her standing in the rain and began my walk home. My flat is about twenty minutes from the parliament building. A nice walk too if it hadn't been raining. I'm from Wales originally, born in Aberystwyth – my father was a lecturer at the university – so I'm used to rain but nothing quite assaults you like a downpour in Edinburgh. I don't know if it's the stone that darkens like a bad mood or the fact that the pavements flick it all back up at you but whatever it is, the first thing I did when I got home that afternoon was light the log burner.

Home. It's not really home. It's a one-bedroom flat on the ground floor of a three-storey townhouse in central Edinburgh. It was unfurnished when I took out the lease and it's not much different now. I have a sofa, a desk pushed up against the bay window that looks out onto the road and a bed, our old bed, in the room at the back. But it's mine, it's a place to scurry to when it's raining outside or reporters ask too many questions. My phone rang just as I was closing the door to the stove.

'Jamie.'

'How did it go?'

'Horrible. Sad.'

'I'm sorry I couldn't be there.'

'It's OK. I'm glad you weren't there, to be honest.'

'Did they mention Tilly?'

'No. I did, though.'

'And?'

'And they nodded their heads. Some reporter stopped me outside.' I carried the phone to the kitchen, put it on speaker and filled the kettle. 'I'll be fine. I just need a day or two to right myself. And a cup of tea.'

The kitchen was the room I loved the most, it was the reason I took the flat. The large sash window that opened on to the communal gardens – it told its own story. Before the digital radio balanced on its narrow sill, the small folding table beneath its panes, the IKEA roller blind screwed into the reveal above it, the window was just right. It belonged in this room in this way. It was the house's way of shouting, above the din of eight flats each with their own electricity meter and letterbox, I was once better than this; I was proportionate. I like that. I like it when echoes of the past will not be silenced.

'Seren, listen. I need to talk to you.'

'What is it? What's wrong?'

'Nothing's wrong. It's just – it's coming up for five years.'

'I know that.'

'But – I mean the maintenance order. We need to talk about it.'

'You mean Claire wants you to talk to me about it.'

'I don't want to just pull the plug, you know. But we've bought this house and then, well the thing is—'

'When does it end?'

'What? The order?'

'Yes, I forget. When is it, June or July?'

'July.'

'OK.'

'Look, Seren, if you're in difficulty, of course we can talk about extending it. Until you're on your feet again.'

'I'm on my feet.'

'You are? You're writing again?'

'Sort of.' I looked over at my desk, at my closed laptop, a box for some trainers I bought months ago, a packet of postcards I'd bought in the botanical gardens and an empty wine bottle.

'That's great.'

'Yes exactly. Pretty great. Don't worry about me. You and Claire – you do what you need to do. I'm fine.'

I have tried to write again. About six months earlier, I tried writing a short story about a woman who makes artisanal soap, selling the stuff at craft fairs. It was going well enough until I sensed a darkness in my main character. A jealousy of her friend that threatened to tip over into some act of calculated violence. I couldn't finish it.

I could sit before a parliamentary select committee, I could be interviewed by journalists on the events of that night. It wasn't like I couldn't talk about what happened to Tilly because I could. Matilda Ann Doughty was born on the 9th of December 2013. A much-loved child, she was murdered on the 17th of June 2017 by her uncle-through-marriage, Johan Teuling. These are the facts. They are objective and true. I could recite them and (sometimes) face questions with reasonable equanimity.

What I couldn't do, in the years after she died, was write creatively. I couldn't get close to strong emotion like fear or jealousy or anger and, of course, that makes life difficult for a writer. What stories don't have those elements? But if I did manage to sustain an idea for long enough to reach a moment of crisis, I felt something move inside me. It was not unlike a pregnancy, albeit an unwanted one. In fact, a psychoanalyst I once saw – a year or two after Tilly died – told me I was effectively carrying a dead baby around inside me. That I would have to give birth to my grief if I was ever going to write again. Needless to say, I didn't return for another session.

I was still getting royalty payments from *Indigo Lights* but they were becoming sporadic and never more than a few hundred pounds – nowhere near enough to keep up the rent on my flat. I decided to email my agent.

From: Seren Doughty
To: Charlotte Kinsella
Date: 17 March 2023 at 16:32
Subject: Hello


Charlotte, I need to write something. Have you got any ideas? What are you looking for at the moment?


X


From: Charlotte Kinsella
To: Seren Doughty
Date: 17 March 2023 at 16:52
Subject: Hello

Where have you been? Yes, you must write. Let me talk to Tess. She asked about you at lunch only last week.

C x

She phoned me back early the following week. 'I think we need to meet. Can you come down to London?'

I looked around my flat; at the bare walls with nothing on them besides scuffmarks from chairs and sofas long since moved out and then never back in again. On the floorboards, dust balls that I had come to know, recognise. The biggest one by my left foot – it frequently attached itself to my sock. 'Yes, probably.'

'When?'

'I don't know. Next week?'

'The sooner the better. Tess is very keen to see you. She wants to see you writing again. As do I.'

'OK. That's good, I guess.'

'What's changed?'

'Honestly? I can't afford the rent on my flat.'

'Well, it's as good a reason as any. Let me talk to Tess and get back to you with a date. But next week, OK?'

Tess Gallagher was the editor who bought my first novel. She was 'passionate' about it, full of enthusiasm for my story of a little girl with synaesthesia, a condition that meant, from a young age, Indigo was able to 'see' emotion as colour. Like the gradings on a pH scale, Indigo could read joy, sadness, disgust or jealousy according to how strong or weak it was.

I had thought it would be a happier time, the publication of my first novel. Tess was not only my editor but also publishing director of the imprint so she held a lot of sway. It was quite a coup, Charlotte told me, that Tess had bought my book.

In the months that followed Tess and I talked a lot about what I'd set out to achieve, where the plot holes were and what had to be resolved in the next edit. As naïve as it sounds, I didn't know there was so much to do on the other side of selling a book. I kind of thought it would be choosing cover designs, listening to the audio recording, changing the odd word here or there but no, Tess was exacting. She wanted perfection.

Jamie and I had just got married, we were living together in a flat in Bonnington, and he frequently came home to find me with my head in my hands. Tess had sent back another huge structural edit that required a complete overhaul of whole characters. It felt huge, massive and somehow, at times, like a rebuke. Like I'd been found out. 'But it's what you wanted,' Jamie said. 'This is what you've been working towards.' I nodded my head. Yes, I thought. I have only myself to blame.

She'd preface emails with phrases like, 'you're not quite ready to wash your hands of it yet'. Sentences that made me think she had seen this before, this antipathy and *dislike* for a book sold and then endlessly edited. I was just so sick of it by the time it came out that I forgot not everyone else had read it close to a hundred times and given up on ever making Indigo's mother a more sympathetic character. I came to view it through a tight prism of changes, line queries and problems that were endlessly refracted back to me at such acute angles that I felt sick to my stomach with each new email from her.

But then it came out and everybody loved it. Well, not everybody. There were a few sniffy reviews in one or two of the broadsheets but people were reading it, sharing recommendations online and then it was picked up by a Radio 4 review programme. 'It's good,' Tess said, in her matter-of-fact way. 'People are talking about it.'

'But are they buying it?' I still, at that point, had yet to receive any sales figures.

'It's your first novel. Don't worry about the numbers. All that matters, at this stage, is that people are reading it.'

And read it they did. In their thousands and then, when the paperback came out a year later, in their tens of thousands. Within a few months, I had earned out of my small advance and began receiving royalty payments. Tess expressed an interest in my next book. Except there was no next book. I was pregnant, we'd just moved to a Victorian terraced house in Morningside, a pretty red-brick with three bedrooms and a room in the attic where I could write. But the last thing I wanted to do was write. I had just pulled off the apparently herculean task of writing a successful work of fiction and what I wanted was some time to wipe down the kitchen cupboards, decorate the nursery and research best push-chairs on *Which?*.

'A follow-up to *Indigo Lights*,' Tess had announced on a call with me and Charlotte. 'Your readers will want to know what becomes of Indigo. It's the obvious next step for a story where your main character is a twelve-year-old girl.'

Charlotte drew up a contract and I agreed to write a sequel, provisional title: *Indigo Flames.* The basic idea was that with the onset of puberty, Indigo's ability to interpret emotion goes haywire. She veers between heightened sensitivity to complete numbness; she misjudges hostility for shyness, fear for guilt and gets herself into all sorts of adolescent scrapes. 'It will appeal to YA as well as all the adult readers who loved your first one,' Tess wrote. Full of enthusiasm, she was.

Except there was no book. I couldn't write it. And I didn't really want to write it. The whole concept felt forced and contrived. With hindsight I should have declined the offer. I should have made the decision to have my baby, stay at home with her for the first year and then, when the time was right, try writing something completely new and fresh.

But instead of doing one thing well, I did two things badly. I stayed up late in the evenings, long after Tilly had gone down for the night, labouring at something I had no love or heart for. If she happened to nap in the day or play with an empty yogurt pot for longer than usual, I'd open my laptop and attempt as many words as I could tap on to the screen. That's all I was doing, writing words and hoping they would, at some point, coalesce into a novel.

I had accepted and spent the first payment of the advance so added to the general unhappiness was the anxiety of having taken money for something I had little hope of delivering.

Jamie grew tired of my complaints and my general absence every evening. Time that should have been ours – precious, ringfenced by the fact that our baby slept at night – time that should have been spent eating, drinking or watching TV together was instead spent apart, me in the other room writing something I knew wasn't very good.

I wasn't lying when I said it sank like a stone. The reviews were lukewarm at best, scathing at worst. This time there was no mention of another. No suggestion that I write about Indigo as an adult. Provisional title: *Indigo Bombs*?

Tilly had just turned two when the second book came out and after reading the first few reviews on Amazon ('utter horseshit' and 'can't believe I paid for this'), I made the decision to largely ignore it, pretend it had never happened. I had a few friends message me to say they enjoyed it but I knew they were lying. I knew they felt they had to acknowledge my second literary offering in some way. The truth? I wished I'd never written it.

But that's not how I feel now, about this book. I've never understood, before today, how writing can be a desperate, urgent thing – not unlike needing a shit, the hair on your arms standing up to join in the chorus of need.

And therefore, by contrast, it's impossible for me not to see that my second book was not pressing or urgent. No. It was written when my baby daughter was alive, curious and delighted every time I looked at her; who had just three years and ten months left to live – it's impossible not to think what a colossal and unforgivable waste of time it was.

Charlotte's offices were on Haymarket. The plan was to meet there, have a brief 'pre-match' chat as she called it and then walk to the restaurant Tess had booked in Soho. It was wet, the rain coming down in the kind of soft drizzle that soaks everything through.

'You need to take this offer,' Charlotte said, pulling the umbrella we were sharing and, by extension, me.

'I'm not flogging the Indigo horse any more. That shit's dead.'

'Oh completely. No, she's definitely not thinking Indigo.'

'What's she thinking then?'

'Ghosts,' Tess clapped her hands together gently. She was a small, neat woman with light, grey-blonde hair cut to her jaw. Her hands were veiny, creamy in colour – they looked like they'd be nice to hold. She wore a ring on the middle finger of each hand so that when she brought them together, they clinked. One of the rings was the kind of thing you might see at a craft fair: silver, inlaid with rose quartz. I thought of my soap story and wondered if I should pitch it.

'Ghosts,' I said. Our main courses had just arrived – I'd ordered fish cakes with a green salad. 'Is that not what you ordered?' she asked, mistaking the look of disappointment on my face.

'No, it's fine. It's good,' I said, picking up my fork.

'Not ghosts that go bump-in-the-night but the inner demon, you know.'

I worked hard to continue chewing in what I hoped was a normal fashion.

'It's a hot topic now. The terror that exists within. Getting on top of internal pain as you respond to the forces without. You'll need a setting that's completely isolated, deserted.'

'Like Robinson Crusoe?' I asked.

'Well, yes. I mean, let's just think about that. Defoe was responding to the zeitgeist. Searching for new land, conquering new frontiers. But now, it's not about physical land but space, head space. Now, in the age of social media and continuous contact, people crave metaphorical silence and distance.'

'I'm not sure this is my genre.'

Tess took a mouthful of her butternut squash risotto. She shook her head as she chewed and then returned her fork to the plate. 'Indigo's powers were transcendental, decidedly not of this earth. You're very good at drawing a line around the amorphous, the spiritual. Saying *this is that*. Rendering the intangible, real and material. I can't think of another writer better suited to the task.'

'Or any other writer with so many inner demons,' I laughed.

Tess interlaced her fingers and performed a shallow nod. 'I'm not going to lie to you,' I saw her tongue move over her molars searching for an errant morsel. 'The tragedy you've suffered, it changes a person, it changes a writer's profile. I'm sorry to be so blunt but it's true. The question for all of us is what do we do with that? Are you just never going to write again? That seems—'

'You need a new project,' Charlotte interrupted. 'You need something to pull you out of this slump.'

'I'm not writing about Matilda. I'm not serving up more of her for those that didn't get enough from the media.'

'No, not at all,' Tess reached across the table and patted the top of my hand with her own. 'Fiction. This is a work of fiction. But your own experiences, your own tremendous skill as a writer – I just feel you are uniquely suited to the job. To producing something powerful.'

What if I'd like to remain in the slump? It had been almost six years since Tilly died. Was that too long? Not long enough? There's no manual for grief. And even if there were, would it include a chapter on how long you should remain inert and creatively blocked if your daughter, your *only* daughter, is collateral damage in a psychopath's plan for revenge? Perhaps I should be the one to write it.

These were the thoughts passing through my brain when the waiter came over to ask if we were happy with our food and so the moment passed with all of us apparently nodding our heads in assent.

'The bottom line is, nobody else is going to offer you a book deal. The balance on your second book is pretty eye-watering.' We were walking back towards Piccadilly, having said goodbye to Tess outside the restaurant. The rain had stopped. The pavements were slick with the splash of cars and shoes that still carried the rain with them. 'You should bite her hand off,' Charlotte said.

'I thought that once before.'

'She's offering a modest advance.'

'How much?'

'Ten. I might be able to get her up to twelve.'

I nodded. We had approached the stairwell down to the station.

'It's money in the bank. An opportunity to do something new. Tess has put this proposal together for *you*. She wants to see you writing again. Take it, Seren. Go and live somewhere else for a while, find a remote place and write a new book.'

A man and a woman walked up the steps towards us, side-by-side, both with headphones on. There was no way to tell if they were together. We were standing to one side of the stairwell but still, the man made a big show of having to alter his path to accommodate us. 'It's all about being unpeopled,' Charlotte said.

'Unpeopled.'

'Do you have any ideas?'

The Western Isles had been the destination of choice for every summer holiday of my childhood. We'd start in Stornoway and make our way south, always stopping at the campsite in Castlebay and – if the weather was kind to us – using the port there as a jumping-off point for the remoter islands: Vatersay, before the causeway was built, Pabbay, Sandray and Finish.

It didn't always work out. Some years the wind and rain would blow in with such force that we would be – all four of us – compelled to wait it out in our tent, playing endless games of gin rummy and patience. But more often than not, the boats ran and we made it down. Of all the islands we visited, it was always Finish that made my dad shake his head and swallow a lump as the first glimpse of its western cliffs and headlands hove into view. It was big and alive and just always there. As difficult as it is to recollect the feelings of a child, that's what I felt. It endured and remained, even if the people it once supported no longer wanted it.

Alana and I would lean over the side – my mum always opting to sit inside the cabin and huddle her jacket around her, enjoying the final minutes of comfort – waiting for the boat to drop anchor near the beach on the eastern side.

Finish Island. In the late eighties and early nineties, it still showcased the crumbling buildings of a settlement abandoned by its human population in the summer of 1912. 'People here lived simple, hard, blameless lives,' my dad explained. That last word stuck with me. Blameless. Even then, before I'd learnt to feel blame, or real blame I should say, I remember thinking how lucky the islanders were. To feel like they'd done nothing wrong.

He told us all about crofting, explained how it worked, how the islanders were, for centuries, completely self-sufficient: spinning wool, catching fish, birds, cutting peat for fuel. He made it sound so wild and *romantic*, I guess. I fell in love with the idea of doing for yourself, for your family and neighbours – surrounded on all sides by the sea and the sky. But then he told us of the schoolteacher who grew tired of the wind and rain; who, despite having the most comfortable house on the island – built for him by eager islanders who hoped he would stay, take a wife and raise his own family among them – decided he could not live in a place unreachable for seven months of the year. How this decision forced the hand of another family who could not, in turn, resign their children to illiteracy. And finally, how once the balance had been irrevocably tipped, all the remaining men, women and children – born and raised on Finish – climbed aboard boards on a sunny morning in July and fought back tears as they said goodbye to the land that had supported them and generations of their families for centuries.

Finish Island was the obvious setting for my new book. It was also, quite simply, a place to go. The rental agreement on my flat was up for renewal at the beginning of May and there was no way, without Jamie's payments, I could afford to extend it. When I got back to Edinburgh that evening I emailed Charlotte to say yes, draw up the contract.

# Two

THE OFFICES OF NATIONAL Trust Scotland were not easy to find. They're not meant to be, the building is clearly their corporate headquarters, located a train ride and a walk through an industrial estate from the town centre. I signed in at reception and waited for a woman called Elspeth who was, she told me over the phone earlier that morning, the Properties Executive.

I followed Elspeth to a small room on the first floor, where she invited me to sit down with a cup of vending machine coffee. On the table were forms, a clutch of black biros, a ring binder and an old-fashioned brass key. It was all way more formal and administrative than the key-in-an-envelope and *good luck!* I had been expecting. 'And what is it you'll be doing on Finish?' she asked, pen in hand.

'Writing. I'm writing a book.'

'I see. And you're aware the bothy has no running water?'

'Yes, I know that.'

'About ten years ago one of our rangers installed a small wind turbine and a couple of solar panels so it wouldn't be correct to say there's no power, but it's not to be relied upon.'

'No, that's fine.'

'The building was the former schoolhouse. Built in the nineteenth century so there is a fireplace.'

'I know. I've been to Finish before.'

She smiled and moved down her form. 'And how long do you plan on staying?'

'I'm not sure. It depends on how I get on. A few months maybe.'

'Months?'

'I think so.'

As she wrote my answer, I saw the slightest shake of her head.

'Is that unusual?'

'Aye, it is a bit. We get people asking to stay overnight or for a few nights but it's not often we get anyone looking to stay much beyond that.'

'I don't know, as I say. Nothing is set in stone. At least until September.'

'Oh aye, I should think so. You wouldn't be able to stay much beyond that. Shall I put the 4th of September for return of the key? That's a Monday,' she said, peering at me over the top of her glasses.

'Sounds good.'

'And can I take the names of those staying with you?'

'I'm going alone.'

'You're going alone?'

'Yes,' I was starting to feel impatient. 'Is that a problem?'

'No, not a problem,' she took her glasses off and folded them gently before laying them on the table. 'It's – it's unusual, I would say that.'

'I'm very familiar with the Outer Hebrides. I went a lot as a child and then later with—' I took a sip of coffee, too much and too quickly. I burnt my tongue. 'With others.'

She nodded and smiled. 'So you've never seen one then.'

'Seen one what?'

'A ghost,' she mouthed, her hand to her mouth, miming some great secret.

'No,' I laughed. 'Although it would be handy. I'm supposed to be writing a ghost story.'

'Some say,' she said, ignoring this last detail, 'some say it's the unquiet souls of a terrible massacre that happened there hundreds of years ago. But you probably know all about that.'

The burnt patch felt rough against the roof of my mouth as I nodded that yes, I knew all about that.


I needed to find out about this massacre. Not because I was frightened by Elspeth's scaremongering about unquiet souls, but because it did seem like a rather obvious gap in my knowledge. If I was going to immerse myself in a place I should probably know a little of its history.

It was mid-April. I'd signed the contract and already spent a good chunk of the first payment on train and ferry tickets, a new rucksack, a Berghaus waterproof jacket, hiking boots and a sleeping bag.

What I hadn't done, clearly, was any research.

I spent the first morning of my week at the National Library of Scotland in Edinburgh sitting at a table in the café with an empty notebook open before me, sipping cups of coffee that turned lukewarm as I watched people come and go, observing the clatter of a knife and fork dropped onto a tray, smelling the tang of ketchup sachets torn open and squeezed onto warm plates – that's pretty much all I did. This is the trouble, I thought. I'm not interested in demons, or ghosts or spirits. I like people, I've always been interested in real, living human beings.

In the afternoon I picked myself up and found my way into the General Reading Room. The librarian at the enquiries desk had curly – almost pubic – hair that stopped just below his earlobes. He had olive skin and wore tortoiseshell glasses that he pushed up the bridge of his nose as I approached. 'Can I help you?' he asked – not in a whisper, but quietly.

'I'm looking for information on a massacre.'

'OK,' he nodded. 'Any idea when this might have occurred?'

'No idea. Hundreds of years ago, if that's any help.'

'OK. Do you know how to search the main catalogue?'

'Not really.'

'I can show you?'

'Please.'

He was tall and very slim. Like he didn't eat enough or whatever he did eat just slid through his digestive system and evacuated itself immediately. If I'd had to guess, I'd have put him at twenty-four, maybe twenty-five. I followed him through to the main room where a dozen or so readers of varying ages and levels of concentration sat around a large banquet-like central table. Off to the sides were smaller desks where the rodent few sat behind laptop screens, their cables coiled out behind them like tails. 'Do I need a laptop? To do a search?'

He turned, his hand on the wooden rail of the staircase that led up to a galleried floor above us. 'No. I mean, you can but the computer terminals are up here.' He took the stairs two-by-two and turned to wait for me at the top. I had the odd sensation that he was trying to impress me. He pulled a wheelie chair over for himself and invited me to take the one before the screen.

'You type the search terms here,' he said, leaning across me and taking hold of the mouse. I could smell damp, like his T-shirt hadn't dried properly.

I typed the word *massacre* into the search box and he laughed.

'I think you might need to be more specific.'

As I typed in the word *Scottish*, he coughed and wheeled himself closer. 'Allow me.' I leant back and watched as he typed: *clan battles middle ages.* 'Massacres, like the one you're looking for, were almost always the result of inter-clan feuding. That should give you a few titles – enough to get started anyway.'

'Thanks. Sorry to be such a dufus.'

'You'll get the hang of it. Lots of people have difficulty in the beginning.' I noticed he used his middle finger to push his glasses back up his nose – it amused me how incongruous the gesture was. Like I was being told to fuck off in the way only a librarian can: quietly and politely. 'Is there anything else?'

'How much time do you have?'

'Sorry?'

'It was a joke. Ignore me. I'll have a little play around here. Thanks for your help.'

He found me in the café later that same afternoon. 'Do you mind if I join you?'

'Go ahead,' I said, pulling my cup of coffee towards me.

'How's the research going?'

'Oh, you know.'

'Have you managed to narrow your search?'

'You can only narrow your search if you know what you're searching for.'

'What are you working on exactly?'

'I'm supposed to be writing a book – a novel.'

'OK,' he nodded. On a small side plate was a white roll, a little foil package of butter and a mini jar of strawberry jam. I watched him concentrate on pulling his roll apart so that it split in two. The action gave him a myopic, slightly stupid look.

'Is that lunch or dinner?'

'Late lunch,' he said as he spread the butter and then the jam. When he took his first bite he lifted his upper lip to clear the thick layer of jam. It gave him a mean, albeit very temporary, grimace. 'I guess my first question would be why supposed? Who's making you write this novel?'

'Ostensibly my editor and agent but in truth, me. My circumstances.' I shrugged. 'I need the money.'

He sat back against his chair. I felt his long legs stretch out beneath the table, his trainer brush against the side of my boot. 'You're published then?'

'Trust me. It's not as amazing as it sounds.'

'But still,' he swept the hair from his forehead, held it there for a few seconds and then let it flop down again. 'It's pretty special.' He returned to his roll.

'Maybe. What do you do? Apart from work here?'

'I'm a student at Edinburgh University, starting a PhD in September.'

'What's it in?'

'Soil,' he nodded. 'Ethnoarchaeology to be exact.'

'Ethnoarchaeology? What does that involve?'

'Analysing phosphorus content and pH levels in the soil and then drawing conclusions on how arable land was farmed in Scotland.'

'Sounds fascinating,' I said. It came out sounding sarcastic, which I hadn't intended at all.

'I know,' he laughed. 'To be honest, my mind is not entirely made up. I studied Geology at St Andrews where we did plenty of field trips. We went to places in the Outer Hebrides: St Kilda, Finish and Eigg and, always, it struck me how rich and abundant an island is for any kind of investigation but particularly the soil.'

'Completely,' I agreed. 'I know Finish really well. My parents took me and my sister there every summer and it's funny because I remember thinking about the soil. You know the way when you lift a heavy rock? You see ants, wood lice and all sorts crawling underneath but also this rich, dark soil. I used to imagine doing that with Finish. Like I wanted to know what was beneath it. Where did you grow up?'

'Aberdeen. My dad was a partner in a GP practice there. But he had a small boat, a skiff that he kept in

Cromarty, so always, on a Friday, right after seeing his last patient, he'd come home, pick me up and we'd drive three hours, spend the night in a tent and get up early the next morning to go out sailing, fishing – sometimes mountain climbing.'

'Just you and your dad?'

'My mother died when I was twelve.'

'That's young. To lose your mum.'

He shrugged. 'Kind of. Difficult age. I was old enough to be left alone in the house but not old enough to do anything useful like cook a meal. I spent a lot of time on my own. Or in the library waiting for him to finish work.'

'Is that why you like working here?'

'Probably,' he smiled. 'I can get a lot done while I work. Reading and research.'

'When you're not helping morons like me?'

He smiled and resumed eating. 'I enjoy it. I like helping people.'

He was helpful. A little too helpful, in fact. After that afternoon in the café, I started spending more and more of my time in the reading room, down esoteric rabbit holes: losing myself in stories of beasts on land and sea; pagan rituals involving the moon and stone circles; banshees and lost font stones. Alex often came and found me. He'd make a point of placing a book down on my desk, open to a particular chapter and pressing his index finger down in meaningful, pointed silence. It began to irritate me, the patronising attitude. The chapters were always on that first topic I'd searched for: the massacre. I sound petulant. They *were* useful.

I found the answer to my question, after all. I learnt all about how a galley of armed men from Clan MacNeil set sail from Barra sometime in the sixteenth century, how they slaughtered the entire population of Finish, men, women and children, in a cave – all in revenge for some wrong. It was hard reading.

So hard I decided to turn to more practical matters. My tenancy was up at the end of the first week of May and though I'd sold a lot of stuff, there were a couple of boxes I needed looking after.

Jamie and his wife Claire had just bought a house near Edinburgh Airport, in East Craigs. If you're going to start again, if your mission is to pretend you were never married or fathered a child who died, then probably a new build on the outskirts of Edinburgh is the place to do it.

A waft of insulated air hit me as soon as Jamie opened the door. I smelt something citrus, sharp and manufactured. 'Seren. Come in,' he stepped back into the narrow hallway. 'It's nice to see you,' he said as I planted a kiss on his cheek and walked past him into the kitchen.

It was a light, bright room at the front of the house with a large window that opened onto a rectangle of grass, beyond which – if I stood on tiptoe – I could see the driver of the Prius that brought me here. He was still there, parked by the kerb, tapping away on the phone nestled in its cradle.

Jamie lifted the kettle and with the lid popped open like some urgent thing, prompted me for my decision. 'Normal?'

'What?'

'Normal tea?'

'Oh. Yes. Thanks.'

He filled the kettle and plonked it back on its base before turning to face me. 'You're looking well.'

'Thanks,' I said, trying not to see the *womankind* teabags beside the kettle or the bottle of Gaviscon on the table.

It brought to mind a documentary I once watched. It might even have been with Jamie. It was about a woman who finally – after many failed attempts – learnt to read. She had, during her years of illiteracy, stockpiled books on the shelves in her house: Hemingway, Fitzgerald, Dickens. She had hoarded the big names, pulled them close to her with no realistic prospect of ever discovering what made them so special. The woman cried in the closing minutes of the documentary, inconsolable that her world had become a noisier place. I remember her grief, in a moment of apparent triumph, that something unpleasant had been let in. Yes, I thought, clocking the folic acid on the window sill, I know how you feel.

'So, what's new?' He passed the cup to me, our fingers touching just briefly. I followed him to the table which was wedged in against the far wall. He lifted it with one hand and slid along the bench, throwing a sage and lemon cushion to the wall at the end as he did so. I pulled out a chair on my side and sat down. He looked small and somehow hobbled by the whole bench-and-table caper. 'What's new?' I repeated.

'Oh, this and that.'

'How's Claire?'

'She's well,' he nodded. 'Yeah, she's good.'

'Pregnant?'

'How did you know?'

'I've never known you take folic acid. Or use Gaviscon for that matter.'

'Right, yes. We're expecting.'

'Congratulations.'

'Thank you. That's why I rang the other day. We're going to need the extra money coming in every month.'

'It's fine,' I waved his explanation away. 'I understand. It's been good, actually. Forced me to get my shit together.'

'So, when are you leaving?'

'I've just got here.'

'Come on, Seren—'

'It's a joke. I'm joking. Early May.'

'Are you going from Castlebay?'

'I am. I need to find a guesthouse or a hostel or something. Another thing on my to-do list.'

'What about the campsite? Where we stayed?'

I stared at him, willing him to look me in the eye. He did, finally, and it was a relief. A brief reassurance that she still exists, between us. The pain is a comfort. It bruises him like it does me and I like to see that.

'It's not much,' I said, ignoring his question. 'Just a couple of boxes.'

'I'll put them in the loft. When do you want me to come and get them?'

'Tomorrow? Anytime in the morning would be good.'

We heard the sound of a car pulling up near the front door. I kept my eyes trained on Jamie, saw how he sat up straighter, looked down into his mug of tea – as if the answer to this impossible situation might be found in the murky brown of his drink. I felt sorry for him. I wished I could reach out, put my hand on his and tell him it would be OK.

Claire looked like she was about five or six months. Her bump was perfectly accentuated by a tight, stripy top I recognised from Gap. 'Seren,' she walked towards me and held her arms out. I stood up, submitted to an awkward hug and found myself inhaling the same citrus scent I'd detected at the door. Did she shampoo her hair with it?

'It's nice to see you. You look well,' I said, sitting down again.

'Thanks. As do you. Have you lost weight?'

I felt Jamie look at me again.

'Probably. I was never much of a cook.'

'What will you do for food on the island?' she asked.

I turned my mug in my hands, twisting the handle from one side to the other. 'I plan on taking big bags of rice, pasta, lentils. I want to give fishing and foraging a go too.'

She walked up to Jamie, her bump at his eyeline and waited for him to slide along the bench. 'It will be so strange. You won't be able to just nip out and buy something whenever you like,' she said, pushing her thick, wavy brown hair back from her face. And neither will you, I thought, but I knew it was the resentment speaking. Not for her but for Jamie really – for the having to do it all again. The opportunity he has to keep this one safe.

'No, that's right,' I pushed my chair back and started rooting around in my bag. 'I don't want to intrude.'

'No, stay, Seren,' she reached across the table, careful not to actually touch me. 'We were about to make dinner,' she turned a significant look on Jamie.

'Yes, stay. I'll make something.'

'I need to get back to the library before it closes. Plus, I'm going out this evening.'

'Ooh, anywhere exciting?'

'Just out to dinner. With a friend.' I unlocked my phone and opened the Uber app.

'Going to live on a desert island. Sailing off into the unknown,' she said, lifting her shoulders. 'So exciting.'

I nodded, selected my ride, steadfast in my determination not to serve up the ball she wanted.

'Very different to our little adventure,' she said, apparently happy to serve herself.

The thought of going out with Alex hadn't occurred to me until I found myself lying to Jamie and Claire about my plans for the evening. But on the way back to the library, I thought I should at least see if he was up for it. It wasn't the thought of having sex – though it would be good to experience that at least once this year – it was more the thought of talking to someone new. At forty-two I wasn't old exactly but definitely not young. I suppose I was drawn to his youth and lack of self-consciousness. I found it appealing, especially given my afternoon with Jamie and Claire – all of us smiling around a too-big dining table, pretending life was a series of exciting adventures instead of what it was: a course of obstacles, some surmountable, many not and a few that were just plain catastrophic.

Alex and I had exchanged numbers the previous morning in the canteen. It had become our habit to have lunch together. I say lunch. He persisted with his white roll and selection of jams while I drank my coffee and the occasional goat's cheese tart and suppressed the urge to ask him how constipated he must be.

I texted him from the cab on my way back to Edinburgh. He was waiting for me outside, on George IV Bridge. 'That was a nice surprise.'

'Well, I thought I should probably thank you for all your help.'

'I haven't finished yet.'

'What do you mean?'

'I've been doing a bit of digging. I'll tell you at dinner.'

We walked to a falafel place he knew on a little winding street nestled just below the castle walls. The stripped wood flooring and scrubbed tables with a miscellaneous assortment of chairs made me feel old. It was more like a coffee shop than a restaurant. We had to order at the counter but it didn't seem like there was much ordering to do. Everybody appeared to be eating the same thing. But the smell – something curried with mustard seeds – cut through my reservations. As soon as we took our seats at a table, the waitress brought us two glasses of something cloudy. 'What's this?' I asked.

'Kombucha,' Alex said, lifting the glass to his lips.

'I didn't order this.'

'It comes with the meal. Try it. It's really good.'

'Do you have any wine?' I asked the waitress.

She frowned, her eyes looking up and to the right, like she was trying to remember something from long ago – some ancient commodity like myrrh or snake oil.

'Forget it,' I said. 'This is fine.'

'I'm really glad you asked me out tonight.'

'Me too,' I grimaced, putting my glass back down. It turned out the cloudy stuff not only looked revolting, but tasted revolting too. 'So, go on, what is it you've found out?'

'Your island? Finish?'

'Yes.'

'I've been reading accounts from people who say it's haunted.'

I laughed. 'People say that about all the islands in the Outer Hebrides. Scotland is chock-full of ghosts. There's probably one in the kitchen now, making falafels.'

He looked wounded.

'Sorry. Tell me about the ghosts.'

'After the final evacuation, in 1912, a wealthy landowner bought the island with a view to grazing sheep on it. He installed two shepherds who lived in the old schoolhouse, now the bothy.'

The waitress brought two plates of the generic offering to our table. I was right to predict falafels but also some kind of dahl, brown rice and the curried mixture I'd smelt earlier. 'Vegan and gluten-free,' Alex said, as if these two things were all anybody need ever know about their food. He laid his napkin across his lap in a prim and precise way. I felt my willingness to have sex with him slip away.

'So, what about the shepherds?'

'They reported sightings. Visions.'

'Of what?'

Alex picked up a falafel and bit into it. 'Children.'

'Children?'

He nodded as he chewed.

'I must have been to Finish Island ten times at least. My dad could have written a book on it. I've never heard of or seen any kiddie ghosts.'

He shrugged, popping the other half of the falafel into his mouth. 'I'm not saying I think it's true. Just what I read.'

'OK. But what? What happened to the shepherds?'

'They claim they were tormented by the spirits of these dead children. In both accounts they report their belongings were taken, their flocks led away in the night and then, one night—'

'How do you know all this?'

'They were interviewed by the *Stornoway Gazette* in 1918. It was around the time of the Cottingley Fairies, Sir Arthur Conan Doyle had just come out as a spiritualist – there was a general appetite for supernatural phenomena.'

'OK. One night—' I prompted.

'One night they saw an old woman with long white hair walking along the headland.'

'And?'

'And she was *wailing like a banshee*, apparently.'

'They saw her? Both of them?'

'Yep,' he nodded. 'A clear case of folie à deux.'

'What do you – what's folie à deux?'

'It's when someone experiencing paranoid delusions convinces a second person so that two people come to share the same idea. The new recruit then bolsters the original fantasy by legitimising it with their own belief.'

I shook my head. I had hoped for a more relaxing evening.

'They got in their boat and made the crossing to a nearby island with a lighthouse.'

'Barra Head?'

'Yes, that was it. They got the lighthouse keeper to raise the alarm and they never returned.'

'Why are you telling me all this?'

'I thought it would be good material for your book. The old woman wandering in the night. Very atmospheric, don't you think?'

'I mean yes, but that's not how I write.'

'How do you write?'

I rolled my eyes.

'Come on. I've got a published author all to myself. Tell me, what's the secret?'

'There is no secret. And to be honest, I'm not a good person to ask. I haven't written in a long time.'

'But you must remember. How do you get started? What was your way in with *Indigo Lights* for example?'

'It was just an idea I had. Every book is different.'

'But what's your idea for this one?'

'I don't have one yet. I'm just going to go to Finish, get myself set up and take it slowly, I suppose. I'll probably keep a journal until some idea takes me.'

A bar. A proper drink. I thought I might be able to rescue the evening with some alcohol. He wasn't exactly teetotal but he didn't drink very often. When we got to the bar, it was clear he had no idea what to order. 'Try a lager,' I suggested.

'OK,' he leant on the curved chrome of the bar and peered left and right. 'I'll have a small glass.'

I left him at the table while I went to the ladies. When I returned, I saw a printed document, roughly three centimetres thick with five or six words aligned centrally in size twelve font on the front. My internal organs dropped in disappointment. 'What's this?'

'My debut novel.'

I took a long drink of my wine.

'I thought, since you're about to go off to your island, you might like to take it with you. See what you think.'

I lifted the bottom corner, flicked the dog-eared pages between my finger and thumb. 'There must be three hundred pages here.'

'Three hundred and sixty-seven.'

'I mean, it's nice of you to think of me but, Alex, I'm just not going to have time to read—'

'You can't write all the time. You'll need to take a break. I know I shouldn't be the one to say it but it's really good. A couple of friends have read it and they loved it.'

'I'm sure they did. But I don't know when I'll be back and I wouldn't want to take it and then not get back to you.'

'I have plenty of copies. You can have that one.'

'Right. Thanks. Anyway, cheers,' I said, lifting my glass. 'Cheers.'

'What do you think of the lager?'

'It's nice. Aren't you going to ask me?'

'Ask you what?'

'What it's about?'

'Oh, yes. What's it about?'

'A young boy called Arturo who learns to sail from his father. His dad is a fisherman who goes out every day to catch their supper and enough to sell in the market the next day.'

'OK.'

'Anyway, one day his father never returns. Arturo quickly realises he's the only one who can go out and find him.'

'I take it this is set, like, pre-coastguard?'

'Yeah, fifteenth or sixteenth century.'

'OK. So, he goes out searching for his dad?'

'But on his travels, he spots a small island, home to a colony of mermaids.'

'Colony. Is that the collective noun for mermaids?'

He shrugged. 'It felt right.'

'OK. Wow. I wasn't expecting the fantasy element to come in so quickly.'

'The mermaids aren't like ordinary mermaids. We're not talking Disney here. They're massively over-sexed, aggressive, hungry mermaids. They call to Arturo from the island.'

'So . . . lotus-eaters, basically.'

'Yeah, I guess you could say that. A modern-day version.'

'But you just said it was set hundreds of years ago—'

'Arturo is a young boy, a virgin,' he continued, ignoring me. 'He's sorely tempted.'

'I can imagine.'

'But he's also determined to find his father, you know?'

'Mmm. Difficult.'

'Every creative writing course I've ever gone on, they always talk about conflict. Your main character has to feel conflicted about the decisions they're forced to make.'

'Whether to be wanked off by the nymphomaniac mermaids or find your missing father?'

'You're mocking me.'

I couldn't help laughing. 'I'm sorry. Really, I am. And for the record, I think it's good to take risks. I did that with my first book and played it far too safe with my second.'

And then, against my better judgement, I picked up his manuscript, put it in my bag and promised to read it.

# Three

IT'S A CLICHÉ, I know. Waking up, hungover and regretful, next to the naked body of the person you stupidly fucked the night before. What's less common-place is waking to the sound of your ex-husband ringing your doorbell. I got out of bed, pulled on an old T-shirt and walked down the corridor.

'You said morning,' he said when I finally opened the door to him. The air was cold and it cut straight through my T-shirt, wrapped itself around my legs. I had to squint, push my hair back from where it fell forward on my face. Jamie, on the other hand, looked like he belonged to the moving, noisy world behind him. A small lorry – it looked like a removals van – was reversing in rhythmic beeps, the driver leaning out of his window, looking down at the markings on the road. 'Is that for you?' he asked.

'What? No. There's no way I could fill one of those. Come in,' I said, leaving him to close the main door while I went through my own smaller, flimsier one. 'The boxes are in the kitchen,' I said, walking through the living room, but he didn't follow me.

'You never put a telly up then,' he said, pointing to the black, rectangular brackets above the fireplace where the previous tenant – so the estate agent had told me – had installed a sixty-five-inch flat screen. He had left the fixings in case I wanted to do the same.

'I don't watch TV. Why would I pay to have a big one mounted on the wall?'

From the other room we heard the creaking of the bed and the slap of feet on the wooden floorboards. 'You've got company?'

I shrugged. 'He works at the library. Did you say yes to coffee?'

'You didn't offer. But yes. No sugar.'

'No sugar,' I said. I didn't mean for it to come out as a question.

'Trying to cut down on refined things.'

I led the way into the kitchen. 'You've come to the right place,' I said, putting a filter into the machine.

'Come again?'

'Cutting down on refined things. This place,' I motioned around me, 'it's pretty rough round the edges. Even more so now.'

'What have you done with your furniture?'

'Sold it. What was mine. Or given it away to charity. The landlord's happy for me to leave anything that might be useful.'

'Even that?' he pointed to the coffee machine.

'Yes. Why, do you want it?'

'No,' he said quickly. 'Trying to cut back on caffeine too.'

I don't think I rolled my eyes. But I can't be sure.

'It's going to be uncomfortable, you know. On Finish, alone.'

'Yes. And no,' I leant over to see how much of the water had filtered through, conscious the T-shirt was rising up over my bum cheeks. 'Did you know National Trust Scotland have installed a wind turbine and solar panels in the bothy?' I turned to face him and just caught the quick shift of his eyes back up to my head.

'I didn't know that. But then, why would I? Tilly was much more interested in the abandoned village, remember?'

'Yes,' I nodded my head. We took her there the summer before she was due to start reception. It was to be our last holiday during term time. It was to be our last holiday ever, as it turned out. We were 'making the most of it,' people said. If they'd only known. If we'd only known.

Alex walked into the kitchen, cock and balls swinging.

'Morning,' he said, pushing a matted clump of hair from his forehead. I turned to Jamie, trying to think of what to say. Perhaps to tell him how foreign he'd felt to me the day before, how disappointed I was with his choice of engineered laminate flooring, but Alex was standing in the doorway, waiting for an introduction, and it was clear nothing meaningful could be said as long as his penis was on display.

'We'll give you a minute,' Jamie said, raising the back of his hand to his eyeline.

'Sorry?' Alex said, taking another step into the room. Jamie looked at me, appalled.

'Put some clothes on,' I clarified for Alex. 'We'll give you a minute to put some clothes on?'

'Oh right. Yeah. Can I get a cup of coffee first?' he said, walking over to the machine. 'It smells amazing.'

Jamie threw his hands up as Alex turned his – admittedly very toned – arse cheeks to both of us and poured himself a cup. 'Back in a bit,' he said, sipping as he walked out.

Jamie went over to the window, where he dug his hands into his jean pockets. The lower sash was open a few inches revealing the stone ledge, its cracked and missing patches of paint revealing, like a bad case of psoriasis, a red layer beneath. 'What time is his mummy coming to pick him up?'

'Fuck you.'

'Seriously Seren, how old is he?'

'I don't know. Twenty-something.'

He shook his head.

'I didn't ask to see his birth certificate.'

'Clearly.'

I sensed movement and looked down. A small, brown sparrow landed on the ledge. We watched it hop in surprised, tentative steps from one flaky patch to another, all the while working hard to return its brown feathers to order. 'Sorry,' he said. 'It's none of my business.'

'I'll put it down to shock.'

'I wasn't expecting a naked – what is he? Librarian, did you say?'

'Librarian. And a Gen Z. They don't do shame.'

'Clearly.'

'That's the second time you've said that.'

'What is it you want me to take?'

I pointed. On the floor, nestled in the corner, were two cardboard boxes, one on top of the other. 'Photos, her nursery pictures. The hand prints.'

He bent down and put his right hand flat on the top box.

'I can't put them in storage.'

'No,' he nodded.

'I need to know they're with someone who understands. I've put you down as my next of kin. With the travel insurance company. I hope that's OK.'

'It's fine.'

'I don't have anyone else.'

He straightened up and rubbed his lower lip with his thumb; something he does whenever he's unsure. I've seen him do it a hundred times: when he drove into a busy car park; when someone offered him a beer before five o'clock; when the mortician asked him if he wanted to see her.

I stood before him and waited. I knew he wanted to touch me. I was the closest person to the child who'd produced the things in the boxes. I was her tongue sticking out in concentration; her fingertips white as she pressed down with the pencil; I was her long hair falling forward as she worked. But so much had intervened: people, jealousies, unspeakable acts of violence and then certificates – death, the dissolution of one marriage and registration of another – ultrasounds and folic acid. Things had happened that put us at a remove. A distance that felt impossible to bridge.

Nevertheless, he reached for me. He pulled my shoulders towards his chest and held me there, my breasts beneath the thin cotton pressed to him; my body – unwashed, undressed, unrefined – and his. Somewhere, somehow, in the togetherness of us, our fug, our breath, our heartbeats, was Matilda. Not physical, not tangible anymore, but there, in the curious alchemy of us.

I didn't notice Alex walk back into the room, fully clothed, holding my phone out to me. 'If you unlock your phone, I can give you my email address.' Without shame and also – apparently – tact.

'What?' I asked, confused.

'For feedback on my manuscript? It's much easier over email, don't you think?'

I felt Jamie's hands lift from my back. 'We're kind of having a moment here,' he said, sniffing. 'Do you think you could leave us?'

'Sorry, it's just I have to get going. I'm supposed to be at the library for ten.'

I reached for my phone, unlocked it and handed it back.

'In your contacts?'

'Wherever.'

He nodded as he stood there, his face bent to the screen, his shoulders hunched as he tapped.

'Leave us?' Jamie said.

'Hmm? Oh yeah, sorry,' he said, walking out into the corridor slowly.

'It's not his fault,' I said. 'He doesn't understand any of this.'

'I'm not sure I do,' Jamie ran the fingers of his right hand up and down my spine. 'It just hits you sometimes, you know.'

'I know.'

'And you're going now and what you just said – about not having anyone. It makes me feel, it makes me feel really sad. Like I've let you down.'

'You haven't let me down.'

'I couldn't spend my life alone, you know that, don't you? I had to have – I had to have a family again.'

'I know, I know.'

'But I love you. I haven't stopped loving you.'

'Yes.'

'So, if you need anything, call me or get a message to me. I'll come.'

I looked at him, the tears falling freely down my face. 'She's really gone, isn't she?'

He nodded, too overcome to speak.

'I've added myself as a new contact. I'm under J for Jennings—' Alex's voice again.

'Jesus fucking Christ.'

'Jamie, don't. Alex,' I said, taking my phone back from him, 'you need to go now.'

'OK, OK. I'm going. Good luck,' he said with his arms out, as if there was nothing left to do but hug.

'You too,' I stayed where I was. 'Have a nice life.'

# Four

BEFORE LEAVING EDINBURGH, I went into WHSmith's and bought a pack of three A4 notebooks and some blue Bic biro pens. Given the power from the wind turbine and solar panels was not to be relied upon, pens and paper were a must. I also bought three head torches, a pen knife, a pot of Vaseline, a bar of laundry soap, water purification tablets, a book of crossword puzzles and a couple of paperbacks I'd been meaning to read. I wandered from shop to shop, picking things up. Would I need a potato peeler? What about a bottle opener? The truth was, I really didn't know what I was doing; I had no idea what was already in the bothy. Elspeth had told me there was no inventory of stuff – people left things but what they chose to leave and what to take was in constant flux.

So I bought things I imagined myself using but my imagination was patchy. It was two-dimensional, flat and all of it a massive distraction from the biggest question of all: what was I going to write? I had told Tess I planned to journal when I first got there but could I really draw out quotidian descriptions of grass and stone, rabbits and streams, cliffs and beach into a ghost story of eighty-thousand words?

And then of course there was the ghost stuff. Disgruntled child spirits running amok and old ladies screaming from the headlands. As mad as it is to write this now, in light of all that's happened, I wasn't afraid of any of these predictions coming true. I didn't believe in ghosts or the supernatural. I believed in men who bought ten-litre fuel caddies in hardware shops; men who hosed petrol through a front door letterbox and a back-door cat flap; men who were so righteous in their anger they didn't trouble themselves to find out how many souls were inside the house they planned to set alight.

The worst thing that could happen to me *had* happened to me. What did I care about ghosts and phantoms? No, what worried me as I walked up the gangplank and boarded the ferry in Oban that overcast day at the beginning of May was the giant leap of faith all this was in my ability to write.

The crossing took five hours. It was the best part of the trip. The train from Waverley to Glasgow had been full and noisy but the ferry was quiet with very few passengers. There was a restaurant not far from where I was sitting and, when I woke from my nap, I bought myself a cheese and tomato sandwich and a cup of coffee. It was nice. It felt good to be travelling. I watched little islets float by, their only inhabitants curlews calling to one another and the odd long-tail duck. Five hours. It's the kind of time you can really sink into. I fell asleep again.

I woke to the sight of Kisimul Castle standing alone in the bay and the sound of the captain's voice telling foot passengers to make their way to the designated exit. I decided there was enough time to run upstairs to the viewing deck and get a better view of the castle. Ancient fortress and home of clan MacNeil, it stood proud, strong, impenetrable – all adjectives you'd associate with a castle – and yet . . . and yet, it was out of place. It was somehow ridiculous with its fifteenth-century battlements lording its strength over a town that now boasted an Indian restaurant and a Co-op.

The Bayview Guesthouse was a short walk from the ferry terminal. An Arts and Crafts-style building with three imposing A-frame gables extending wide across the bay, it commanded lovely views of the castle.

Reception was a tall wood-effect counter in a wide hallway. On its surface was a closed A4 ledger and an old-fashioned bell. To my left was a cosy lounge with sofas, low coffee tables and an open fire. Beside one of the sofas, against the wall, was a black Labrador in a big dog basket. She was sitting upright, with six or seven tiny puppies asleep around her.

'You've met Carla then,' a voice behind me said. I turned around to find a woman in her late-fifties with very fair skin and light, delicate features. Her hair which had once been very dark, almost black at a guess, was now shot through with grey. There was something vaguely Irish about the combination – she reminded me of a character from an Edna O'Brien novel. 'She's very proud of her pups, aren't you, girl?'

'They're beautiful.'

'Aye, they are. Just got to find homes for them now. Seren, is it?'

'Yes, hello.'

'I'm Rosalie. Welcome to Castlebay,' she said, the last word coming out thick and quick, more *Cassaby* than

Castlebay. I was still a bit dozy from my sleep on the ferry and, for a worrying moment, thought she had slipped into Gaelic. She opened the ledger and moved her pen down the page.

'Is Kisimul Castle open?' I asked.

'No. It's closed for renovation, I'm afraid. But speak to my cousin, Daley. He owns a boat down at the marina. If you want a little walk around the castle walls, I'm sure he could find time to take you over.'

'Does he go to the islands?'

'Which island were you thinking?'

'Finish.'

'Oh yes, go and talk to him. He'll be more than happy to help,' she said, smiling.


Her cousin looked Australian. Like cartoon Australian. His face was too sun-kissed for the Outer Hebrides. Even before he spoke a single word, I got a strong Brad-off-*Neighbours* vibe from him. He was tall, muscular, with shoulder-length dark blond hair that looked like it had only ever been washed by the sea. His sunglasses hung from a thick cord around his neck and he wore shorts despite the cool temperature and drizzle. It was gone six by the time I wandered down to the marina and the clouds were a heavy, rolling purple.

He was standing in the stern of the *Spes Secunda* (I could just about make out the words painted on the side), counting life jackets piled on the bench before him. He looked up as I approached. 'Can I help you?'

'Your cousin Rosalie sent me. I was wondering if it would be possible to visit Kisimul.'

'Didn't she tell you it's closed? For renovation, apparently. Not that there's much going on at the moment.'

'She said I could have a little wander around the outside?'

'We'd have to ask Roger.'

'Who's Roger?'

'Caretaker. Paid by some government body to look after the place.'

'Do you think he'd mind me looking around?'

'Only one way to find out,' he said, holding his hand out to me. 'Roger's got a bit of a BO problem, I should probably warn you,' he said. 'He's pretty fat too. But what do you expect? Holed up in there all day.' I followed his gaze up the stone walls to the battlements. For a castle it was pretty small: four walls that enclosed a courtyard and tower. A cube and a cuboid, so close to the town it defined and yet far enough away to have nothing to do with it.

It took all of two minutes to reach the castle jetty. Daley roped his boat to one of the pilings. Together we walked up a short flight of stone steps, past a rusted iron grill pinioned to one side and through an opening to the courtyard. The ground was scrubby grass cut across by overgrown pathways that led to a terrace of small, three-storey cottages on the other side. They looked particularly dark and dismal under the heavy clouds. In the distance, a low growl of thunder could be heard.

'The castle is closed,' a wheezy voice shouted at us from the open door of one of the cottages. A short, balding man – as fat as Daley had warned – dressed in faded stonewash jeans and a brown woollen jumper lumbered up the front step into the courtyard.

'Rog,' Daley shouted, his voice startling me. 'Rog, I said she could come in.'

'Why did you do that? You have no authority here, Daley.'

'But I can show her around, like. We don't want to disturb you.'

'Well, you have.'

'Is it dinner time? Is that why you're so cranky?'

'Shut up, Daley.'

'Rog, give me the keys and get back to your pies.'

'Historic Environment Scotland have entrusted Kisimul Castle to me. I will show this person,' he looked me up and down, 'around.'

Daley turned to me and shrugged. 'You're in. You OK on your own? He's kind of a prick.' This last was said in full hearing distance of Roger.

'I'll be fine. Thanks.'

'No worries. Come out when you're ready.'

'You'll want to see the feasting hall,' Roger said, reaching for a ring of keys that hung from one of his belt loops.

'I really do appreciate you showing me around,' I said, trying to atone for the prick comment.

'It's very difficult,' he said as we walked down a long stone corridor, 'when someone like Daley just rocks up with one of his girlfriends. The castle is—'

'I'm not his girlfriend. We met like ten minutes ago.'

'He's a fast mover, I'll give him that.'

Roger, by contrast, was a very slow mover. It took us a long time to amble down another walkway where the only light was what rainy grey could penetrate the arrow slits we passed.

Everywhere was cold and damp. The walls, the uneven stone flags and especially the feasting hall. I had a splitting headache which I had thought was from all the travelling and not drinking enough water but as I stepped down into the feasting hall, a room below ground level surrounded on all sides by walls mildewed in an angry black-green, I realised it was more to do with the humidity and air pressure from the looming storm. The windows, set high in the walls, showed nothing but violet bruised sky. I thought of the Australian outside in his boat, waiting for me.

Against the opposite wall was a long oak table, capable of seating twenty. The surface was dull and soft, like you could easily sink a fingernail in. Why hadn't it been covered over or protected in any way? What was Roger doing all day? There were no chairs around it, just a lectern made of the same dark wood pushed hard up against it. Above the table, on the thick plaques of lime plaster, was an arrangement of six swords, the hilts fanning out from the central point of confluence at the tip.

I wanted to be alone to think about what all of this meant: the absence of anywhere to sit in a room where a lectern and weapons held sway. But behind me all I could hear was the laboured breathing of my guide, standing too close. 'How did you and Daley meet?'

'I'm staying at the Bayview. Rosalie put me onto him.'

'You like him, do you?'

'As I said, I don't really know him. We've just met.'

'He's Australian.'

'So I gather,' I said, taking a step away from him.

'His mother was from here, from Barra. Why you would leave all this for Australia is beyond me.'

'Hmm. Was this room used exclusively for eating?'

'Eating and gathering. This is where the clan chiefs would have come together, where they conducted their business,' he said, frowning a little. 'I expect Daley is used to seeing people wear lighter, thinner clothes.'

'Why are there no chairs?'

'They've been removed as part of the renovation. The table is going next week. He left his wife, you know.'

'Who did? Daley?'

'Aye, left her in some backwater in Australia. To come here, of all places.'

'I should probably get back. It's going to pour down and I don't want to keep him waiting. Do you mind if I take a picture?'

'They were known for their fearlessness, the MacNeils.'

'Yes.'

'If they wanted something, they took it.'

'Is that right?'

'They were absolutely brutal,' he whispered.

'Interesting.' I stepped away again.

'And if someone wronged them,' he shook his head and attempted a whistle.

I raised my phone and took a photo of the sword display. 'What?'

'They were taught a lesson. You didn't want to be on the receiving end of a lesson from the MacNeils, let me tell you.' His breaths were shallow and patchy. I thought I heard him lick his lips. 'The people of Finish learnt that the hard way.'

'What's that?' I asked, turning to him.

'Punished. The MacNeils punished them.' His breath didn't actually smell that bad. It was pretty much the only positive thing that could be said about him.

'But can you give me specifics?'

He looked a little hurt by my question or maybe it was the directness of it. 'What do you mean, specifics?'

'I assume you're referring to the massacre. But do you know why they killed the islanders? I've heard so much about MacNeil "vengeance" and how they could not be crossed. Lots of euphemisms basically. But what was the wrong?'

My question seemed to jolt him. His face dropped and he looked uncertain. 'If the MacNeils wanted something, they took it.'

'You said. But what? What did they take?'

'How much longer are you going to be? It's time I was having my tea.'

'I just want to get one more of the table.'

'I'll let you get on with it then.'

I waited until he laboured up the steps and out of the room before turning my phone landscape. I wanted the entire length of the table, complete with lectern, but just as I pressed the button, the exact moment in fact, the whole room was cracked open by lightning. A second or two later came heavy, loud thunder. I didn't bother checking the image or attempting another. I could hear the rain was already starting to come down so I dropped my phone into my bag and ran up the steps to join Roger, who didn't wait for me to get out of the way before leaning across to lock the door.

'How was he?' Daley asked when I got back to the boat.

'He thought I was your girlfriend,' I said, taking his hand and climbing back into the boat.

'Dirty old bastard. Did you get what you need?'

'I think so.' I sat down inside the cabin as he started the engine. 'The feasting hall was interesting.'

'Ah yeah. Where the clan chiefs met. Pretty far out, eh?'

'Hmm,' I agreed, opening my bag and taking my phone out.

'Rog loves all that blood and vengeance stuff.'

The photo I took was white and over-exposed. Like the old negatives strips you used to get with a roll of developed photos. Had I selected some strange setting? I zoomed in, moved the image right with my finger and that was when I saw it. The shadowy outline of a person at the end of the table – the table itself appearing in relief, white against black. The shadow, basically a cloud of dark grey, almost black pixels, looked very much like the head and shoulders of a man slumped at the table.

There was nothing else in that room that could have made a shadow like that – the lectern was too low and spindly. I thought back to the flash of lightning, the fact that it happened the moment I pressed the red button. It was impossible not to feel a little unnerved.

My room was on the second floor, in the very top of the central A-frame gable I'd seen from the road when I first arrived. There was a double bed nestled in the corner and the floor was carpeted in a trodden-down blue.

The room wasn't in any way modern but there was a general feel of comfort; of objects carefully arranged and furniture – the wardrobe, a small desk against the wall – where it should be.

I put my rucksack down on the bed, pulled out my belongings until I unearthed my wash bag and walked down the corridor to the shared bathroom. I had a shower, brushed my teeth and while putting on some makeup in the mirror, I saw on the wall behind me a coat of arms. In the top left was a boar's head with what looked like some kind of long bone – maybe a shin – in its jaw. In the adjacent quadrant, a sheep with a thick, curly fleece and then, in the lower left was a baby lying cradled in an open hand. Below it all, written in an ornate Celtic font, was the name MacKinnon.

When I opened the door, I came face-to-face with an old woman. Not simply waiting in the hallway outside, she was actually on the threshold, her toes and nose must have been touching the door while it was closed. I gasped and stepped back, expecting a similar reaction from her, but she just stood there, unmoved, like she'd been waiting for me.

'You frightened me,' I managed. Her eyes were unfocused and cloudy, like she had cataracts. Her hair was long and white and straggly. 'Are you staying here?' I asked.

Her eyes moved every time I spoke, circling my voice. I stepped towards her, expecting she would step back, but she didn't. 'Do you need me to help you find your room?' I asked, attempting to side-step her into the hallway, but she moved – quickly – and blocked me.

I was trying to work out what to do – push past her? – when I heard Rosalie's voice coming up the stairs. 'Mam?' she called.

'Here,' I shouted.

Her steps came more rapidly then. 'I'm sorry. Were you in there?' she asked me, pointing at the room behind me.

'I was. It's fine.'

'Mam, you know you mustn't come up here,' she said, taking her mother by the arm. 'This used to be her bathroom,' she explained to me. 'She gets confused from time to time. Come with me now, we'll get you something to eat. That would be nice, wouldn't it?' I was watching them walk away, back towards the top of the stairwell, when Rosalie turned to me. 'Dinner's being served now, in the dining room. Come down when you're ready.'

I found myself a small table at the front of the house, near a window. The old woman, Rosalie's mother, had been seated by the time I arrived, on her own, near the swing door through to the kitchen. Rosalie and a young woman with very long hair were busy moving back and forth, serving guests at the other tables.

There was a quiet, practised efficiency about the whole operation – not unlike the hush of first holy communion. Every interaction involved both Rosalie and the girl leaning in, listening intently to whatever words were spoken, and then the girl would turn to Rosalie for translation.

'Would you like something to drink?' Rosalie asked me when they came over. The girl hung behind her, waiting for me to speak.

'A glass of wine, please,' I smiled. 'The house red looks fine.'

'No problem. Olena will get that for you.' She turned to Olena, pointed to a large red square on her notepad and mimed lifting a glass to her lips. 'And what would you like to eat?' she asked, once Olena had been sent off on her errand.

'Is she deaf?' I asked.

'No. Ukrainian.'

'I'll have the salmon, please.'

'Salmon,' Rosalie repeated, writing it down.

'Can I ask you something?'

'Of course.'

'Upstairs in the bathroom.'

'I'm so sorry about that. She's—'

'No, no, not that. I wanted to ask about the coat of arms on the wall. MacKinnon?'

'Aye, Mam's a MacKinnon. Or she was before she married.'

'There's a picture of a baby in a palm?'

Rosalie stepped back so that Olena could come forward and place the glass of wine before me. The gesture was so ceremonial and solemn, I felt laughter bubble up in the back of my throat.

'She was a midwife,' Rosalie continued. 'I was too before my late husband and I bought this place. It's in the MacKinnon blood.'

'Really? You believe that?' is what I wanted to ask but, just like the laughter, I managed to stifle it.

'It's a gift,' she nodded. 'Passed from mother to daughter. On an island like Finish, you can imagine, it was a lifeline.'

'Finish?'

'Mam's people, they were all from Finish. Her mother, mine and Daley's grandmother, was the last baby born there. Before it was abandoned in 1912.'

'I interrupted you. You were saying—'

'What was I saying?'

'How it was a lifeline?'

'Aye, you're right,' she agreed, as if I were the one who had suggested it. 'Nobody on the island dared interfere with a woman in her child-bed – their only job was to call for the midwife. And do you know what? No woman attended by a MacKinnon ever died. She would stay up with them for two, three nights, however long it took. And all the children born into her hands would call her Granny. Isn't that something?'

'Granny,' I repeated.

'That's right, uh huh. Will you be wanting boiled potatoes or chips with your salmon?'

There was a knock at the door. Rosalie excused herself and went to the hallway where she opened the front door. I heard what I thought were American accents and looked up to see an older couple, early sixties perhaps, both with grey hair, exclaiming against the weather. Rosalie looked harassed as she led them to the table next to mine. 'I'll be back to take your order in a moment.'

'Good evening,' the man said and I thought, maybe Canadian. 'I'm Cameron and this is my wife Linda.'

'Nice to meet you. I'm Seren.' His wife, who was busy arranging her napkin on her lap, simply smiled back at me.

'Seren?' Cameron puzzled. 'That's Welsh, isn't it?'

'It is.'

'You're not from round here then?'

'I've come up from Edinburgh.'

'Cameron's from here,' Linda announced, raising her eyebrows in her husband's direction.

'Really? You sound . . . Canadian?'

'No, dear,' she laughed. 'That's just his accent. His great-great—' I noticed Cameron nodded each of the *greats* through as she spoke, 'grandfather was from Finish Island. He was part of the evacuation to Canada during the great potato famine of 1846.'

'Is that right?'

'I've always wanted to come see it,' he said. 'Had to wait until Linda here retired. She was in Retail Credit Risk Management at the Bank of Canada.'

I sipped my wine and prayed to God that neither of them would try to explain what that meant. When it became apparent there would be no note of interest from me, Cameron pushed on. 'But as soon as you did, I booked the tickets, didn't I?'

'The very next day,' she nodded. 'Now all we need is to find someone who can take us down there.'

'My cousin Daley's your man,' Rosalie said, appearing with Olena and two menus. 'He'll run you down, no problem. Seren here's looking to go too, aren't you?'

'I am.'

'Oh, you are?' Linda asked, all smiles now. 'Are your people from Finish too?'

'Haven't you been listening?' Cameron said, raising his voice a little. 'She said she's from Wales. That's nowhere near here.'

'Why are you going then?' Linda asked, puzzled.

'I'm going to live there for a while.'

'No,' Linda shook her head, laughing. 'You can't live on Finish.' She turned to Olena and tapped the side of her glass. 'We'll take a bottle of the Sauvignon Blanc.'

'Uninhabited,' Cameron enunciated for the group, as if we were all hard of hearing. Olena, who must have thought he was clarifying his wife's wine order, looked at Rosalie, confused.

But Rosalie wasn't interested in clarifying a drinks order. 'How long are you staying?' she asked me.

'A few months,' I said, twisting the stem of my wine glass. 'I have permission from National Trust Scotland.' It came out more primly than I intended.

Linda shook her head as if all she'd heard from me this evening was lies. 'But it's haunted. You don't know that?'

'That's only a problem if you believe in that kind of thing.'

'And you don't?'

'Not really, no.'

'A lot of ancient blood spilt,' Linda said, turning to Rosalie, who leant down with her pad and pen. 'We'll have the salmon with boiled potatoes. A glass of water for Cameron, no ice. He needs to take his statin.'

Rosalie nodded and left us, Olena trailing slowly behind her.

'You better tell her,' Cameron said.

'Tell me what?' I asked.

'There was a massacre there,' Linda began.

'I know.'

'You do? And do you also know that, in the Celtic tradition, when blood is spilled, particularly the blood of children, there must be a reckoning. Shall we share the cheesecake?' she asked Cameron, glancing down at the menu.

'I was thinking the brownie?'

'You know what eggs do to you.'

'I'll leave you to your dinner,' I said.

'Evil acts, Sarah,' she said.

'It's Seren.'

'Committed by evil men. That kind of violence, it leaves a trace.'

The swing door opened and Olena walked towards us, my salmon in one hand and a bottle of their white wine in the other. Linda pursed her lips as Olena put the plate down before me. 'It's one thing going during the day,' she said, holding her glass up while Olena poured into it. 'But it's a known fact that spirits roam the land at night. Anyway, bon appétit,' she said, raising her now full glass to me.

# Five

IT WAS A RELIEF to take my glass of wine and go upstairs to my room. I thought I might open my laptop, watch a film or something, but the window – I'd been so rattled by Rosalie's mum at the bathroom door I'd forgotten to draw the curtains before dinner – was too much of a spectacle. It looked down at the bay, at the reassuring bulk and ambient lights of the Caledonian MacBrayne ferry, waiting to set sail for Oban first thing in the morning and then – with startling, almost transcendental clarity – Kisimul Castle. I was standing there, looking at the stone walls, thinking back to the photo I'd taken – of the shadow figure slumped at the table – when my phone buzzed with a new message. Alex. It had been a mistake to give him my number; this was the third in a series I'd so far ignored: *I expect you haven't got much reception on your island but if you do get this, I'd love to know your thoughts on my book!*

I put my phone on 'do not disturb' and got into bed.

I woke to the sound of a loud, piercing scream. I tapped the screen on my phone and saw it was 2.34 in the morning. I sat up in bed, wondering if I'd dreamt it but then it came again, a scream that vibrated through the bones of the house.

I got out of bed and opened the door. It sounded like it had come from downstairs. I peered out. Another noise but this time, less of a scream and more of a howl. Like someone was in terrible pain. I walked along the corridor and saw, as I went, lights come on under the closed doors of other guest rooms. Hearing their movements and voices within made me feel braver. Clearly, I wasn't the only one who'd heard it.

I crept down to the first floor and closer to the source of the noise and now it sounded like choking sounds. Like someone was trying desperately to clear their throat.

I approached the door to Rosalie's rooms, the one marked *Private.* I went right up to it even though I had no idea what I was going to do once I got there. In my uncertainty, I just stood at the threshold, not unlike the position her mum had taken outside the bathroom a few hours earlier.

I heard Rosalie's voice. 'You'll hurt yourself,' she was saying. This was followed by more crying and then a rasping, scratching sound. 'Get back into bed, Mam. Please.'

'No,' came the answer. It was the fitful, shaken voice of an old person struggling to speak. And then: 'it can't be helped'.

I put my ear closer to the door and heard the same voice say something about her knee. It was difficult to make out. And then there was no more making out because the door next to my ear was suddenly opened and Rosalie was staring at me in surprise.

'I'm sorry,' I mumbled. 'I heard choking.'

'She's not choking.'

'No.'

'She's fine. Just a little confused.'

Beyond Rosalie, sitting on the end of her bed, dressed in a light-blue nightgown with her long white hair around her shoulders, was her mother. She was dragging a large wooden brush through the strands of it with grim, focused attention. 'I didn't mean to intrude. I just thought – I thought you might need help.'

'We're fine. She's calmer now. I'll let her carry on with her brushing a wee while longer.'

'If you need me.'

'We don't. You go on back to bed now. We'll be fine.'


I woke early and exhausted the following morning – I felt like I'd had very little actual sleep. In the milky grey morning, the noises from the night before felt like a dream, like an implausible story I'd told myself.

I decided to go for a run. It was cold as I stepped outside the front door, the wind coming off the sea biting and I had to fight the urge to tiptoe back upstairs and into bed. But I didn't. I didn't because Tilly was on my mind.

I can think of Tilly when I'm doing something physically exhausting like running. I can let my mind wander carefully, tentatively in the direction of the hot, painful thing. If I'm sitting still or staring out of a window, I won't. I'll read a book or strike up a conversation with the person next to me. But that morning, as I laboured up the hill with views out to the north Atlantic, I allowed myself to remember.

I walked up to the fence post that separated the campsite from the coastal path. I couldn't recall exactly where our pitch had been, only that we'd woken somewhere near where I stood, in our tent. Tilly in a small sleeping bag between us. What I remember most clearly was how the light, filtered by the blue canvas of the tent, revealed the dimensions of her face; the rise and fall of her chin, her rosebud lips, how they led to the cleft that ran up to her nose. Her face was formed perfection; it was of me, once upon a time at one with me and yet there we were – she sleeping, me watching – entirely separate. It felt miraculous.

But from where I stood, that morning, it was more myth than miracle. It was hard to hold on to the fact that she had once been alive and here with me. That she had once been flesh and blood and beating heart beneath my hand.

I thought of the shadowy figure I had seen yesterday and took my phone out. I snapped a picture of the large family tent pegged there. I zoomed in on the picture, searched right and then left. Nothing. Nothing but longing. The wind scorched the moisture on my cheeks and when the pain became too great to stand still any longer, I continued my run.

Further up the coastal path – a mile or so from the campsite – I met Daley coming out of his house. It was a small bungalow, the type you'd imagine a couple in their seventies moving into, all crazy paving and white UPVC windows and doors. A completely incongruous choice for the Brad-off-*Neighbours* persona I'd assigned him. 'Morning,' I shouted.

'Hey,' he said, looking up. 'Starting early?'

'Something like that,' I stopped and tried to catch my breath. 'I'm glad I caught you actually. I wanted to talk to you about Finish.'

'Yeah, I'm taking a couple at Rosalie's down there in a few hours. You want to come?'

'Definitely. But, I don't know if Rosalie's told you, it's kind of a one-way deal.'

'You're staying out there?'

'For a few months. At least until September.'

'Ah yeah, you can't stay much beyond September. Unless you're prepared to hunt rabbits.'

'So I hear. But am I right in thinking you visit the island regularly? Through the summer?'

'Yeah, this time of year I'm down there once a week, sometimes more, sometimes less.'

'So you could bring me deliveries? Fresh food, anything I might need? I'd pay you of course.'

'Yeah, I can do that. The Co-op opens in about twenty minutes,' he said, looking at his watch. 'If you go and buy what you need, tell them I'll come and collect it. I can get it in the boat ready for later.'

'That's great. Thank you.'

'You'll want a lot of dried stuff. Pasta, rice, flour, that kind of thing.'

'Yep,' I nodded.

'And a sharp knife. There isn't one in the bothy. You'll want that for preparing food.'

'I'm really glad I bumped into you. What time are you leaving?' I asked.

'I told them ten.'

I nodded. 'I'll meet you down at the jetty.'


I did as Daley suggested and then ran back to the guest-house where I had a shower, packed my bags and decided there was time for breakfast before I had to be down at the marina. Rosalie was sitting at the same table her mother had been at the night before – the one nearest the kitchen swing door. She was wearing her glasses and was typing something on a laptop. Before I could approach, Olena quickly intercepted, asking what I'd like to eat.

'A cooked breakfast, please,' I said. 'My last big meal,' I said patting my stomach.

'You want big?'

'No, Olena,' Rosalie shouted from her corner. And then, inexplicably, she continued: 'Seren is going to live on one of the abandoned islands.'

'Bad island?'

'No. ABANDONED,' she shouted. 'No people.'

Olena turned forty-five degrees in my direction, a frown forming between her eyebrows.

'It's fine,' I smiled. 'Could I have my eggs fried, please?'

'She won't be able to cook,' Rosalie continued, apparently determined to hammer home this point of spoken English.

'No cook?' she said to me, now thoroughly baffled.

'This breakfast?' I pointed to her notepad. 'Please cook,' and invoking the universal language of emoji, brought my hands together in prayer.

'OK. I do,' she said, smiling now. She pivoted in the direction of the kitchen, her thick knot of a plait just missing my face.

'Sit down with me,' Rosalie said. 'Have some tea.'

'Thank you.'

'Fetch a cup from that table, would you?' she said, lifting the teapot in readiness. 'I just wanted to say how sorry I am about last night. For disturbing you.'

'No, please. I'm sorry. I shouldn't have intruded like that. How's your mum this morning?'

'Exhausted, as you might expect. These – well, episodes for want of a better word – they take a lot out of her, you know? It's very painful, but there you go. We have to live with it.'

'Does she do that a lot?'

'The crying?'

'And the brushing of her hair.'

'Not a lot, I wouldn't say. But from time to time. She says it feels like she's being taken over, you know? I had her tested for epilepsy but the doctor thinks it's more likely dementia. I don't know. We do what we can.'

'It must be difficult.'

'It is,' she nodded, taking her glasses off. She smiled at Olena as she put my breakfast down before me. I had hoped to go and eat by myself in the corner, as I had the night before. 'That was the thinking behind Olena. I thought she would be able to lighten the load down here a bit. Free me up for Mam. But, it's not your problem,' she said, glancing down at my plate. 'Didn't you ask for fried eggs?'

'It's fine,' I said, quickly eating a forkful of the scrambled eggs. 'I need to get going anyway. Daley said to meet at ten.'

'You'll be wanting a packed lunch in that case,' Rosalie said, getting up from the table. 'I'll leave you to eat your breakfast in peace.'

In the daylight, I could see that Cameron used hair gel to engineer a crunchy grey quiff. I watched it not move, despite the persistent breeze coming off the water, as he told me once again that Linda had worked in Retail Credit Risk Management at the Bank of Canada.

'My first husband died,' she added, as if this were a crucial piece of knowledge I needed in order to understand her job title. I noticed Daley behind them, carrying life jackets, then a first aid kit and finally a rectangular, electronic box – it looked like some kind of surround sound audio system – out from his office and onto the *Spes Secunda*.

'He was a terrific man. We used to play squash together,' Cameron said, shaking his head. 'Boy, did he have a strong backhand return.'

'Oh yeah,' Linda agreed. 'He sure did.'

'I had two daughters with him and then, after he died, Cameron came to see me,' she said, giving her husband a coy smile.

'Did he?' Much like booking this trip the day after she retired, it seemed neither of them were prepared to wait around.

'I did,' Cameron agreed. 'And we were blessed with our own daughter, weren't we?'

Linda nodded. 'I was forty-three when I found myself a newly married widow so neither of us held out much hope for a third child.'

'No, ma'am,' Cameron shook his head.

I called over to Daley, who was now carrying my Co-op shopping to the boat. 'Do you need any help?'

'Nah, you're all right,' he shouted back.

'We were over the moon, weren't we?' Linda beamed. 'Oh yeah.'

'Must have been difficult though, having just lost your husband and all?'

She waved my concerns away. 'He would have wanted me to be happy again.'

'He was a terrific man,' Cameron agreed. 'The way he used to return a volley drop? Oh, he would have wanted us to be happy, all right.'

'All set?' Daley called, from inside the boat. He held his hand out to me, 'stick one of those on,' he said, pointing to the pile of lifejackets on the stern bench.

'Did you hear the crying last night?' Linda asked me as she stepped aboard.

'What crying?' Daley asked.

'The owner's mother. She set up this terrific wail in the middle of the night.'

'Is she OK?'

'It was some noise,' Cameron said, deliberately not taking Daley's hand to board the boat. 'We thought someone was dying, didn't we, Lin?'

'The woman you heard crying is Daley's aunt,' I said to Cameron, who was chin down and oblivious to everything as he attempted to fasten his lifejacket.

'What was she doing?' Daley asked me.

'Crying. And brushing her hair.'

'Shit. She does that when she feels like she's being taken over.'

'That's what Rosalie said.'

'You spoke to her? To Rosie?'

'A little while ago. She said . . .' I paused, realising I didn't know his aunt's name, 'Mrs MacKinnon was just really tired this morning.'

'Her name's Kathleen. Or Kitty. We all call her Kitty.'

'Have I got this on tight enough?' Linda asked Daley.

'Let me see,' Daley said, reaching across me to pull at one of her straps. It had the effect of turning her, like a sprung doll in a jewellery box, towards us.

'She reminds me of one of those white-haired witches,' Cameron said. 'What are they called, Lin?'

'Banshees,' Linda supplied, sitting down on the stern bench.

'That's it, she reminds me of a banshee.'

I looked at Daley but he just rolled his eyes, climbed into his seat and started the engine.

'What is it they say? About the banshee?' Cameron asked as he shuffled over to his wife.

'When the banshee cries, someone dies,' Linda sang merrily as we motored out into the open water.

# Six

AND THEN, THERE IT WAS. Finish Island. I'd never approached it from the western side before; the boat companies we'd used in the past had always opted for a beach landing, on the eastern side of the island. But Daley said he wanted to show me something.

The green, hummocky slopes extended like thick, misshapen fingers into the sea that lapped and waved against them. The land looked timeless. It *was* timeless. Insensible and untouched by the fact that people no longer wanted to live on it. I had the impression of a huge, sleeping animal – a dog or a bear perhaps – waking to the sound of our visit as a furry ear flaps at a fly. We were fleeting, inconsequential. The real people, the people who mattered, had left long ago. And so there was nothing to do but sleep.

'That there,' Daley said, slowing as we passed a huge sea stack on our left, 'is Finamuil. In low tide you can cross to it from the island.'

'Are we getting off?' Cameron shouted. Linda broke off half a ham sandwich as he spoke and passed it to him.

'Not yet,' Daley shouted back. 'Hold tight.'

He turned the boat around and went back, briefly, the way we'd come – back past the sea stack and right, under a rocky arch. 'Get ready for this,' he shouted. Above our heads was a low, heavy roof of glistening gneiss. It altered everything: the light, the sound of the boat, the colour of the water – which became a tame azure. It was as if we'd been let in a back door, told to come in out of all that noise.

'Is this the natural arch?' Linda shouted.

Ignoring her, Daley pointed to a rocky ledge at the bottom of a two-hundred-metre drop. It was nine, maybe ten metres from the sea stack he'd just pointed out. 'That's what I mean. You can walk or wade at low tide.'

'And at high tide?' I asked.

He shrugged his shoulders. 'It's possible but you've got to watch the currents. There's a chance you could be swept out into the Sound.'

'OK,' I replied, not entirely sure why we were having this conversation.

'And the descent here—'

'Are we getting out?' Cameron again, this time his mouth full of chewed sandwich.

'Yeah, we're getting out,' he said, lowering the anchor. 'If the eastern side is choppy—'

'East. That's the side with the beach?'

'Exactly. If that's choppy, you can also land a boat here.'

We left Linda and Cameron to their photography of the natural arch. I followed him along the rocky platform, past Finamuil on my right until the ledge we stood on became very narrow, hugging the precipitous cliff-face. Daley offered his hand and I took it. He stopped and pointed up the cliff-face, all the way to the jutting green of a headland. 'That's Ceum a'Mhaide up there,' he said, reaching for the sunglasses that had been resting against his chest.

'I know Ceum a'Mhaide,' I said. 'Lovely views. I've been to Finish quite a few times.'

'What, here?' he asked, pointing at the wet rock beneath our boots.

'No, the beach and the headlands.'

'This is your route down,' he continued. 'These stepped ledges. It's the easiest, quickest way to get here without specialist climbing equipment.'

'Why would I need to get down here?'

'For that,' he said, turning to face me and pointing behind me, to Finamuil.

I turned, looked over my left shoulder and saw that the innermost side of the sea stack, the side that faced the island, contained an opening: a pitch-black V of an entrance that led inside. It was strangely obscene, the way Finamuil – viewed from this point and this particular angle – lay before us, open and in practised welcoming. 'Chulainn's cave,' Daley said.

'Chulainn?'

'She laid down her life when the island was being raided. So the story goes.'

'When you say raided, do you mean the massacre?'

'Probably. They got everyone – men, women, children – in the cave and set fire—'

'No, I know,' I said quickly, my palm up to stop him. 'I know the details. Who is Chulainn though? What did she do to try and save them?'

'No one knows for sure. We're talking events from hundreds of years ago. It's the stuff of legend now.'

I thought of the bottom-left quadrant of the MacKinnon coat of arms, the baby cradled in the open palm. 'Was she a relative of yours? Of your aunt's?'

'She was the midwife, so yes, probably. All midwives on Finish were MacKinnon born.'

'Rosalie said. She was a midwife too?'

'And my mum and Kathleen.'

We stood together, the ledge forcing an intimacy that felt apt, given the view. 'They named the cave after her,' I said, squinting at that deep V of the entrance again. 'I can see the gynaecological connection.'

'For sure. Looks like a Map of Tassie.'

'What's that?'

'Not heard of that one? Tasmania. If you look at it on a map, it looks like a,' he coughed, 'well, like a huge vagina.'

'Always difficult saying huge vagina to someone you've just met.'

'It's not been easy. Anyway, it was named after her because it became a place of shelter for anyone who needed sanctuary on the island.'

'Like a womb.'

'Exactly. Just in case you ever get caught on this side of the island and need shelter, now you know where it is.'

We got back in the boat and rounded the southern tip of Finish before heading to her eastern side. Daley anchored the boat around thirty metres from the shore and, in a rubber dinghy, took us over to a rocky outcrop where we had to climb up and over huge barnacle-covered boulders. It was slow-going for Linda and Cameron, older than me by a good twenty years and wary of slipping on the rocks. I followed their path towards the damp, wave-flattened sand and the dusty dunes beyond and then, out of nowhere, like a gull flying directly at my face, I was hit by a memory of Tilly.

It could have been the talk of midwives, of caves that looked like a gateway to a womb, that brought her to me in such vivid shape and motion but as I followed Linda, I saw Tilly in her red wellington boots, holding Jamie's hand as she squelched through the same shallows. I kept my eyes trained on Linda's grey waterproof jacket as this footage of my lost child played out. Her little hand in his, the crown of her head, the long, windswept tendrils of blonde hair.

'There's the abandoned village,' Linda said, nudging Cameron, who immediately, on cue, brought the view-finder of his camera to his face and began clicking away. One, two, three, so many exposures it was impossible to count. They will have lots of pictures, I thought. They'll look at them and then move on. It felt unfair, that I was clinging to a fragile, transitory memory of another visit, another time. I closed my eyes and saw Tilly running towards the ruined walls, saw her attempting to climb them with Jamie's protective hand at her back.

We had reached the ruins of the village and Cameron was crouching down to get a close-up of the stone work, blown through by sand.

'Mummy, can we live here?' Tilly had asked, standing on the same wall.

'You want to stay?' I said, reaching out to steady her.

'We need to build a roof,' she said, tucking her hands under her armpits.

'And we'd need electricity, clean water, food,' Jamie had said. He was reading the map, looking for Cnoc fiacail, the tallest point on Finish – so-called because it looked like a giant's tooth.

'We can drink the sea,' she had said, ever the pragmatist.

'Don't you think so?' Linda prompted.

'What's that?'

'That it must have been awful. To be so deprived of comfort?'

'They didn't know any better. I mean, that stands to reason, doesn't it? You only know one thing by the absence of another.'

'Oh, they knew,' Cameron said. 'My great, great grandfather, he was the one who emigrated to Canada? He was a fisherman here and he travelled in the summer, up to Stornoway and the mainland. He saw how other people lived.'

'But that's what I'm saying, seeing how others lived, the comforts they had. It made life here increasingly intolerable. But until that happened, well, they were probably quite content. It is a beautiful place to live, if you don't know any better.'

'It's a nice theory,' Cameron smiled enigmatically and I hated him then. Hated his proud pounding greats every time he spoke about this island. He called Linda away and a few minutes later I heard him agree with Daley to meet back at the beach in two hours.

We continued our walk directly east, up from the beach to the bothy. Daley brought with him the rectangular box

I'd seen earlier, explaining as we went that it was a battery to store the energy produced by the wind turbine and solar panels. 'So, I will have power?' I asked.

'A little. Some of the time. Nothing you can rely on.'

'So, pen and paper, then.'

'Pretty much. There it is. Your new home.'

There it was. I'd seen it many times before but never, obviously, with a view to living in it. The old schoolhouse, the bothy, the place where I write these words now, was a corrugated iron roof resting on four walls. It was altogether more 'constructed' than the small cottage walls we'd just seen. But even so, the bothy was effectively a house drawn by a child: a central black door flanked on either side by symmetrical sash windows. On the right, the northern gable end, just as Elspeth at National Trust Scotland had said, was a chimney stack and cowl – all of which gave me hope of comfort on cold, damp evenings. 'Have you got the key?' Daley asked.

I opened the smallest zip compartment in my rucksack and handed it to Daley.

The floor was made up of thick stone flags that had been cut in uneven, coarse strokes and then cemented together. To my right, the gable end with the chimney, was a small living area. The whole of the downstairs was one room deep with most of the far wall taken up by the immense stone surround of the fireplace. Above the fireplace, a thick wooden lintel – perhaps oak, it looked like a strong, dark wood – and I could see that it had been scratched and marked by the names of people who had stayed here. Positioned in front of the hearth was a rocking chair.

It is strange, difficult even, to describe the bothy and see it as I saw it that morning, with Daley beside me. I had no idea what life would be like on this island, in this building. I didn't know then what visions would play out, what company I would keep. What terrors I would know.

On the shelf above the fireplace was an empty wine bottle with the stub of a white candle and wax drippings down the side; a can of lighter fluid and a small upturned lid from a jam jar. In the two alcoves to the left and right of the fireplace were big boxes of wood and kindling. Daley, I remember, went straight to one of them, the one on the left of the fireplace and crouched down. 'This should last you about a week. And there's always peat.'

'Who's Pete?' I asked, alarmed.

'Peat. P-E-A-T.'

'Oh. Right. Yes,' I laughed.

'There are some tools out back. I better show you.'

But before we went outside, Daley led the way to the other side of the room, the area to the right of the still-open front door. There, under the window, someone had nailed a piece of plywood to serve as a makeshift kitchen work surface. Beside it was a small rectangle of a table with two chairs positioned either side. On top of the table was a single burner camping stove as well as a stack of plastic bowls, a set of cutlery, an enamel mug and a wine glass. 'I can bring you fresh cannisters when I come.'

'We should probably talk about that. How does this work?'

'It's up to you really. I can bring you whatever you want, within reason, like. You can either email me if you've got power or hand me a list when I come for next time.'

'Should I give you some money now?' Weirdly this conversation felt more awkward than the one about huge vaginas.

'You could give me – what – a hundred? A hundred pounds. Just to cover anything you might need. We can always reckon up at the end.'

I picked up one of the bowls. 'I'm going to need some washing-up liquid and a sponge.'

'There are a couple of six-litre containers out back too. You'll need to collect your drinking water from a stream, there's one not far from here. I'll show you that too.'

A stone staircase led off the kitchen, up the far wall and into the roof space. Daley was happy for me to lead the way on this bit of the tour. I quickly discovered, as I neared the roof, that there wasn't enough room to stand up – I had to walk, stooped over, to what would be my bed, an old-fashioned iron bedframe with a thin off-white mattress, pushed up against the wall. God only knows how they had got it up the narrow winding stairs. Beside it was a small three-legged stool intended as a bedside table. 'What do you think?' Daley had hold of a roof rafter and leant in from the staircase.

'I wasn't expecting such comfort,' I said, patting the mattress.

'No second thoughts, eh?'

'Not yet.'

I followed him back down the stairs. Outside, round the back of the bothy, was a small, lean-to wooden shed. Inside was a jumble of miscellany: discarded plant pots, wellies in various sizes and colours, an orange bucket, the empty water containers and a stack of what looked like ancient tools. Daley proceeded to point out the pleadhag (dibble), a treisgeir (peat cutter), a caschrom (foot plough), a racan (rake) and an axe – all in perfect Gaelic. But at the time I knew nothing of tilling the land, or how to cut peat or the best place to plant seeds. I just stood there, nodding my head as he explained how to use the L-shaped metal fixing at the bottom of the treis-geir to slice the row of peat and extract the bricks. 'Do you want me to show you?' he asked.

'I can use my hour of internet to watch a YouTube video on it.'

'Better stick some logs on that list of yours.'

We left the bothy and walked northwest to the stream. Daley had drawn a circle around a confluence of blue lines on his OS map. 'It's a bit of a climb so you need to plan for that. Over there is the burial ground,' he pointed to a mound a few hundred metres to our right, a short hike up from the beach. I could just about see two grey heads bobbing among the stones and long grasses. 'He's nuts for his great greats, eh?'

'I won't miss any more tales of his ancestors.'

'He's probably down there digging them all up. Speaking of the burial ground,' he said, stopping, 'use it to orient yourself. It can be tough out here, even in the summer months. Fog can roll in from the sea and before you know it, you're lost.'

'Right, OK.'

'You'll need to fill up every other day. It's up to you what time you set off but remember to give yourself plenty of daylight to get back. You need to allow time for purification too, if you're going to drink it. How many tablets you got?'

'Six packs.'

'I can bring more if you need them. And don't go wandering around here at night.'

'Because I might bump into a ghost?' I laughed.

'Because of the dark. You might twist your ankle, injure yourself.'

'Yep. Of course.'

'Keep this map with you,' he said, handing me the folded rectangle of the OS. 'Especially the first few times you go out.'

Back at the bothy, Daley shared his flask of coffee with me. I opened the foil package of sandwiches Rosalie had made me that morning. 'Want one?' I pulled the rocking chair round and sat back in the dip. My weight set the rollers in motion so that it looked like I was taunting him: offering a sandwich and then taking it back again.

'Comfy, eh?' he said, reaching for one.

'The whole place is really comfy. I think – with the exception of having to trudge up a hill for drinking water – it's going to be pretty easy.'

'It'll be sweet all right.' He pulled out the chair that was tucked under the desk below the window. 'That view, eh?'

'I wrote my last book with a view of loft conversions and soil pipes.' I took a big bite of my sandwich. 'This is a definite improvement.'

'Going to be lonely, eh.'

'Hmm. Maybe. I think there's a difference between being lonely and alone.'

'It's easy to talk about the difference when you're sitting here with someone, eating a sandwich and drinking coffee. But it gets to some people. It's harder than you think.'

'Easier for me, though.'

'How's that?'

'I've got you. You'll be coming every week or ten days?'

He didn't answer, just frowned. Like he was listening for something. 'You hear that?'

'No. What?'

'Nothing,' he shook his head. 'What was I saying?'

'How often you'll come.'

'In high season, yeah. When the kids go back in August, everything gets quiet again—' he stopped. This time I heard it too. A voice in the distance. We paused, neither of us saying a word.

It was the sound of a woman screaming.

We stood up at the same time. Daley dropped his sandwich and ran to the door. I followed him as he ran outside and stood still, waiting for the voice, strained and tense, to reach us again.

'Over there!' I shouted, spotting Linda out of the corner of my eye, halfway between us and the beach. She was waving her arms frantically.

He knew the terrain and was much faster than me. By the time I got to the spot where Linda had been standing, they were several hundred metres ahead of me, inside the burial ground.

As I approached, out-of-breath, I saw Daley was kneeling down, his curtain of blond hair covering the side of his face as he rocked to-and-fro, performing chest compressions on an unconscious Cameron.

I put my arm around Linda, tried to pull her away but she wouldn't budge.

'Get down to the boat,' Daley shouted. 'Radio for help.'

I did as he told me. The woman on the radio told me the air ambulance was on its way and to continue chest compressions until further help arrived. By the time I'd rowed back to the rocks, spent a frustrating ten minutes trying to work out where I could tie the dinghy so it wouldn't drift away, scrambled back over the rocks and up to the burial ground, I could hear the helicopter in the distance.

My relief was short-lived when I saw Linda's ashen face. She was sitting in a heap on the wet grass while Daley continued with his compressions, drops of sweat now falling from the tip of his nose.

'The air ambulance is coming,' I said. Neither of them looked up at me. Why would they? A helicopter with medical professionals and life-saving equipment on board wasn't going to make a blind bit of difference.

Anyone could see he was dead.

# Part II

*Saturday 6th May*
My first morning and it's fitting that the sky is overcast and grey. What happened yesterday, at the burial ground, it feels like a huge cloud. I don't want to say omen. He was sixty-nine, taking statins for a heart condition – I heard Linda relaying all this to the paramedics as they tried the defibrillator on Cameron – so it was not inconceivable that he might just keel over like that. The fact that it happened here, on Finish, in the graveyard where his ancestors are buried, is a coincidence. A pretty painful one, but a coincidence nonetheless.

After several more attempts to shock Cameron's heart back into action, the paramedic got to his feet. The pilot took over then, explained they would take Cameron's body to Benbecula where a doctor would officially pronounce him dead.

After that there was very little to say or do. Linda, who had just a few hours ago been telling me about her short widowhood at forty-three, was now facing it all again. Except this time there was no Cameron waiting in the wings. Or off the squash court.

Daley and I spent the rest of the afternoon carrying bags and supplies from the boat up to the bothy and then it was time for our own goodbye. I don't think we would have hugged had it not been for what happened.

*Late morning*
Everywhere is a mess. And cold. The walls are damp and thick with it. I boiled some water on the gas stove and

managed to make a cup of coffee but then couldn't find the milk so just drank it black. I also lit the fire – anything to chase this cold away. It definitely helps. It's amazing actually, how quickly the place warms up.

The table is covered in packets, boxes and tins of food – all the stuff Daley and I unpacked yesterday: tuna, mackerel and sardines as well as tins of vegetables like carrots, peas and potatoes; six cartons of semi-skimmed UHT milk and a few tins of condensed milk; two-kilogram bags of plain flour, porridge oats and red lentils; a couple of blocks of salted butter, a chunk of Stilton, some fresh tomatoes and a bag of apples. I also bought two gas cannisters, some toilet roll, three bottles of red wine, a bottle opener (though I've just found one on a windowsill), a tea-towel, teabags and the sharp knife Daley recommended I buy for food prep.

I thought I might try putting some of it away but no, there's nowhere to put any of it. No cupboards or drawers. There's the plank of plywood under the window. It'll do. To sum up then: I've made coffee, lit the fire and moved shit from one surface to another. That's been my morning's work.

I made another cup of coffee but this time I remembered the cartons of milk were on the floor under the table. So now I have my coffee and I'm sitting at my desk, looking out of the window and I don't know what on earth I'm going to write.

'It's not about physical land,' Tess had said. 'But space, head space.' It's a good thing it's not about physical land – I can't even see the landscape. All I can see are long beads of rain, whipped horizontal along the glass pane and in between the lines are varying brushstrokes of grey.

Of course, it's still only day one. I haven't even unpacked my rucksack, haven't worked out how I'm going to brush my teeth with no running water or what to dry my clothes on (in front of the fire – but on what?) but I feel the need to get started. I need to make this ludicrous venture purposeful.

All of this is really just a distraction from the obvious. A man died here yesterday. He stepped off Daley's boat with a beating heart and was loaded into a helicopter with a still one. I just can't get my head around it. He was alive, curious, excited – annoying – but alive and then he wasn't. Then he was something to be transported and certified.

It's stopped raining and I can see a break in the clouds above Cnoc fiacail. I'm going for a swim.

*3.20 p.m.*

I hesitated down at the beach. Fear of what the cold water might do to my heart but also the thought of getting in trouble, being pulled away by a rip tide, the fact of being so alone here – I'd be pretty much fucked.

But what's the point of being here if I'm too afraid to swim? I took my clothes off and walked into the water. It was amazing. Fucking cold but amazing. I stayed close to the beach and was careful to keep my boots and ruck-sack in sight at all times but still, it felt great to lie on my back and watch the birds – kittiwakes? – fly over. I need to do some proper research on the birds around here.

I'm writing this on one of the rocks near the beach. I'm dressed, my hair is wrapped in a towel and I can see, about twenty metres out from the shoreline, the heads of several seals waiting like impatient dogs. What's she doing? their twitching noses ask. Is she coming back in? Shit or get off the pot, lady.

Time for lunch.

*7.23 p.m.*

It is not an omen. It has no significance beyond the immediate impact of a sudden death on the people who witness it. I cannot let myself go down that rabbit hole.

And despite everything, it has been a good day. The impatient seals were a definite high point but so too was lunch: sardines on crackers followed by a handful of dried apricots and a mug of Cabernet Sauvignon (not a legally recognised unit of measurement). I went upstairs to my little garret bedroom and slept it off on my 1940s hospital bedstead and mattress, waking up just after three. It felt a little bit like I'd woken up in an abandoned sanatorium. All the nurses and starched uniforms gone and just me, left behind with the run of the place.

I spent the afternoon turning over the soil on the patch of land to the east of the bothy. There is another, bigger one, round the back but it's west-facing so the soil won't get much sun until evening. I thought of Alex and his PhD on ethnoarchaeology. What had he said he was doing? Analysing pH levels in the soil or something. Dull. Very dull. Was it any duller than what I am doing though? Writing about turning over soil? I crouched down and grabbed a moist, stony chunk of it, hoisting a fat, pink, wriggling worm with it. Tilly had loved the garden, she had loved pointing with wrinkled-nosed amazement at the creepy crawlies that fled – in panic – beneath her fingers.

I got up, put the tools back in the lean-to and went inside. Time for dinner.

*10.06 p.m.*

I heard a voice. A man's, judging by the depth of it. Down by Chulainn's cave.

It happened after dinner. I decided to walk up to the Neolithic stone circle, also known as Crois an fionnadh. Thirteen tall, lozenge-shaped stones standing vertical around a central flat one, known as the font stone. The monument was designated a World Heritage Site by National Trust Scotland in the early 1990s, I can't remember what year exactly and I don't feel like getting my notes out now. I want to get this recorded while it's all still fresh in my memory.

Remembering Tilly in her wellies yesterday, the worms in the garden today – it felt like an obvious place for me to go. I'd read in the library how the font stone – flat, rectangular with a long gash/crevice running from top to bottom – was where precious water collected. Lixivium, they called it. It's basically a combination of rain and sea water but the islanders believed its contact with the sky and sea transformed it into some kind of divine elixir – a deterrent to evil. Girls were anointed with it the night before their weddings, pregnant women were encouraged to rub their breasts and swollen bellies with it and mothers bathed their newborn infants in it. They believed – fervently – that the Lixivium in the font stone kept their young ones safe.

Like I said then, an obvious place for me to go.

The sun was setting, its last rays falling flat across the grass. I sat down on the end of the font stone, the whole time thinking: I'm too late. I'm six years too late. But still, something, some instinct – superstition perhaps – made me dip my fingers in the crevice and rub it between my eyebrows.

That was when I heard it. A loud, booming call that seemed to come up from the centre of the earth. I felt the stone beneath me move, buzz with transferred energy. I stood up and again, the same call but this time I was able to make out a word. It sounded like 'thall' or 'vall'. It was coming from the western side of the island.

I walked towards Ceum a'Mhaide, less than half a mile from Crois an fionnadh. By the time I reached the headland, the sun had well and truly gone down though there was still a low glow on the horizon, out to sea. I turned my torchlight on the cliff-face below, searched right and left, across the mouth of the cave, looking for a boat, a man, a loud speaker?! Ludicrous, I know, but someone made that noise. I couldn't find anything and, as the minutes passed, the darkness was becoming more and more complete.

I am writing this still wearing my boots and jacket. I haven't taken them off yet, haven't so much as rekindled the fire. The only thing I could think to do was record what I heard.

I've done that and now I'm going to bed.

*Sunday 7th May*

I woke with the sunrise again. It's strange because there are curtains on the downstairs windows but there's no blind for the Velux in the bedroom. The very room in which you need darkness. So, first thing I did this morning, even before coffee and lighting the fire, was hunt around in the lean-to for something to nail up over the window. I found some old sacking but the fibres are so loose and coarse it hardly seems worth it. I could always repurpose the curtains down here but it feels a bit drastic. And anyway, it's not like there aren't benefits to waking with the sunrise. I'm here after all, at my desk, writing these words.

'Thall' means 'over there' in Gaelic. I've just looked it up. Perhaps the voice I heard was a tour guide, someone like Daley (I'm pretty sure it wasn't Daley – shouting in Gaelic definitely isn't his style), pointing out the natural arch or the cave to a boatload of punters. Finish Island at Sunset or some such bullshit. It just felt bigger, the voice I mean. It felt deep and sonorous but perhaps I'm attaching more significance to it because of what I was doing and what I was feeling when I heard it.

Connecting to the internet was a mistake though. I've just seen the following email from Charlotte:

From: Charlotte Kinsella
To: Seren Doughty
Date: 5 May 2023 at 15:17
Subject: Fwd: Seren Doughty

Who's Alex?? Apparently he's keen to hear your thoughts . . . !

Hope the writing is going well.

C x

Begin forwarded message:

Dear Ms Kinsella,

I'm writing to ask if you would be so kind as to forward this message to Seren Doughty, who I understand from your website is one of your authors. I had the pleasure of meeting Seren last month when she was visiting the National Library of Scotland in Edinburgh. As a senior research assistant, it was my pleasure to provide her with information that will, I trust, prove essential to her written endeavours.

During the course of our acquaintance, Seren expressed an interest in reading my, as yet, unpublished novel, *The Siren Calls*. We exchanged numbers but, as I'm sure you're aware, there is no mobile phone reception on Finish Island – though I believe she may have internet access. I am keen to hear her thoughts and would be very grateful to you for passing on this message.

In the meantime, please find attached the first three chapters of the afore-mentioned novel and accompanying synopsis. I hope you enjoy it and, if you'd like to read the full manuscript, please don't hesitate to let me know.

With best wishes,
Alex Jennings

During the course of our acquaintance? A tutorial on how to search the main catalogue, coffee in the library canteen and a vegan dinner followed by self-conscious, dreary sex wasn't exactly an acquaintance that could be mapped.

His manuscript. Until last week it had been at the bottom of my rucksack, where it had been since I packed it – reluctantly – on my last morning in Edinburgh. In order to make my rucksack useful for hikes around the island I'd jettisoned everything, including his manuscript, which had fallen down the side of the box containing firewood in the alcove. I've read your book and it's my belief it would make excellent kindling.

I should reply to Charlotte. Or better still, email Alex directly – I have his email address now – tell him there will be no feedback and to please leave me alone, but I can't be bothered to think about that right now. I want to go for a swim before my porridge.

*1.47 p.m.*

My vegetable patch is really coming together. I spent the morning – or what was left of it after another long swim in the sea – planting seeds: runner beans, courgettes, carrots and tomatoes. The tomatoes are not quite done yet, I've planted up seven pots and there are five more in the lean-to but I was starting to feel tired from the early-morning start and swimming. I'm eating a bowl of pasta and butter at my desk while I write this. It feels good – the fatigue that comes from doing something. I'm going upstairs to have a little nap.

*PM*

Just dreamt of Tilly. I must get this down before I forget.

She was up at Crois an fionnadh, very close to where I'd been last night, except she wasn't alone. I was aware there were other children nearby but I didn't look at them. I didn't dare take my eyes from her. She was wearing a dark dress; it was made of heavy wool, the sections sewn together in an outdated style.

She was taller, visibly older, her hair darker at the crown, but I knew it was her. 'Tilly,' I wanted to say. 'You've come back to me.' But I didn't. I knew it was a delicate balance. Don't move, don't speak – let it play out. I hoped she would say something. I longed for her to open her mouth, to see if her milk teeth had been replaced by adult ones and what her smile was like now.

But she was distracted. She kept looking to the headland where, I could sense, the other children were waiting for her. It was now or never. If I wanted her back, I would have to do something. I opened my mouth to call her but instead of my voice and my words, the ground beneath us shook with the vibrations of that deep, booming call of 'thall'. It was not my word, it was not what I wanted. 'Over there' was a distraction I could do without. But there was no point in saying anything at all. Because she was running, they all were, a merry band of kids similar age and height to her. They were running for the headland, arms out wide, building up a momentum that would make it difficult to stop in time.

I woke up, drenched in sweat.

*Later*
It's the first time I've dreamt of her since she died. Strange, almost unbelievable but it's true. It's the reason Jamie

convinced me to see the psychotherapist who likened my grief to being pregnant with a dead baby. I agreed to see her, the psychotherapist, but I was going through the motions. I knew why I didn't dream of Tilly. I certainly had my own theory, anyway.

Tilly was burnt up in that house. And I don't just mean her body. I saw the smoke that rose up into the sky that night. I mean she was burnt up. Her essence, her spirit, the thing that made her eyes shine and her fingers clutch mine. It went up and away from me, it travelled in that white, heavy, granular smoke far, far away. I could never properly explain this to anyone. Not to my mum who was grieving a daughter and granddaughter, not to Jamie who was as dumbfounded, as devastated by the appalling details of her death as I was and certainly not the psycho- therapist who was so pleased with her own metaphors.

It was strange enough to say that I never dreamt of her but to add that it was my belief her very soul had vanished was too much for most people's sympathy. So I never talked about it. Even when our family liaison officer put us in contact with a support group for other grieving families, even as they shared their dreams – often deeply haunting; endlessly repeating the events they'd endured – I kept quiet about how my daughter's absence was so complete it had failed even to penetrate my subconscious.

*Monday 8th May, afternoon*
It's rained all day. My vegetable patch is completely water- logged, the seeds probably washed away. I've done nothing except read up on birds and sit before the fire.

*Tuesday 9th May*

Much better weather today. Still overcast but dry. Sunset is at 9.24 p.m. this evening. I plan to go up to Crois an fionnadh again. See if I can't hear that voice again. I'll take my notebook with me. Also, a torch. Probably a good idea to light a couple of oil burners and leave the curtains open – make the bothy more of a beacon in the dark.

*9.20 p.m.*

Fucking midges are out in force tonight. There's no rhyme nor reason for it. The other night, the night I heard the voice, there were none and tonight, now, they're dancing around my pen. Of course I forgot to spray myself.

No voice. Going home before I get eaten alive.

*PM*

Someone has been in here. I know it. My things – pens, laptop, notebook – they look like they've been moved around. I don't know what to do, what to make of it. Could the boatman have come looking for me? But there was no boat tonight and no call either.

But there is something else. Something that has unnerved me. As I approached the bothy, on my way back, I noticed the curtains were closed.

I left them open. I know I did that. It's written here, just above this entry, that I'll '. . . leave the curtains open. . .'.

And then there's the OS map. It's not folded up like it was. Someone has opened it and then hastily tried to force it back between the cardboard covers.

I've just opened it up, spread it flat on my desk. Instinctively, I looked for the Finamuil sea stack and there, above it, pressed hard into the blue of the Finish Sound is a big, heavy-handed: X.

*Thursday 11th May*

I don't know what I was thinking. The whole curtains-closed-curtains-open thing and the weird cross on the OS map. I'm actually ashamed to read back what I wrote on Tuesday night. I think it's being alone. It's almost a week since Daley left me here and I'm not used to it. I thought, mostly because I've lived alone since my divorce, that I'd be used to it or, at the very least, better able to cope but this is different. It's silence and yet it isn't. Because you can hear the wind and the waves and the birds calling. It's not quiet. There is sound. But the absence of human voices and sounds that make sense, that is unnerving after a while. It also means, I'm guessing, that the voice inside my head has got louder. And it doesn't always make perfect sense. I think that's what makes this journal so important. It's beneficial to externalise my thoughts and impressions. And right now, it would appear, I'm all about phantom boatmen coming into the bothy and doodling on my map.

Of course, it's obvious. The cross is exactly where I thought the booming call came from. I must have written it myself and just – just not remembered.

Anyway, Daley is due. Probably today or tomorrow. I need to get my shit together. I'm going up to the stream to wash my knickers.

*11.29 a.m.*

I slipped and fell at the stream. Nothing serious, I haven't actually injured myself – just a very bruised arse.

The stream is about half a mile north-west of the bothy, at the base of Cnoc fiacail. The ground around it is green and boggy, peppered with rocks and stones. I took my clothes off but, because the wind had risen since this morning, pinned them under a rock. I stepped down the rocky banks until my feet were covered by the shallow margins on the stream. Further in, the water runs deep and there's a spot, right in the middle, where you can sit down and the water will come right up to your collarbone. That's what I was heading for when I heard a scream. High-pitched, it rang through the air. It came from behind me, from the rocks that skirt the base of Cnoc fiacail.

I swung around but lost my footing and landed heavily on a jagged rock on the stream bed. I think I must have cried out because a second or two later, a bird – a guillemot, I think – flew overhead. It came from behind me, from the rocks, unleashing, as it went, the same high-pitched, staccato scream I'd just heard.

I should have known. I've been using what few kilowatt hours are available in the battery to read up on birds. Finish is known for its guillemot nests, built on the rocky western cliffs. Those sides offer very little in the way of foothold or landing place and many islanders – young ones included with their small agile limbs – fell to their deaths in an attempt to capture the eggs.

Something else I read: female guillemots sacrifice themselves to hunters; they go willingly into the net in order that their hatchlings might survive.

The maternal coda.

I washed my hair, felt the bubbles skim my forearms as they travelled downstream with all the other dirt, dry skin and bacteria. The water is seriously cold but you feel seriously good afterwards.

It's hard not to feel disheartened. I've learnt a bit about birds, I've described a few sunsets but most of my writing this week has been about how cold the water is and how hard it is to dig a vegetable patch. Groundbreaking stuff. Christ, I'm resorting to puns now. I need to do more. Go further. And I would do, except my bum hurts and I need to get these knickers dry.

*Friday 12th May*

Daley's coming today. That was my first thought as I took a shit this morning. It's been a week and I'm down to my last toilet roll. I could always cut the sacking I found in the lean-to into squares and wipe my arse with those. Or, of course, there's always the stream or the sea but it would be nice to open my bowels without having to then wash in freezing cold water.

I also forgot to buy sanitary towels. It was all such a rush that morning in Castlebay: pulling things from the shelves in the Co-op before returning to the guesthouse for breakfast and checking out. I packed a bloody potato peeler and book of crossword puzzles but no towels. When I imagined life on Finish alone, I saw solitude, time to reflect, uninterrupted hours of writing. What I didn't foresee was an attractive Australian visiting every week to ten days or having to explain to him how all the dried apricots and mixed nuts meant I was getting through the toilet roll at an alarming rate or – better still – that I had very heavy periods and would he mind picking up a few packets of the super maxi plus for me?

I had a quick wash in the sea (body up to armpits) and then back here for breakfast. I went through my clothes, sniffing for a passable T-shirt. I should have taken a bag of clothes up to the stream yesterday.

I used the camera on my laptop to apply some eyeliner, mascara and, I hesitated before smearing it on, lip gloss. I rubbed my lips together so that they became pink and sparkly. Ridiculous move. In the background, the iron fender, the stone flags – all strong, solid, functional things. I was sitting in a building that had been constructed with the sole purpose of educating the island's children; a place that stood for learning, for pupils who arrived at the door barefoot and eager to return to the sheep shearing or peat cutting or whatever task was most pressing at that particular time of the year and yet, there I was, smearing a product full of lanolin – the very thing they worked hard to harvest from their wool – for no reason other than the fact I'd like to make my lips look plump and sparkly for some bloke I'd quite like to fuck. No. I rubbed the back of my hand across my mouth and felt, there was that word again, ashamed.

What's wrong with me?

*Later*

I was down at the beach, waiting for him. He sounded the horn and waved as he got closer, which made me feel a bit shy. I literally haven't spoken in days. I coughed to check my voice still worked. What would I say? How's it going? I rehearsed speaking. In the bone-dry morning air, the words came out with an Australian twang. He'd think I was taking the piss. No, better stay quiet until he speaks. 'How're you going?' he asked, handing me one of the large shopping bags.

'Good. Yes, good.'

'Managing OK?'

'I think so.'

'What you been doing?'

'Writing. Gardening,' I remembered with sudden enthusiasm.

'Good work.'

'Yes, except it pissed down the day after I sowed my seeds. But I've got a few shoots. I need to make climbers for them. Squash and carrots too. Fully organic. You'll have to come for dinner and try them.'

I felt him turn to look at me as we walked up the dunes.

'When they grow, I mean,' I added.

'Sounds good. What else you been up to?'

'Err, sunsets. I've been up Crois an fionnadh a few times at sunset. Did I say it right?'

'The stone circle? Ah yeah, it's beautiful up there. Treacherous in the dark though – you've been taking your torch with you?'

'Yep,' I nodded, opening the bothy door.

He followed me inside and we put our bags on the table.

'Have you got time for a coffee? Or,' I laughed, too loudly, 'I should say: have you brought any coffee?'

'Yeah. It's in this one here,' he said, tapping the side of the bag he'd just put down. 'You OK?'

'Completely,' I dug around in the bag, found the packet and then proceeded to hack into it with a knife. I took a deep lungful and sighed. 'Oh my god,' I said, holding it out to him. Except I misjudged the distance between us and brushed his nostrils with the torn fragments of the packet. He pulled his head back. 'Yeah, it's nice.'

'Sorry. I'm just excited to see someone.'

'You been filling up the water containers OK?'

'Yes. Yep,' I nodded, spooning coffee grains into the percolator. 'I went up only this morning in fact.'

'And you're using the purification tablets?'

'Yes. Why, do I sound like I'm not?' I laughed.

'You're a bit – well, jumpy.'

'I'm just pleased to see – someone. Turns out, a week on your own is a long time.'

'What's going on?'

'Let me make these coffees and I'll tell you.'


'It must have been a horn from a nearby boat.' This time he was sitting in the rocking chair with the OS map on his lap and I was in my desk chair. He'd lit the fire while I made coffee.

'Except there was no boat. Not that I could see anyway.'

'You wouldn't be able to see a boat under the arch from the Ceum a'Mhaide headland.'

'And it wasn't a horn. It was a word. I heard "thall".'

'People still speak Gaelic in these parts. It's not unusual to hear words like that shouted out. You said it was a calm evening?'

'It was actually, it was lovely.'

'That'll be it then. That's like 101 for boat tours here. I'm telling you. A sunset stop at the natural arch. The tourists love it. That's what you heard.'

This was good. He was backing up everything I'd told myself.

'And the map?' He looked down at his lap. I hadn't refolded it since spotting the cross. 'God knows how many passengers have borrowed this,' he said, lifting it up. 'I could have made this mark myself. Are you getting enough sleep?'

'Yes. I mean, I'm waking early, with the sunrise but I'm not sleeping badly.'

'Listen, the loneliness – it can be hard. Harder than people think. What about coming back to Castlebay for a few days? I'm sure Rosalie would put you up.'

I remembered Kathleen's cries the night before I left. 'No, I'm fine. I'm good. It helps actually, to say all this stuff out loud. Plus, I'm making good progress with my writing,' I lied.

'What exactly is it you're writing?' he rocked forward, the soles of his boots landing flat on the stone flags.

'At the moment, journal entries. But the ultimate plan is to write a ghost story.'

'Banshees and all that stuff Linda was spouting?'

'No, nothing like that. I'm more interested in the history of the island, the massacre and the role of Chulainn, for example. All of that strikes me as a good foundation for a tale of the supernatural.'

'All the more reason to come back with me today. Speak to my Aunty Kitty. She'll be able to tell you much more than I can.'

I thought about those clouded eyes of hers, circling as I spoke. I shook my head, 'I need to stay here. The whole point of this project was for me to be alone, explore the island, record my experiences in the kind of detail that might reveal a way in.'

'Whatever floats your boat but just remember, you can always send me a message. If you've had enough, like, or need a break. Oh, before I forget,' he rocked forward again and half stood so he could reach into his back pocket. 'Rosalie asked me to give this to you.'

It was a letter, addressed to the manager of the Bayview Guesthouse, Castlebay. 'What's this?'

'One of your mates, I think. Looking to get a hold of you.'

Dear Seren,

Please forgive the scattergun approach. I have tried, unsuccessfully, to get in touch with you by other, more direct, means.

I understand you are busy and I really don't mean to take up too much of your time but I wanted to let you know that I've had some very encouraging comments from various literary agents about my book.

One in particular has commended my writing style and asked to read the full manuscript. With that in mind, I'd really appreciate your feedback. Certainly a few pointers on where it could be improved would be very helpful.

I trust you have my contact details but, just in case, please find them below. It goes without saying, I would very much like to hear from you.

In the meantime, I hope all is going well on Finish Island and that your writing is proving fruitful.

With very best wishes,
Alex

I balled it up and threw it on the fire.

*Saturday 13th May, late morning*
Woke up this morning with an uncontrollable urge to clean the bothy. It helps that it's pissing with rain outside.

I stripped down to my underwear and started scrubbing. I wiped the walls down with a bowl of soapy water, swept up ash, mud, bits of glass, dust, fingernails and god knows what else – all the detritus that has accumulated on the floor, in the corners, on the window sills since the bothy was built, probably. It could have been Daley's offer to take me back to Castlebay, his concern that I wasn't coping or maybe it was the writer in me procrastinating (I better just scrub this bit of grout between the flags before I write another sentence) that drove me to my hands and knees this morning but, whatever the reason, I feel pretty good now.

The bothy is clean, my vegetables are growing, I have a kitchen full of supplies thanks to Daley so there's no excuse. I need to write something. Make some attempt at a plot.

The rain has stopped and I can see some blue in the distance. I'll have some lunch, perhaps a little sleep and then, if this weather holds, I'll go visit the cave.

*6 p.m.*

I'm sitting on the rocky ledge at the bottom of the western cliffs. In front of me, on the other side of the exposed shingle beach is the Finamuil sea stack and the long vulva-like opening of Chulainn's cave.

It's windy down here. The distance between Finamuil and Finish, which (presumably) didn't exist once upon a time creates a kind of wind tunnel. The pages of my notebook keep lifting and flapping as I try to write this.

I can cross over. I should cross over.

The tide is out and there are only a few inches of water above the rocks.

The drop in temperature is sudden and shocking. It is total: this movement from the outside to the inside. With the light from my head torch I can see the walls are made up of what look like long striated spears, I guess, for want of a better word. Their points converge at some distant apex in the darkness above me. It reminds me of the sword display in the feasting room of Kisimul Castle.

Water drips regularly, rhythmically, somewhere in the back of the cave. I have found a kind of seat, a bench really. It feels like it has been carved out of the wall. It's quite comfortable. I guess this is where they might have sat, the islanders who hid in the cave, awaiting their fate at the hands of clan MacNeil. How long were they down here? Unimaginable. The fear, hiding from someone you know means you harm.

I'm sitting on something. A small rock or stone. Or perhaps a twig. I reach behind me. It's small and tubular. Up close and under the glare of my head torch, it looks like a bone. I put it against my little finger. It's exactly the same length as one of the small phalanges there. Could it be? A lot of people died in here.

Impossible not to think of Tilly. Of her hiding in the wardrobe. I need some air.

The tide. The inches of water I walked through earlier was the tide coming in, not out. The Finish Sound has risen up, it's right up at the mouth of the cave and I'm worried if I make an attempt to swim across I'll get swept away, like Daley warned. Shit. What's wrong with me? I don't know enough about wild places like this. I don't know bird names or bloody tidal times or even when to spray myself with midge repellent. Choose a deserted setting, isolated, far from anyone else, Tess had said. And I'd nodded along. All very easy when you're eating fishcakes in a Soho restaurant but the truth is, you can't just have a go at this. You need to know things.

And then there's Tilly. Dreams and memories that are painful, so painful. They stop my breath.

I have no idea how long I'll be here. Hours? The whole thing is completely batshit. I better turn my torch off, save the battery.

Woken by noises. They're coming from the other side of the cave. An animal? The tide is still high. I need to calm down.

Just heard it again. It's the sound of someone shifting position on the dusty ground. Limbs moving. Not wings or paws but limbs. The boatman? 'Is somebody there?' My voice sounds strange to me – trembly and uncertain.

Nothing. No answer but also, no more sounds of movement. If I hear it again I'm going to take my chances in the water. I don't think my heart can take any more of this.

Movement again. This time closer. Something is coming closer. And then a long, slow exhale—

*5 a.m.*

How to describe what just happened. I need to. I know I need to. But I'm afraid. Afraid that if I write it down then I also acknowledge it as truth. And from where I'm sitting right now, alone in this bothy (albeit with the fire ablaze and every candle and oil burner lit) that really is terrifying.

I can't bring myself to write it.

I got out of there. I grabbed whatever came to hand – this notebook, my torch, thank god I didn't take my boots off – and I crawled as fast as I could towards the opening. I feared whatever had been moving and breathing in that cave with me would follow and maybe it did but I wasn't about to look behind me for confirmation. No, I kept my face forward, my eyes trained on any sliver of light, any perceptible lifting of the pitch black that might lead me out.

It was the glimmer of moonlight on the Finish cliff-face, the gneiss rock washed bright and gleaming by the waves from the sound, that finally caught my attention. I scrabbled through the dirt, passed the opening and launched myself, expecting to meet water, onto the hard shingle of the beach that separates the Finamuil sea stack from the island. I had no idea of the time or how many hours had passed since I last looked out of the cave – all I knew was that the tide had been and now it was gone. I could go home.

Still can't sleep. There's something else. Something I'm fearful of recording here.

After the exhale. I heard it. Whispered, raspy. A female voice. She said just one word.

Fan.

### Monday 15th May

Yesterday was a write-off. It rained the whole day. I did nothing, wrote nothing. I managed a few crackers and an apple at lunchtime and then fell asleep in the rocking chair, in front of the fire just after six. I woke up aching and sore a few hours later and took myself upstairs to bed.

But this morning, waking up in my bed, under my corrugated iron roof, I find myself thinking of a girl I once knew, called Ash.

We were friends, briefly, when I was fourteen. Her full name was Haight Ashbury but, for obvious reasons, she went by Ash. Her mum was a hippy, a kind of cartoon stoner: fervent anti-vaxxer long before it was fashionable. They lived in a communal squat a few roads away from my secondary school. Ash was only in my form for a few terms.

I remembered that her mum's favourite book was Khalil Gibran's *The Prophet*. I was fourteen, self-conscious and keen to model what I saw as a more truthful, honest way of existing. I had grown critical of my parents; I wanted to be different, to wash in just water, to eat no meat and do no harm, to tread lightly and carry a book full of moral parables around with me wherever I went.

My parents accepted the friendship with easy tolerance but I didn't like her to come to my house. I was embarrassed, naturally, by their comfortable, conventional lives – even Alana's devotion to Janet Jackson filled me with shame.

Ours was a short-lived friendship. In the September of Year 11, Ash's mum heard about a new commune up near the Cairngorms and, without any notice – without so much as a goodbye – they packed up and left. Naturally we didn't stay in touch. It was 1994 and she had no actual address. I didn't hear from Ash for years; we'd had a brief kiss in my first year of university, when we'd found ourselves, drunk and elated on coincidence, in the same student union bar at Nottingham University. But that was it.

And then, on the day of Tilly's funeral, she sent me a copy of *The Prophet*. It was conspicuous, a book-shaped package among all the flowers and teddy bears. The story had dominated the local news and appeared – albeit briefly – in the national media as well so obviously she knew what had happened.

Ash had marked the chapter on Joy and Sorrow with a little Post-it note and written one word at the top, underlined twice. Light.

The chapter had nothing to do with light. It was about how you can only know joy because you've known sorrow and vice versa. I knew all that. I'd read it several times as a teenager and, more to the point, I knew – more than anyone – that Tilly had been my deepest joy and her dead body the only sorrow that would ever matter. But I remembered that word. Light. And for a long time, I just thought Ash hadn't read the chapter properly. It even annoyed me, the lack of attention, the misnomer. But it remained in my memory – pretty much the only thing that did from the messages and gifts of that time.

But Saturday night. In the cave. The relief I felt at emerging from the darkness of the cave into the bright light of the moon. The delirium of escape – it was undiluted. It was pure. It was light, underlined twice.

*Wednesday 17th May*
Weather still awful. Torrential rain since Monday. I found a few thumbtacks pressed into the plywood work surface in the kitchen which I used upstairs to fix the sacking across the window. It's worked – a bit. It's certainly dimmer up there now and this morning I slept past seven but difficult to call the venture a success given how grey the sky is.

I also did a few crossword puzzles and finished one of the paperbacks I bought in Edinburgh. Hoping for better weather tomorrow but can't check as there's been no sunshine and very little wind.

Just read the above. What the fuck am I doing? I need to write a novel.

*Thursday 18th May*

Clear skies. Finally, some juice for the battery.

First thing I did was look up the word Fan. It means 'stay' in Gaelic.

Am I losing my mind? Is it madness that before I've had a wee or put on any clothes, I am downstairs on all fours, breasts swinging, searching for the cable to connect my laptop to the battery? Is it crazy to sit with your bare arse cheeks on a chair, shivering with the urge to empty your bladder, praying there is enough power to connect to the internet just so you can type three letters into a Gaelic–English dictionary?

She asked me to stay.

*Evening*

I had been asleep. At some point during my time in that cave, I was deeply asleep. I know that because I didn't realise the tide had gone back out, I wasn't aware of the hours that had slipped by. So, it follows that what I thought was a voice was really just a dream. I've been having pretty vivid dreams since I arrived on the island, after all.

*2 a.m.*

But I heard something move, several times. And each time, it sounded like someone shifting their weight, getting more comfortable.

I need to stop thinking about this. I'm going to drive myself mad.

*Friday 19th May, morning*

Bit of a late breakfast this morning. I've made my porridge but it's still too hot so I've left it cooling on the desk beside me. Like Goldilocks. I can't imagine Goldilocks sitting down to her morning pages with any regularity. Too impulsive a character. Too attached to comfort.

I read *The Artist's Way* back in 2013, when I was trying to write *Indigo Flames*. I was desperate for inspiration, for some steer on what the hell I should be doing with a character I felt no sympathy for any more and I remember feeling encouraged by the idea that all you have to do is get up and write two pages first thing – when you're still a little wild from sleep. It was an easy prescription: take these pills, apply this cream, write two pages every day.

I haven't followed instructions. I'm late to my desk this morning because I've already been out to my vegetable patch but ten lines of writing are better than none.

The good news is that my runner beans have finally sprouted. Delicate green leaves – veined, like foetal hands reaching up to the sky. I've found some bamboo sticks in the lean-to so when they're a bit taller, I'll make some A-frames for them to climb. String, actually – have I got string? Another thing for the list. My carrots have also emerged, many more of them than I imagined and just more – confident? Can you say that about a carrot? That they are a more confident vegetable than the timid runner bean?

The squash and courgettes need very little from me but still, I pruned a few of the dead leaves away.

It feels good to be busy.

*Afternoon*

I just went to tear a page from my notebook. I wanted to write a shopping list for Daley – he should be coming in a day or two, especially now the weather has improved – when I saw two names, written on a random blank page.

Ruaridh and Catriona.

Written in the same Bic biro ink, all caps. I don't know a Ruaridh and Catriona or Rory and Catrina, even.

I bought the notebook in a WHSmith in Edinburgh. Perhaps someone – boyfriend and girlfriend, brother and sister – was trying a pen out?


*9 p.m., ish*

I need to go back to the cave and get my torch and rucksack. Not right now. Obviously. I've felt my grip on sanity slip a little during the last few days but not enough to convince me crawling back into Chulainn's cave in the dead of night is a good idea. Could I ask Daley? But then, how would I explain the fact that I'd left them there in the first place?

I'm worried he'll suggest I return to Castlebay again. The thing is, despite it all, the strange noises, the dreams, the unexplained marks on my OS map, my notebook . . . I don't want to leave.

I can feel myself changing. I don't mean I'm on a 'journey' or that I anticipate these entries will be valuable in any commercial (or even publishable) way, I just mean I'm remembering things, picking up memories I've long neglected, thinking about Tilly and Jamie in a way that felt impossible just a few short weeks ago.

*2 a.m.*

Why would you write two names though? If you're trying out a pen, would you really write out two names, all in capitals? Surely you'd do a loop, a scrawl, a signature? Something that allows you to test the ink properly?

*Sunday 21st May*

I slept late. It's gone nine. The sacking is clearly working though I'm a bit annoyed with myself as I wanted to go and have a wash up at the stream. Daley coming today. If I skip breakfast, I can probably fit it in.

*4 p.m.*

He brought me flowers! Well, not flowers but seeds. Verbena. 'I thought you could do with a little colour in your garden,' he said, holding the packet out to me. Even the presence of the packet, with its bright pink, white and purple flowers, immediately brightened up the drab grey and brown of the bothy. 'They'll draw the bees and butterflies too, which I thought you might like.' His hair, I noticed, has grown longer. He's looking more and more like Brad-off-*Neighbours* – I wonder if he's intuited the image in my head.

I made coffee and we sat before the fire and talked about life in Castlebay. Kathleen's doctor has given her new medication to try to help her sleep through the night; Olena is doing the lunch shift on her own now. I nodded my head and pretended to have an active interest in the comings and goings of the Bayview Guesthouse.

'Have you got a seed tray?' he asked, taking his empty coffee cup over to the table.

'I saw one in the lean-to. Shall I go and get it?'

'Yeah, I reckon I've got time to plant them up. If you want me to?'

'Yes,' I swallowed. It was hard to disguise my happiness but I felt I should. Daley is not a man for extremes of emotion. 'That would be great.'

Outside, he got to work, carefully spooning the compost into the compartments of the seed tray with his fingers while I weeded. Maybe it was because we were both busy, working side-by-side and not facing one another, that he opened up and started telling me about the wife in Port Lincoln. 'I don't know what I was thinking,' he concluded.

'About getting married?'

'We didn't even like each other that much. Used to fight all the time.' He stood up. 'Do you mind if I smoke?' He searched in one of his many pockets and pulled out a packet of tobacco.

'Go ahead.'

He rolled a cigarette, put it to his lips and lit it. 'The sex was pretty good,' he said after a deep inhale, 'but it wasn't a good relationship, you know?'

'Can I have one of those?'

'Have this one if you like?' A surprisingly intimate thing, sharing a cigarette with someone, putting your mouth where theirs has been. I held out my fingers, took my first puff while he rolled another for himself. The mention of sex and the now companionable silence while I waited for him had altered something.

'Did you have kids?' I asked.

'Nah. No way. I knew that would be the end. I'd never get out. It was like I was on a bloody big boat and

I knew, I knew if we dropped that anchor, I'd be stuck. Does that make sense?'

'That you'd use a boating metaphor, yes absolutely.'

'What about you?' he asked on a strangled exhale. 'Never wanted kids?'

'I had a daughter,' I said, squinting at the stonework of the bothy.

'Ah, man. I'm sorry.'

I shook my head. 'It's OK. It's a logical question to ask. I started it – by asking you.'

'Do you want to tell me what happened?'

'Not really.'

'No problem. Hey—'

'Not because I don't want to talk about her. That's not – that's not what's going on here.'

Another long silence grew. It reached up from the soil between us, like the tender green runner beans that I loved and cared for, disproportionately.

What is going on here? That was the question. But neither one of us was quite ready to ask it.


*7 p.m.*

I've had dinner early because I didn't have any lunch. Daley was here and it didn't cross my mind to make lunch. What would I have offered him anyway? Sardines on crackers? Or, a recent speciality of mine, sardines and penne? I was starving by the time he left.

It's like a virus. That first attraction to someone. It's like that first tingle in the back of your throat, that tells you – with absolute certainty – you're going to get ill. And it's pleasurable, cold or fancying someone, because – when it comes down to it – it feels good to submit. You know what's coming, there's no avoiding it so you may as well relax and let it happen.

*Monday 22nd May*

I was woken by a knock at the door. I don't know what time but the sun was properly up.

I put a T-shirt on over my knickers and there he was, on the doorstep. Sunglasses hanging from a string around his neck, khaki shorts, black T-shirt and a completely straight face. No smile, no words. He just looked at me. I must have stepped back to let him in, I must have done. Because then he was really close, his boots next to my bare feet and his hands under my arms and round my back. I kissed him back, of course I did, only stopping to let him pull my T-shirt off.

He smelt so good. Shower gel and fresh air. I took his hand and led him upstairs, his other hand on my lower back all the way up.

*Tuesday 30th May, 8 a.m.*

I'm supposed to be writing a novel. That was the brief. Write about a character who has to get on top of internal pain in order to respond to the forces without. I'm going to have some breakfast and then I'll go write up at the top of Cnoc fiacail. I will write a few chapters if it kills me. And if it's boring as shit? So be it.

It's been a week of glorious sex. Thank god for all the people who want to visit the Outer Hebrides. Yesterday it was a family of four from Stockport and today I think he said he's got a boatload of Japanese students who have travelled up from Cambridge.

Cnoc fiacail is the highest point on Finish. From up here I can see right across the island, the white sandy crescent of the beach – like a fallen moon – and then, right at the other (southern) end of the island, the stones of Crois an fionnadh and the Ceum a'Mhaide headland.

There are too many people for one trip in the dinghy. I can see he's left some of them waiting in the *Spes Secunda* while he motors the first lot over. They're all wearing red and orange lifejackets and watching them climb over the rocks on their hands and feet makes me think of a cast of crabs. This is my problem in a nutshell. Forget ghosts and spirits, my interest is in people. Real, living people who remind me of crabs.

He will come looking for me. That's been our MO in the last week. He brings people to the island, tells them a time to meet back at the rocks and then he makes his way up to me in the bothy.

I could stay here. I could attempt some opening description of the bay, the seals strung like sausages across the damp sand, but the second group are in the dinghy now.

*Saturday 3rd June*
Six years on, it's a Saturday again. I don't know enough about leap years and how this affects the pattern of days and dates, I only know it was a Saturday then and it's a Saturday now.

We spent the day in Edinburgh, shopping for a new water bottle and then lunch in Pizza Express. I offered to stay but she was adamant: 'I want to sleep at Aunty Lana's on my own.'

I should have been more forceful. I should have gone with my instinct. But I swallowed it down. I didn't want to upset Alana or disappoint Tilly. 'OK, Buzzy,' I said.

I said OK and lost everything.

*Afternoon, sometime*

How can that be? How can it be that one moment, one decision, one OK can blight your entire life forever? Because it has. It absolutely has. There is no getting away from that. It doesn't matter what happens now, what diversion there is to be had with Daley, what plot outline or opening paragraphs I write for this book, my life – my real life – ended on a Saturday in June in 2017.

Nothing will ever matter again because all I'm doing is waiting for the day when I join her. I don't mean some blessed tableau in which we eventually meet and hold hands and walk off together. I mean do the same. Pass through the same process and leave this life.

*Early hours*

About an hour after I wrote the above, I heard Daley's boat in the bay. He's asleep upstairs right now. Our first night together and always the worst day in any year for me. It felt like a test. The timing. Like, I just had to pull myself together and become public-facing Seren again.

I've just made myself some coffee. I can't sleep. Not least because the bed is too narrow for both of us but also because my mind is full. I keep thinking of Tilly and then, inexplicably, Chulainn. It's like the two of them are connected in some way. What did she do to have the cave named after her? What did she withstand in service to those children?

On my desk, as I write this, the small finger bone I found in the cave.

If only bones could speak.

*Sunday 4th June, after lunch*
He held it between his fingers as carefully as you would a small vial. 'Where'd you get this?'

'In Chulainn's cave.'

'What were you doing down there?'

'I thought the atmosphere or the mood of the place might kick something off.'

'And?'

'And I shit my pants and left most of my stuff behind.'

He wasn't looking at me any more. He was sniffing the bone. 'Difficult to say where it comes from.'

'But a finger maybe? It's the same size as this,' I said, placing it alongside the phalange of my little finger.

'You need an expert. I'm no expert.'

'But it could be? From the massacre?'

'Could be. Hard to say but, yeah, it could be. A lot of people died down there.'

'What happened to the other remains?'

'Whatever was found in the cave was gathered up just before Finish was finally abandoned. Aunty Kitty thinks they were interred in the graveyard. Under Chulainn's headstone. The great big one that faces out to sea.'

'I should go and have a look at that.'

'Just make sure you go during the day.'

'You think I found something they missed?'

'It's possible.'

'Why did they do it?'

'Stop trophy hunters.'

'No, sorry – the massacre. Why did the MacNeil men come here and kill everyone in the first place?'

'Nobody knows for sure. But the story goes that the people of Finish sent the firstborn son of MacNeil of Barra back to him in a boat. He'd come to the island unannounced, did something he shouldn't – I don't know for sure – and the islanders caught up with him. Broke every bone in his body. Then, when they'd done that, they threw him in a boat and kicked it away without any oars.'

'They wanted him to die slowly?'

'Yeah, except – you got the map?'

'On the desk.'

He got up from where we were sitting at the table, walked over to my desk and returned with the map. I hadn't looked at it since the last time he was here. I got up and joined him on his side of the table.

His index finger was on top of the Finamuil sea stack, very close to the cross. 'If you launch a boat here, in the Finish Sound, there's a slope current that'll draw—'

'What's a slope current?'

'It's a kind of flow, a drift, that draws warm water northwards. The speed of it decreases in deeper water but here, near the shore, it would have been quite fast.'

'So, the slow death was not to be?'

'I mean, he would have been in pain no matter where he ended up. But the islanders might have supposed he'd drift out this way—' he moved his finger westwards in the direction of Greenland and that's when I saw it. Something so unexpected, so unaccountable. I can still feel the shock of it now.

'But in fact the slope current took him up north towards Kisimul,' Daley continued, oblivious, his finger moving again. 'Unfortunately, for the people of Finish, he drifted to his family at the castle – in time to tell them what had happened. Their fate was sealed really, from that point. You don't come back from torturing the son of a MacNeil. You OK?'

'Yes.'

'You look upset.'

'No, I'm OK. Just tired. And it's grisly, isn't it? All this talk of bones and torture.'

'Stick to the here and now, I'd say. Much less complicated.'

I tried to laugh. I must have been reasonably successful because he started gathering up his things, saying he'd be back mid-week. I nodded, helped him find his keys, his sunglasses and did my very best to pretend I hadn't seen what I had.

A cross. Another one. On top of the cave this time.

*Wednesday 7th June*
A puppy. From Rosalie's dog's litter. I can't bring myself to write bitch. Some people – horsey types, vets, farmers – they can pull off that kind of gender noun but not me.

Daley found me up at the stream this morning where I was washing myself. It was still too early to be warm but the sun was there, performing a reluctant fanfare behind thin clouds. Enough to convince me I could sit down on the rocky bed and soap up my armpits.

'G'day.'

I hadn't seen his boat in the bay, hadn't heard him approach above the sound of the flowing water and the squawking gulls. I gasped, shifted deeper into the stream and then gave a little cry as the cold water closed around my throat. 'Sorry, mate. Didn't mean to creep up on you like that.' Mate? 'I want you to meet someone.'

He was holding a small, black furry thing in his arms. 'What's that?'

It curled closer to him, nestling against his peppermint polo shirt as he crouched down on the bank. 'She's one of Carla's, Rosalie's bitch. Nine weeks.'

I felt too naked and stuck for this conversation. My nipples resembled the hard pebbles between my toes. 'Could you pass me that towel over there?'

He stood up but didn't look away as I dried myself with the towel. I decided not to run it between my legs. 'Are you adopting it?'

'Her. She's a lady. No, not me.'

'Daley—'

'You need company.'

'I don't need company. Please don't tell me what I need.'

'I've got a stack of puppy food with me.'

'I don't want a puppy.'

'You'll change your mind when you get to know her. She's a sweetheart, aren't you?' he said, rubbing his nose against the top of her head.

'I don't know how to look after a dog.'

'You feed her, stroke her, talk to her and when she's a bit bigger you take her for long walks.'

'I didn't ask for this,' I said, the panic rising. What I wanted to say: I can't look after small, vulnerable beings. I'm not good at it.

'Loneliness is your enemy here, I'm telling you. I've seen it. Writers, artists like you, they think they can cope, they look forward to it, but then, before you know it, they get scared, or paranoid, start thinking too much about the past, leaving all their stuff in caves.'

'But I'm not lonely. I have you.'

'I can't be here all the time. And come August, when the kids go back to school, I won't be here as much. But Beau here—'

'Beau? That's her name?'

'That's a name. I think it's cute.'

I reached out and touched the top of her head with my fingers. Her fur was unutterably, indescribably soft. 'Why Beau?'

'It means cow in Gaelic. They loved their cows on this island. Slept with them in winter.'

'I cannot imagine sharing the bothy with a cow.'

'In French—,' he continued, 'in French, it means beautiful. And she is a beaut. Don't you think?'

'Daley . . .'

'What?'

'I don't like it when things are forced on me.' I picked up my knickers and pulled them on.

'Hey, I get it. If you don't want a dog when you leave here, that's fine. I'll have her. No worries.'

I shook my head as I dried under my arms.

'Let's get her back to the bothy. You'll change your mind when you see how much nicer it is having her with you.'

'Are you staying for lunch?'

*Evening*

It's not like I haven't been thinking of that second cross. I have. It just strikes me that there's a choice to be made here. I could tell myself that cross was hard-handed onto the map by the unquiet spirit of Chulainn or the ghost of one of the children murdered on this island but if I do that, if I go down that path, not only do I join the ranks of Linda and Elspeth at National Trust Scotland with their whispered, theatrical, eyes-wide-tale-telling, but I will also – realistically – number my days here.

And the truth is, I like it here. I've had the best day of my life today. By life, of course I mean life-after-Tilly. I want more days like today. I can only get that if I'm prepared to put thoughts of that cross from my mind.

And there's also the small matter of the ghost story I've been paid to write.

We walked back to the bothy together. He held Beau in his arms so carefully, so lovingly, I found myself wondering – albeit very briefly – if it was too late for us. I am forty-two. Unlikely but not impossible. He told me about how he works part-time from August, when the summer holidays are over and bookings drop off, as a labourer for a builder he knows in Castlebay. He does as many repairs to roofs, walls and windows as he can before the end of November when any work undertaken has to be internal. 'Don't you miss home?' I asked him. 'This is lovely and everything but Barra in the winter – it's pretty bleak, I'm guessing.'

'If you want the rainbow, you've gotta put up with the rain – Dolly Parton.'

'Can't you enjoy the rainbow and then just board a Qantas Flight? Have the best of both worlds?'

'If you're Russell Crowe or Hugh Jackman. Not if you're barely breaking even on boat rides and fixing soil pipes for lollies. Thing is I didn't intend to stay here as long as I have. After things with Tanya went south, I thought I'd come over and see what it was all about. Mum had talked about life on Barra for such a long time and I knew Rosie and Aunty Kitty were here so I had family but then Covid hit and I couldn't have gone home even if I'd wanted to.'

Back at the bothy, he baulked at the tin of tuna I produced. 'Hasn't anyone ever taught you to fish?'

'Why fish when you get regular deliveries of tuna?'

'You live on an island in the Outer Hebrides. You're surrounded by fish. What about some flounder?'

'I'm a writer,' I countered. 'And before that I worked in a bank. I have never been fishing. I have no idea how to fish.'

'There's no time like the present.' Beau looked up in alarm as he handed her to me. 'Back in a bit.'

He was gone for around forty minutes. When he returned, he was carrying a bamboo fishing rod, the little guide holes for the line looked glued on. 'Did you make that yourself?'

'My old man wouldn't buy a fishing rod. We always made our own.'

'Is he—?'

'A tight arsehole? Yes.'

'No, dead. You talked about him in the past tense.'

'Mum won't let him die. It's not like he hasn't tried. He's had lymphoma, a hip replacement and last year he had a fight with a western brown.'

'What's a western brown?'

'Snake. For flounder, you need to roll your seagull feathers.'

'My thoughts exactly.'

He looked at me and then down at Beau, who was curled up in my lap. 'We've got our work cut out here, mate.' I smiled, happy that Beau was a mate too.

Down at the rocks, I couldn't help but notice how much fitter and more rugged he looked, casting the line out. The lines I'd noticed as I lay next to him in bed, the deep cuts that fanned out from his eyes when he smiled, seemed to smooth out and disappear in the warm afternoon sunshine.

We tried for over an hour, me holding the rod, him taking it back whenever I detected tension. I was hungry and starting to feel frustrated. Tuna on crackers or pasta might not be everyone's cup of tea but it was something. What do they say? A bird in the hand is worth two in the bush?

But then, then the pull came.

'Steady,' Daley shouted. 'Keep it steady.' He was actually bellowing at me. And then, in a rush of movement, his hands on mine, his body behind me, he pulled back and – slowly, with a kind of creeping rhythm – he reeled the line in and then yanked hard, in an upward motion and raised a flashing, silvery, writhing mass from the water.

He showed me how to hold the fish firmly in one hand and grasp the hook with the other. I watched as he tugged on the sharp, silver hook, retracing the path of its entry, removing it with a circular and – what felt to me – almost apologetic motion. 'Everything's soft and slippery,' he explained. 'You can't afford to mess around. Hold him tight and do what you've got to do.' He dropped my flounder into the bucket.

My first fish. I was elated, disproportionately over-joyed. He saw the look on my face and laughed. 'Pretty good, eh?'

'This is better than sex.'

'Steady on.'

'What do I do now?'

'Cast out again,' he said.

'I didn't know it would be such a high.'

'Catching your first fish, there's nothing like it.'

It would be a lie to say I caught another. But Daley did. Daley with his body and hands on mine; Daley wearing me like a costume and then congratulating me on my performance.

Back at the bothy he showed me how to gut them and then, instead of frying the flounder in a pan over my gas stove, he searched around the fireplace, in the alcoves on either side, and then went around the back of the bothy to rummage in the lean-to. He returned with a large flat stone, over the top of which arced a large circular loop. I watched him lift an iron rod from two hooks above the fire. He held it out to me and, without saying anything, I picked the stone up by its loop and slid it along the rod.

'The bannock stone,' he explained, lighting the fire beneath it. 'But you can also use it for grilling meat or fish.'

We ate our late-lunch-early-dinner cross-legged on the floor before the fire. I kept looking up at him, forking the morsels of white fish into his mouth along with a hard, under-ripe courgette from the vegetable patch and I felt happy. Happy to be eating food taken straight from the soil and the sea. I felt, that afternoon – alone with Daley and Beau – that the island was accepting me; that it was offering up this episode of happiness so I would stay. And it was impossible not to hear that word again, whispered in the pitch black of the cave: Fan.

He left late in the evening, before the last of the light disappeared. He offered, as he gathered his things, to take Beau back with him, 'in case you need a bit more time?'

'I think we'll be OK,' I said.

'I've left a stack of puppy food and a lead in the lean-to. And the fishing rod too. Keep practising.'

'I will.'

'Oh, before I forget. I went down to the cave earlier. Found your rucksack and torch. I left it with the fishing rod.'

'You didn't have to do that.'

'I know I didn't. I wanted to. Take care, OK? And take care of this one,' he leant down to give Beau another kiss on the head.

*Later*

The silver, flashing fish being pulled from the water like a baby being pulled from its mother. Slippery, writhing, alive. An end yes but also a beginning.

*Friday 9th June*

Woke up this morning to the sound of rain knocking on the window above my bed. Behind it, like uniformed back-up, was a grey, cloudy sky.

I've come downstairs to make coffee and think about the day. I had a wash yesterday so no need to head up to the stream today. I can use the bucket to save myself from going outside for a wee. Not sure about a shit though. That might be a step too far.

*After lunch*

Daley here. He came in his skiff and anchored it down by the natural arch, climbed up the Ceum a'Mhaide steps so he could surprise me. He's brought a bottle of champagne, some Stilton and a pack of four eclairs.

So glad I didn't shit in the bucket.

*Saturday 10th June*

Blue skies this morning. Beau began whining as soon as Daley went downstairs so he's taken her out for a short walk. I said I'd meet them down at the beach in fifteen minutes. We're going to have a swim.

I didn't think I could ever feel this happy again.

*Sunday 11th June, PM*

He's just left. Said he had some things to do before tomorrow but that he'd be back before the end of the week.

We spent a lot of the weekend in bed, working our way through the champagne and then a bottle of red I'd been saving. Beau was content to sleep at the foot of the bed while I told him surreal details about my life in Edinburgh. Because that's how it felt. Describing the communal gardens outside my flat, I felt like I was making it up, like I was reciting some ancient tale about a place where land is measured out, fenced off and made pretty with flowers – crocuses and tulips in spring, geraniums and cosmos in summer – a place where benches are positioned under trees that blossom pink and white, on paths that lead to a water fountain where small stone angels urinate into a wide pool beneath their feet. And who can enjoy this beautiful place? Only those who hold a special key. To all others it is forbidden.

It's because the contrast with Finish is so great. So – astounding, really. Here, everything is raw and unrefined but given freely. You want to bathe in this stream? Go for it. You'll freeze your tits off though. You want this fish? Help yourself. You'll have to fashion a rod and reel the slippery little fucker in yourself though.

And it strikes me, as I write this now, that if what I feel is the strangeness of things – going from a place where everything is fenced, regulated, managed to this rugged, isolated place – what must the islanders, travelling the other way, have felt? The strangeness of having to say goodbye, yes, but also fear. They must have felt very afraid.

Yesterday, after our swim, we climbed the rocks on the southern edge of the beach to an escarpment about fifty metres above the water. He wanted to show me where they had once built a derrick, a kind of crane used for lifting supplies from boats. 'The trouble was, you could only position a boat correctly if the bay was completely calm which, as you know, is not often.'

'When was this?'

'Beginning of the twentieth century, sometime. A few years before they evacuated.'

'Too little too late.'

'What this place needed,' he said, rubbing his thumb at something in the stubble around his mouth, 'was a proper landing place or a – a breakwater, at the very least. A real solution to the supply problem, you know? But nobody wanted to invest that kind of money or manpower in a small island with a hundred-odd people living on it.'

I looked up at him, watched him watching the sea, tracing perhaps the route the islanders would have taken that morning in 1912 when they gave it up and finally set sail from this difficult place that nobody wanted to make any easier. 'Easier to get to America,' he said.

'What?'

'That's what the medical officer for Inverness-shire said once. It's easier to get to America than Finish. Says it all really.'

*Tuesday 13th June*

Sunshine and showers all morning. I took Beau down to the beach during a sunny spell but we got soaked hurrying home. Lit the fire to warm up and dry out. I'm writing this while sitting in the rocking chair. Beau is asleep beside the hearth.

It's nice, watching a dog sleep.

*Thursday 15th June*

Cloudy with no rain. Weather is now an event in my life. Spent most of the morning in the garden, weeding and thinning out the carrots. Clearly, I wasn't vigorous enough when they first came up.

Daley coming tomorrow.

*Sunday 18th June, AM*

He had to leave early this morning. Rosalie wants him to fix a leaky pipe in the kitchen.

This thing with Daley. It has made the time when he's not here, difficult. The hours are stretching out before me. It's ten thirty and I've already taken Beau for a walk.

*Wednesday 21st June*

Summer solstice. I think I'll go up to Crois an fionnadh tonight with a bottle of wine. It's 8 a.m. and the skies are clear. If it stays this way, the sunset will be spectacular.

Email from Tess:

From: Tess Gallagher
To: Seren Doughty
Date: 19 June 2023 at 09:53
Subject: ghost story

Dear Seren,

I hope the weather has been good enough for these words to reach you and I'm sorry to disturb your island solitude but I thought I should check in. Frankfurt

Book Fair is getting closer and the sales team are excited to start talking about the new novel. I know it's still early days but would you piece together a short synopsis for me?

No pressure – just excited to hear how it's coming along.

Best wishes, as ever,

Tess x

What can I possibly reply? I've been keeping a journal that's mostly an account of a new sexual relationship with a man who looks like a character from *Neighbours*. I've heard some strange noises: some real, some imagined and I found a bone.

And some doodles in a notebook and on a map. It is hardly the stuff of Stephen King. Or Shirley Jackson. Editors pitch by comparing authors. I wonder who has Tess been comparing me to?

Beau needs feeding.

From: Seren Doughty
To: Tess Gallagher
Date: 21 June 2023 at 11:32
Subject: ghost story

Hi Tess,

Lovely to hear from you and yes, you're right – communications on Finish are very much in the lap of the gods. Or the Beaufort wind scale, depending on your value system. Either way, I've been lucky and have had a lot of sunshine in the last couple of days.

The book is coming together but, exactly as you say, it's still early days. I'll try and put something together for you. Leave it with me.

Best,
Seren

*Midday*

Daley said the son of MacNeil had come to Finish unannounced. He thought he 'did something he shouldn't'. It must have been pretty bad for the islanders to react the way they did. Was it something to do with the names in my notebook?

The islanders wanted the MacNeil boy to suffer. That's what Daley said. They broke his bones and kicked his boat away because they wanted him to suffer. What did he do?

*4 p.m.*

Of course, there is one efficient way to kill a large group of people. I know that well enough. Hitler and Goebbels knew it. My sister's estranged husband knew it too, albeit on a smaller scale.

But knowing and describing are two very different things. Looking up at the outside of a house is not the same as going inside.

I think I'll have a swim in the sea before dinner.

*Early evening*

Daley was right about Beau. My little black cow. She is affectionate and curious and though I know her heart belongs to Daley and that she would choose him in a heartbeat over me, I love her temporary loyalty; the way she gives herself to me until such time as Daley returns. I am, in the meantime, the woman who will have to do.

Sunset is just before half ten this evening. I've poured some rosé into an empty water bottle, packed some biscuits and treats for Beau, this notebook, a head torch (already on) and a hand-held one just in case. Beau is waiting – patiently, I should say – by my desk. We never normally go out at this time so it's not like she expects it but she knows something's up.

*9.50 p.m., Crois an fionnadh*

We walked up from the bothy just after nine. It's quite a steep incline so I carried Beau in my arms, my rucksack on my back. The sea is a silty, restless grey with crests that clap together, sharp and peremptory, like an audience that has been kept waiting too long. Let's get this show on the road, it seems to say.

I look to the west and wait for – what? The sunset? I need to be honest with myself. Why have I come here?

Thirteen stones. They are not like the sea or the sky. They have not been here forever but they may as well have been.

I put Beau down beside the font stone and reach for the Lixivium with my fingers – there is plenty there – and wipe it between my eyes. She clambers on to my lap straightaway, eager to sniff my hand. 'It's for Tilly. She's here,' I say and, even though it's the first time I've said it out loud, it's something I've felt for a while now. Ever since that first dream of her. 'It's for her protection,' I tell Beau and it feels good to use the present tense again.

That's what this island has given me: Tilly in the present tense.

*Later*

I need to light the fire and settle Beau. She's shaking and unsettled. As am I.

I knew something would happen tonight. I think I walked – subconsciously is too generous, wilfully ignorant probably closer to the truth – towards some new echo from the island. I knew that shout of 'thall' when I first arrived was no sunset boat tour. I've always known it. I just allowed myself to be convinced otherwise.

I should start at the beginning. At the font stone, sitting there with Beau, I looked up to see a chorus of kittiwakes fly overhead, shrieking as they passed and then, before I had time to turn and watch their progress across the sky, that sound, like a sonic boom: 'thall!' It shook the ground, the solidity of things. Beau yelped and instinctively I held her to me but, shaken as I was, I was determined to see where the sound was coming from this time. With Beau against my chest and my torch in the other hand, I ran to the headland. The sun had just gone down. Everything was suffused with the kind of rose-gold glow that cannot last. A light that becomes redder and more resigned as it dies.

There was no boat or sign of one having been anywhere near the arch.

I waited and waited and when I felt Beau shiver against me, I unzipped my jacket and tucked her inside. But the failing light was a real problem. I didn't fancy scrambling home in the dark, encumbered by Beau and my rucksack. I turned my head torch on and started for home.

I must have gone two or three hundred metres when I heard the first note. It was a lone, low voice at first: melodic, sad and slowly joined by others.

I couldn't make out the words but I knew the meaning, knew it was a lament. The notes of the song, deep and mournful, fingered some tender, scarred tissue in my heart and pressed down on it. Pressed hard.

I turned around and began running back, past the stones towards the headland. It was difficult with Beau on my front and my rucksack on my back, the ground beneath my feet was uneven and boggy but still, I ran. And then, rising up beyond the headland, a thin trickle of smoke that stopped me in my tracks.

I couldn't go any closer. I didn't want to see how the voices I heard connected with the smoke. The truth? I didn't need to see.

I knew, like a well-rehearsed play, what happens next.

*Thursday 22nd June*

Woke up to grey skies and steady rain. It hasn't stopped for the hour I've been awake.

When I came down this morning Beau had done a poo under the table. Poor thing. She's still shaken up from last night, no doubt. As am I.

The island feels big and vast most of the time but on days like this, when the four walls and roof of the bothy are all that keep us from the elements, it feels small and isolated. Isolated island. Technically a tautology but there's something in it. In the uncertainty that comes from being cut-off. The uncertainty, or fear I should say, is two-fold: what are you missing out on and/or what's coming for you?

I keep thinking of that voice, rising up from the cave last night. Giving voice. Calling out for all to hear.

The beginning of the end?

*Afternoon*

Working hypothesis: MacNeil of Kisimul, receiving the almost dead and broken body of his son, sends a small army of men to wreak revenge on Finish. Except they can't find any of the islanders anywhere. They don't know about the cave. It's not visible to anyone passing the western shores. You have to climb down from Ceum a'Mhaide, skirt along the rocky ledge and then, only then – when facing the Finamuil sea stack – can you see the opening. The islanders knew this, they knew it was the perfect hiding place.

They hid in there but something, some unforeseen event, happened to trigger a sighting, that booming shout of 'thall'. From that moment, it was all over. Every soul was already gathered in the cave. A massacre made easy.

*Saturday 24th June*

The seals are out in force this morning, glistening in the sunshine. It's a beautiful morning – not a cloud in the sky. This weather is great for Daley's business (he sent me an email last night to say he had six people book on to his boat for this morning) but not for the poor seals. I watch them begin their arduous belly flop back into the water as the *Spes Secunda* rounds the rocky outcrop of the bay.

Down at the beach there are two distinct groups: three climbers, two men and one woman (they all look to be in their twenties or perhaps early thirties) and a couple with their little boy. He looks around six or seven.

I'm writing this on a rock, several metres back from where they've gathered, in a horseshoe formation, around Daley. 'We meet back here at three. There's no reception anywhere on the island so please don't be late. If you're late, I have to go looking for you and then everyone's delayed.'

The couple nod their heads solemnly but the climbers barely acknowledge what Daley's said. The two men immediately turn to the equipment, start dividing it up while the woman dips her chin and plaits her long blonde hair behind her. When they're ready, they put their helmets on and begin walking in my direction. They wave as they pass me on their way, presumably, to the headlands and cliffs on the other side of the island.

Not far behind them, Daley.

*Early evening*
The family were from Stockport. They walked with us up to the bothy. The man, he was a teacher, asked if he could look inside the bothy.

Their little boy, Jacob, was delighted by Beau. I forgot to warn them actually. I've never had a dog so it's still new to me – the etiquette of what you do when strangers come into your home. I needn't have worried. Jacob immediately got down on the floor, stroking and petting Beau and issuing optimistic commands like 'sit' and 'paw'.

'I haven't trained her,' I explained.

'She's beautiful,' Jacob's mother said. 'We have a Yorkshire terrier at home. Well, kennels right now. But dogs are great for kids. You miss Doodle, don't you, Jacob? Do you have kids?'

'Yes,' I said, keeping my eyes trained on Jacob, who had his nose on the top of Beau's head. It's not the first time I've been asked this question. You don't want to deny the existence of your child but, at the same time, you don't want to go into the details.

I didn't have time to add anything more to my 'yes' because Beau didn't like the weight of Jacob's head on hers. She ducked back and down and made a little yelping sound. I reached out, lifted her onto my lap.

'He won't hurt her,' the woman bristled. 'He's very good with our dog. Aren't you, Jacob?'

'What year was it built?' her husband called. He had his back to us, looking up at the chimney stack stonework.

'Late nineteenth century,' Daley said.

'It's a beautiful spot up here. Tantalising for the poor kids, eh?' he said, moving over to my desk and looking out of the window. 'Having to learn their grammars with a view like that? They must have been desperate to get out.'

'Something like that,' I agreed.

'They cleared all the old cottages to build it,' Daley said.

'Did they?' I stood up, keeping Beau pressed against me. 'You never told me that.'

He looked at me in surprise. 'You never asked.'

'Why did they do that?'

'They had to attract a teacher to the island. Had to make the job attractive. So they chose the best spot on the island, built the wall to enclose the schoolhouse with its own land. Seren's planted up a vegetable patch on the north end, you'll see it as you go out. It's impressive. Courgettes and—'

'Were there many cottages on this site then?' I interrupted.

'They demolished at least a dozen on this site, built new ones, closer to the beach – the walls that you can still see now.'

'A lot of upheaval for a new school,' the husband chimed in.

'The old cottages, the ones on this site, they needed updating anyway. They didn't even have chimneys. The islanders used to light a peat fire, right in the middle of the floor, and it would vent through a hole in the thatch. So the new cottages were built with chimney stacks. And windows. It was an opportunity to rebuild with all mod cons,' he winked.

'Fascinating. We should leave you to it,' the woman said. 'Jacob, come on. Boo doesn't want to play with you.'

'It's Beau,' I said.

But she was already at the door, as keen to leave the bothy as the bored students her husband had just been describing.

'Why didn't you tell me about the cottages being moved?'

Daley, his naked bum cheek tensed with the effort of levering open the Velux window above us, turned to me.

'I would have if you'd asked. Why is it important?' He dropped back down to the bed, rolled a cigarette and passed it to me.

'Because it means someone else already lived here, on this spot.'

'Someone has always already lived here, on this spot. Take Port Lincoln. Founded in the 1800s but that patch of southern Australia had been worked, lived and died on by native Australians for tens of thousands of years before. Historians and writers,' he raised his eyebrows, 'tend to forget that.'

'No, I get it, but for my purposes, writing a ghost story on this island – it's kind of significant that someone else lived on this site.'

I thought of all the unsettling things that had happened: the night the first X appeared in the OS map being a good example. Someone felt sufficiently comfortable and at home in these walls to close the curtains when I'd deliberately left them open. But how to tell Daley that? Daley, who talks about the efficacy of chimney stacks and how to gut fish; who showed me how to cut peat and dry out driftwood; who comes more often than he runs tours; who gave me Beau because he feared I was too lonely. He'll think I can't cope. Nothing will kill this – what is this? romance is the wrong word, sexual dalliance? – faster than the whiff of mental disorder. 'You know who you should talk to?' he said, taking the cigarette from me.

'Who?'

'My Aunty Kitty. What that woman doesn't know about this island isn't worth knowing.'

I thought of her cries that last night in Castlebay. Of her small, stubborn body on the threshold of the bathroom door. 'Is this another attempt to get me to come back to Castlebay?'

He shrugged as he exhaled. 'She might be up for one last visit. I'll speak to Rosie. You never know.'

He left just after two o'clock. Said he had some stuff to do on board the Spes before everybody returned. We kissed goodbye and I had just sat down to write this when I heard a knock at the door.

It was the woman, Jacob's mother. She was on her own, breathing heavily – her face flushed. 'I've just come up from the arch,' her voice was tacky with saliva.

'Come in.'

'No,' she shook her head.

'Where's your son?'

She shook her head and swallowed.

'Let me get you a glass of water.' I was about to walk to the kitchen when she stopped me.

'You need to get down to the arch.'

'Why? Has something happened? Did you see smoke?'

'What? No, no smoke.'

'Is your husband with him?'

'He's had to leave him. Daley told us we had to be back by three.'

I shook my head. 'I don't understand. Why would you leave your son on his own?'

'I haven't. It's your son I'm talking about. He's down by the arch. You shouldn't leave a child that age alone. He could get swept away. So close to the waves.'

I felt a cold shiver, from the top of my spinal cord all the way down to my feet. 'What did you see?'

'I didn't see anything. It was Jacob,' her voice sounded less certain now. 'Jacob said he saw him.'

'Saw who?'

'A boy. A little boy with black hair. He was down by the arch, looking out to sea.'

By the time I got within twenty metres of Crois an fionnadh, I saw Jacob and his dad walking towards me. It was two forty-five. Jacob's cheeks were red, he was running two quick steps to every one of his dad's – who was powering ahead of him. 'Your wife said you saw a little boy?' I said, expecting him to stop but he didn't.

'I didn't. Jacob did,' he said curtly, all bonhomie and friendly curiosity gone. 'Tell the lady what you saw,' he shouted to Jacob.

I began walking with them, back in the direction of the bothy, where I could see the woman was waiting for them. 'He was standing on the rocks and he almost fell off,' Jacob reported matter-of-factly.

'Where was this?'

'Down in that natural arch,' his dad interjected. 'We went in the cave, my wife and I. We wanted to see inside. Jacob didn't want to come so we told him to wait outside.'

'You said he nearly fell? Is that right?'

I saw a tiny, almost imperceptible nod as his mother drew level with us.

'We have to get moving,' she said, reaching for her son's shoulder and pulling him to her side.

'But what was it, Jacob, that made him fall? Or nearly fall?'

Jacob, walking alongside his mother, shrugged at me and I thought that was it. That I wouldn't get any more out of him. But then he stopped and turned around. He looked thoughtful – and a little sad. 'It was the man on the boat. He shouted really loud.'

*Thursday 29th June*

It's been five days. I've been busy – or at least, I've kept myself busy. Working on my vegetable patch, harvesting runner beans. There are loads of them actually – I've been sprinkling them on my porridge in the morning. Delicious.

Of course, there's Beau to look after. She gets me out every day, which is a good thing. I think, without her, I would have retreated inside completely.

Daley came on Monday with a hiking group from Mallaig. Six of them, all retired. I spotted them up at Crois an fionnadh, white-haired heads milling around among the stones, taking photographs, sipping from their Thermos flasks.

What they see of this island. Standing stones, a beach, a bothy, cliff, caves. Things. Tangible, itemisable things. But for me – for me, Finish Island is now something entirely different. Why is that? And why was it Jacob – a child – who saw what he did? Perhaps children are born open and susceptible to the supernatural world and, like the soft bones in their skull, that opening fuses over and becomes hard with age. But me. What am I doing here? Writing a work of fiction, or attempting to do so. Why have I come? Money? The promise of success? The nostalgia of visiting a special place?

I'm looking, like Hansel and Gretel, for the steps that have led me here. And, just like them, I'm having trouble locating the trail.

*Evening, after dinner*

I am trying not to let fear in, I want to stay and write the story of the massacre, but it's hard – being so alone physically and also mentally.

I thought about telling Daley what happened the afternoon Jacob and his parents visited. But I would have had to tell him all of it: that Jacob had seen something his parents hadn't, that it had clearly shaken him up and then, at some point, I would have to concede – ludicrous as it might sound – that I believed the account of a frightened child.

It's not that I'm averse to saying these things and defending my new position. It's more that I don't know enough about what my new position really means.

It's coming. The story of what happened here, it's coming. But it's not here yet.

Why was the little boy that Jacob saw under the arch? Did someone send him out on an errand? Perhaps he was a scout, told to go and find out if the coast was clear? If so, what terror he must have felt at being discovered. Enough to cause a slip.

Is it possible a slip into the Finish Sound would have been preferable to the fate that awaited him in the cave?

*Friday 30th June*

It's a new day. Beau wanted me to know it just after five this morning. She waits until sunrise, ridiculously early this time of year, and then paws the floorboards near my bed, always looking slightly surprised when I lean over – blurry-eyed and mumbling – to pick her up.

Downstairs, I pour some kibble into her bowl before sitting down to my desk. She always looks disappointed when I do that, pausing slightly in her munching to cut a little side-eye, 'oh, you're doing that again, are you?'

'Morning Pages, Beau. They're a gateway to greater creativity.'

'But are they a gateway to a dog walk?' her eyes ask. It's not an unreasonable question.

I must do better. I want to be better. Perhaps my story will begin at the end. A little boy spotted under the natural arch, a booming call from a departing boat, full of men who were leaving the island shores, defeated by the fact that none of them could find anyone to punish. All of the islanders, meanwhile, waiting anxiously inside the cave – two of them, Ruaridh and Catriona – inked out in my notebook for special attention.

But what about the photograph I took of the feasting hall of Kisimul? Who is the man slumped at the table? What had he done? Did he light the fire? Did he see the boy?

Beau wants to go for a walk.

*Afternoon, 3 p.m.*

I need a wash. I've just smelt myself. It's bad. I've been putting it off for a few days now – making do with a flannel and hot water in a bucket – but I need to go and have a proper body wash in the stream. It's a little cloudy but the sun is coming out intermittently. Not a bad day for it. I think I'll take some clothes and do a bit of laundry too.

*Saturday 1st July*

I'm worried if I don't get what happened yesterday down, I'll forget the details. Details are everything.

I was up at the stream with Beau. In the end I didn't go until early evening. The clouds had gone and the sun, though on its way down, was at least unobstructed. I told myself that would make a difference. I basically spent yesterday afternoon trying to convince myself my body needed more than a bucket wash.

At the stream, I took my clothes off and left Beau to her favourite bit of elevated bank, where she can get her tongue down to the flowing water but no part of her body wet. I waded down the stony sides to the deepest part of the stream and tried arranging a bed of rocks it would be comfortable to sit on. I did a half-arsed job: the water was so cold and I was so tense that the stones I did manage to pull together were loose, mismatched and moved apart as soon as I sat down. What I needed was one big stone, smooth and wide enough for two bum cheeks.

I was busy scrubbing at my clothes with the soap when I heard what sounded like a young woman crying.

In films and books, it's always the dog that first notices the presence of the supernatural. They start barking, whining or backing away, but Beau didn't move. I looked to her for corroboration, or even comfort, but she was completely still – rigid, in fact. Behind me, over my left shoulder, was the base of Cnoc fiacail, where the ground rises up to the tallest point on Finish. Around the foothills, skirting it like pubic hair, is a collection of rocks and boulders where, in the past, I've found empty crisp packets, discarded wet wipes and coiled human turds – no doubt Daley's day trippers using the place as a bin or toilet.

It was from over there I heard the sound. I looked at Beau, waiting for some indication of what I was dealing with, but she met my gaze expectantly: what are you going to do now? she seemed to ask.

There were no birds in the sky, no guillemots to blame the noise on this time. Had it even been a guillemot last time? This sound, the crying, it couldn't be mistaken. It was human. It was sobbing. I stood up from the water and felt the gush of it fall from me, loud and conspicuous and somehow announcing me, heralding the beginning of action. But what action? What was it I could hear and what could I do about it?

Beau was unwilling to cross the stream to follow me. I left her and walked – naked and dripping – towards the noise. The sun was now low, behind the cliffs, taking with it all semblance of normality. Of reality, really.

Further up, bending around to the right, the crying got louder. It was rhythmic, punctuated, pained.

A man's voice. I couldn't make out the words; they were blurred, distorted by the crying – more piteous and defeated now. And then? Then a forced silence. A shut-up-or-I'll-hurt-you-more silence. It was the silence of someone cornered, someone unable to escape but desperate to. I stood there, feeling cornered myself, fixed in place by my own fear, my own shivering nakedness. I was, selfishly, terrified I would give my presence away.

And then Beau did give me away. She began barking – loud and troubled. I ran to her, ran back to the stream, my feet landing heavily on the rough, stony ground. I look mad, I thought. Naked, running, stumbling. But what was I running towards? Or, more to the point, what was I running away from?

Beau stood, waiting beside the rock I'd used to hold down my dry clothes while I bathed. As soon as she saw me, she stopped barking. 'What? What is it?' I asked, but she just looked at me, her head cocked to one side. 'Beau,' I said, wading across the stream towards her, my feet stinging from the sudden re-immersion in cold water. She nosed at the upturned rock beside her and that's when I understood.

My clothes had gone.

I searched. I looked under other rocks, behind them, in the stream, all the time telling myself I must be mistaken. They must have blown away. But I knew. I knew. Something else was at work here. The crying and the clothes. Someone had conspired to distract me, to lead me away from my simple chore – the act of washing myself and my clothes – to witness some horrendous reconstruction.

The darkness was closing in, the sun was almost down in a gesture of this-is-nothing-to-do-with-me. But I had no clothes. I had a pile of wet laundry and not a stitch of anything dry to wear for the walk back to the bothy.

I heard laughter then. Children laughing. I heard it come from behind the rocks, where I'd heard the crying just a few minutes before. Sniggering, repressed amusement.

'Who are you?' I shouted, but that only made the sniggering louder. 'Who the fuck are you?' I cried, tears mangling my voice.

I don't know how long I stood there, numb and humiliated. Too long. I knew I had to get walking; I knew it was crucial I get back to the bothy and safety during the minutes of twilight that remained. But instead, like a twist in the bowel, an uncontrollable itch in the nostrils, I felt rage, grief, mania rise up and I started crying. Loudly. Like a child. With my fists clenched and banging against my thighs, I cried my throat raw. I shouted and screamed and hacked up whatever phlegm I could scrape from my throat against a world that could see my daughter, my only daughter, taken from me in such a way. A world that could allow her to burn up like so much fuel – too far from my protection. I cried because in the same lifetime, the same span of years allotted to me, I found myself alone, naked and shivering, in front of some kids who had taken it upon themselves to steal my clothes and laugh at me.

Beau barked again. She was several metres away, running in the direction of the bothy. I remembered Daley's words: don't go wandering around here at night. I had to get moving. Hypothermia was a very real consideration. I had no torch and very little chance of finding my way back in the dark. So I followed Beau. She led the way, my clever, beautiful dog. She saved my life that night. I would have thanked her too. I would have knelt down once we were back inside the stone walls of the bothy and kissed the top of her head, perhaps rubbed her soft, furry ears. I would have done all these things if I hadn't seen, from a distance, that the bothy was illuminated by candles I hadn't lit and in the air, the smoke of a fire I hadn't started.

Someone was inside.

*Later, sometime after 4 p.m.*
I've just had lunch (tinned tomato soup with a handful of almonds) followed by a sleep. I thought it would make me feel better but, if anything, I feel worse.

I knew it wasn't Daley in the bothy. He never comes at night and he certainly wouldn't make himself at home like that if I wasn't there. No, had it been Daley, he would have come and found me and Beau first.

So that left another possibility. The same possibility I encountered the night I came back from Crois an fionn-nadh to find the curtains had been closed. Whoever or whatever had let themselves in that night had obviously felt the need for privacy.

But as I approached the bothy this time, I could see the curtains were not closed and the door was ajar.

Candles were flickering, the interior of the bothy lit up as if for a medieval church service. The warm fingers of the fire reached out for me, for my hands, my mottled, shivering limbs and pulled me into the room. The pull of these things – light and warmth – was so strong, so powerful I was able to overlook the man crouching before the fire with his hands spread wide.

A man with brown, curly hair.

He turned sharply and stood up. Alex. He was tall. I didn't remember him being so tall. 'What on earth?'

I had forgotten I was naked.

He reached a hand behind his head, pulled his jumper off, revealing a washed-out grey T-shirt underneath. The hair on his stomach looked especially dark in the dim light. He held his jumper out to me but I didn't move towards it.

It was Beau who stepped forward.

'Who's this?' he asked but I noticed he didn't bend down to her. Instead he stayed where he was and shook the jumper. 'Please. Put this on.'

What could I do? When you're naked and cold – and I mean the kind of cold that's cellular – everything is a reflex. I took the jumper and put it on. The wool fibres felt so good, so substantial and alive against my skin. I pulled the front of it down and felt the back rise up over my arse.

'Who's this?' he repeated.

'My dog. Her name's Beau.' My words sounded strange, like my voice box had been grated.

'Where did you get her?'

'Castlebay. What are you doing here?'

'I thought I'd come and see you. I'm glad I did. You look – you look like, well, like something's happened.'

'I lost my clothes. Up at the stream.'

'You lost your clothes? All of them?'

'They were taken.'

'Taken?' he laughed. 'Taken how?'

'Does it matter?'

'No, I suppose not. Come and sit here. By the fire,' he said, motioning to the rocking chair.

'I've got no – I need bottoms.'

'Where are they, upstairs?'

I thought about it. Thought about the impossibility of walking up the stairs with my undercarriage completely exposed. I told him where he could find my pyjama bottoms. He ran up the stairs and returned a minute later with them.

I didn't want him there but, at the same time, I did. He was a person, another human being who was doing things for me: he brought me a cup of hot tea that was so sweet it must have been twenty per cent sugar. He followed my instructions for feeding Beau, stoked the fire and made sure I was comfortable under my sleeping bag in the rocking chair. 'What are you doing here?' I asked again.

'I told you. I wanted to come and see you. I tried all the traditional ways of getting in touch.'

'So, you thought you'd try breaking and entering instead?'

'It's not – is that what you think? That this is breaking and entering? I did knock and there was no answer. And then I thought it would be nice for you to return to a cosy cottage.'

'It's a bothy.'

'Have I done something to offend you?'

'It's a bit weird, don't you think? I ask you for help looking up a book in the library and the next thing I know, you've followed me to a remote island in the Outer Hebrides.'

'I think you're missing a few stages in between.'

I stared at him.

'We slept together? That feels like an important part of the narrative. You asked to read my manuscript? You're shaking your head. That didn't happen?'

'No. I mean, yes. We had sex. But I didn't ask to read your book.'

He nodded. 'Is that why I found it in the log box? Only good for kindling?' He was smiling but his eyes, I noticed, were not.

'Oh, that. No, I was emptying my rucksack and I just put it there.'

'You haven't read it yet then?'

'Not yet,' I said, feeling guilty about the whole manuscript-as-kindling thing. I nodded my head towards my desk, to my open laptop and notebooks. 'I've been busy with my own writing.'

'So I see.'

I took another big gulp of tea. It really was delicious with so much sugar.

'But you've had time to plant up all those vegetables.'

'It's called basic subsistence, Alex. I eat what I grow.'

'No need to get defensive. I'm impressed, it's impressive what you've done here.'

I leant my head back and closed my eyes.

'Do you want to tell me what happened?'

'Not really.'

'OK. Would you like me to make you something to eat?'

'I'd like you to tell me how – no, forget how – why you're here. And don't tell me it's for feedback.'

He took a deep breath and again, that patient, forbearing smile. Like he was dealing with a patient with Alzheimer's. 'I'm about to start a PhD. I think I told you back in Edinburgh when we first met.'

'Ethnoarchaeology.'

'I didn't think you'd remember.'

'So, what? You're doing it here now, I suppose?'

'I was thinking I'd do the research here. Gather soil samples, organic matter, all the physical evidence I need and then return to Edinburgh in September.'

'I thought you wanted to be a writer?'

'I do. The two things are not mutually exclusive. I can gather information during the day and write at night. Ever since you expressed an interest in my writing, I've—'

'I didn't.'

'OK, but you packed my manuscript, brought it all the way here with you.'

'Only because you were so insistent.'

Silence. We both stared at the fire. He was the first to speak again. 'It sounds like you've had a difficult day. You look exhausted. Let's talk some more in the morning.'

I didn't want to agree with anything he said but I was tired. Every time I closed my eyes I felt myself sinking. 'I think you should sleep down here,' I said, rocking forward to get up. He held the roller down so I could ease myself out of the seat.

'Good night,' he said.

I grabbed my papers and pens from the desk, said goodnight and went upstairs. In the quiet and privacy of my room, I opened up the map.

A new cross. On the stream at the base of Cnoc fiacail.

*Sunday 2nd July*
Woke early this morning. Not because of Beau pawing or Alex making any noise (he's still sound asleep), just

the awareness, I suppose, of someone else in the bothy with me. It's been nearly two months of completely solitary living and I guess I've got used to it.

I came down and made coffee. There is enough in the pot for him but he's still curled up and snoring in his yellow sleeping bag. It has horizontal ridges on it and makes him look like a caterpillar.

I hate caterpillars. I hate how fat and undulating they are. Their little hairs. They make me feel sick.

*11.30 p.m.*

Over dinner tonight, he told me more about how he travelled from Vatersay on a small boat with an outboard motor. We were sitting at the little table in the kitchen. 'It's my dad's old skiff,' he said, hoovering up the penne and sardines.

'Where are you staying?' I asked him.

'Where am I staying?'

'Yes.'

'I was staying at the campsite. Right near the beach.'

'OK. And you're going back, when?'

He looked around him. 'I can't stay here?'

'No.'

'Why not?'

'Finish is mine. I got here first.'

He laughed then. Actually threw his head back and laughed. He reached for a piece of kitchen towel and wiped his mouth while nodding, like he was preparing to enjoy whatever was coming next.

'I mean it,' I said.

'No, I don't doubt it.'

'I've checked the weather for tomorrow. Mild breeze but generally calm. You should have no problem returning.'

'Can I just check my understanding? You're saying that this island and this bothy, both of which belong to National Trust Scotland, cannot be visited or used by anyone other than you?'

'No, that is not what I'm saying.'

'OK. What are you saying then?'

'You're welcome to come to the island during the day, gather your soil samples or whatever it is that you need and then go home, go back to Vatersay.'

'Thank you for that. Can I ask you a question?'

'Sure.'

'Why are you so keen to get rid of me? Have I done something to upset you?'

'I came here to be alone, Alex. You know that. You've always known that.'

'OK.'

'So why are you here?'

'Contrary to whatever you think about finders keepers, this island does not belong to you. I have as much right to be here as you. I'm sorry to be so blunt but it's true.' I noticed how his voice rose and became shrill when he was agitated. 'Look, this is not what I wanted. It's clear I've done something to offend you and if I have, I'm sorry. I apologise. I should not have let myself in last night. I can see how it looks, but in my defence, it was getting dark outside—'

'Finish is haunted.'

He opened his mouth and then closed it again. Beau, made anxious by the sudden silence, licked my toes and the top of my foot. I leant down and picked her up, put her on my lap.

'It is,' I said.

'I'm not disagreeing with you.'

'When we went out that night in Edinburgh? You mentioned those shepherds? You said they were freaked out by the sight of children running around?'

'Yes.'

'Well, I think,' I stroked Beau's body, 'I know, now, there's something in that. In what you found.'

His eyes narrowed. He took off his glasses, held them by the arm and with his other hand rubbed his eyes. When he put them back on, the skin around his eye sockets looked raw, like they'd been peeled. 'Is any of what you're telling me related to the condition I found you in on Friday night?'

'You didn't find me. I returned.'

'OK. You returned. But is it?'

'Yes.'

'You said your clothes were taken?'

'By kids,' I nodded. 'I heard kids laughing at me.'

'Kids? As in children?'

'Yes, Alex. I'm pretty sure there were no goats involved.'

'I'm just asking because the shepherd who reported the sightings, the one interviewed by the *Stornoway Gazette*, he specifically said children. I'm trying to clarify things, that's all.'

'You can't clarify. You can't understand. What's going on here – it's not something you can cross-reference or look up in a computer. It's – it's beyond that.'

'Clearly.'

'I'm just trying to get you to understand that this is not a good place for you.'

'Which begs the question: why is it a good place for you?'

'Because – because – it's very difficult to explain. The spirits, the visions, I don't know what you want to call them, I have no words for them—'

'The ghosts?'

'They want me to stay.'

'They want you to stay?'

'Yes.'

'And no one else?'

'No. I don't know. I realise this makes me sound completely mad.'

'Perhaps all of this is precisely the reason why I should stay. It's clear that, with all this going on, you need help and support. I have a boat, I can fetch supplies.'

'I already have someone who does that.'

'Who?'

'Daley.'

'And he's flesh and blood?'

'Fuck off.'

'I'm sorry,' he laughed.

I stroked the soft downy fur of Beau's ear. 'Something is playing out for me. Some performance, some re-enactment – whatever you want to call it – and it's important I stay here, to write it all down.'

'The island is your muse.'

I felt tired by the conversation. Exhausted by having him in the bothy with me. 'Something like that.'

'And you're not willing to share your muse with anyone else.'

*Wednesday 5th July*

He has a tent. This is not something to be overlooked. Granted, it's not as good as him disappearing off to Vatersay every evening but it does mean I get the bothy back to myself. He's taken the patch of land behind the bothy – the area I disregarded for my plants because it would only ever get evening sun. We've agreed he can come inside during the day, use the kitchen, warm himself before the fire if it's particularly cold or wet but at night, he sticks to his tent.

He's spent the last three days channelling Tom Hanks in *Castaway*. I saw him, yesterday afternoon, climb the rocky outcrop that frames the southern edge of the beach. He was barefoot, in shorts and wearing a red T-shirt, and was carrying what looked like Daley's bamboo fishing rod on his shoulder.

When was *Castaway* made? He probably wasn't even born when that film came out. Tosser.

I can't help but feel a stab of jealousy for his easy ways; his acceptance that the tent is his home; his natural under-standing that the sea is full of fish we can eat. I had to be shown and taught and, even then, this is the first time the fishing rod has been used since Daley left it for me.

My jealousy was not helped when he returned a few hours later with a bucketful of flounder and saithe. He cooked them over an open fire he made near his tent. When he invited me to join him, I begrudgingly accepted. The smell of grilled fish was maddening.

He puts me to shame with his foraging. Razor clams, samphire, blaeberries – he even managed to make some sort of cordial from a flower I thought was nothing more than a weed. It's called meadowsweet and it looks just like a dandelion clock. He crushes it in a pestle and mortar, adds lemon juice, some water, a few spoonfuls of sugar and calls it a mocktail – which annoys me. Still, you've got to hand it to him. He knows how to get by in the wild.

Aside from the odd lunch and to use the internet every once in a while, he doesn't come inside the bothy very often during the day. We eat together most evenings.

I haven't written for a while. I feel wiped out by what happened up at the stream, plus Alex's appearance so soon after – life has been quite unsettled. But this morning I got up early, made myself a coffee, fed Beau and brought this journal up to date.

I think I'll take Beau down to the beach today. It's not as warm as yesterday (my barometer for wind chill is how reluctant I am to pull down my pyjama bottoms and do a dump in the morning) but there's no rain forecast. That's another thing: I have to walk further to go to the toilet now that Alex is camped behind the bothy.

From: Seren Doughty
To: Daley MacKinnon
Date: 5 July 2023 at 10:27
Subject: pants


So it seems, as well as being unable to catch fish or cut peat bricks, I am also shit at weighing down wet laundry. It's a pretty niche skill but there you go, it's important to admit one's failings. I lost almost all my pants up at the stream last week. Would you mind ordering me some from M&S? I've copied a link below. Please add it to the bill.

Also – I have a visitor. A guy I knew, briefly, in Edinburgh. The one whose letter you delivered a few weeks ago. More on that when you come but suffice to say, I'm not over the moon about it. He's sleeping in a tent outside.

Looking forward to seeing you,

S x

From: Daley MacKinnon
To: Seren Doughty
Date: 5 July 2023 at 16:03
Subject: pants

Is this your idea of foreplay? Lucky for you, I find multipack cotton briefs very arousing.

I've got a booking next week (Tuesday 11th) so I'll meet the newbie then. Have you given any thought to a dirty protest?

D

*Thursday 6th July*
A light drizzle this morning, nothing that would prevent a walk. Yesterday, on our way down to the beach, Beau

started pulling towards the burial ground. And I remembered, I said I'd go and take a look at Chulainn's headstone.

Alex has just walked in and asked if there's any coffee going. It's the third time he's done that this week.

*Friday 7th July, 10 p.m.*

The evening started off well enough. He offered to make dinner (kedgeree with chunks of flounder, courgette and peas from the patch – it was delicious) and I opened a bottle of Co-op Chianti I'd been saving – for what I don't know, Daley never drinks if he has to return the same day.

He was keen to tell me all about the parts of the island he's explored; how he wants to do some climbing on the western cliffs but didn't bring the right equipment with him.

'You could probably get what you need in Stornoway.'

'If I didn't know better, I'd say you were trying to get rid of me.'

I took a sip of wine and put my glass down slowly. Neither of us said anything for a while.

'Charlotte's nice.'

'Charlotte?'

'Your agent, Charlotte Kinsella. She never replied, of course.'

'What were you expecting? She's hardly going to disclose my location to you, a perfect stranger.'

'No, I mean on my book. I sent her the first three chapters and she never got back to me.'

'Oh, right.'

'Not for her, I know that's what you're going to say. Still, a simple refusal would have been nice.'

'The thing is – the nymphomaniac mermaids—'

'Sirens.'

'Yes, sorry, sirens. It sounds a bit—'

'What?'

'Well, adult. You know, soft porn? Charlotte's list is commercial literary fiction.'

'How do you know?'

'How do I know? I'm on it.'

'No, how do you know what my book is about? You haven't read it. You told me so yourself.'

'Fair point. But I got a pretty good idea from your description of it that night we went out.'

'You think a five-minute drunken outline in a bar merits a synopsis?'

'You had, like, half a lager.'

'And you've read how many pages?'

'I'm just trying to offer some explanation as to why she passed on it.'

'Well, for your information, I think I'm close with another one.'

'Really? Do they specialise in erotic fiction?'

'Very funny. No, he's quite well-known actually. Rupert Wentham?'

'His list is quite established, mostly male writers. You've done well to attract his attention.'

'He really liked the island setting.'

'It's very on-trend at the moment. I hate using that word but it's apt in this instance. Everyone is obsessed with digital detox. Islands are the perfect metaphor for that.'

'Doesn't it frustrate you though? The homogeneity of modern fiction; the way the gatekeepers are all, essentially, like sheep, commissioning more of the same until the market is saturated?'

'It's a setting, Alex. That's all. And a fairly broad one at that. You're still free to make your story unique. I'm just not sure a horny teenager set upon by a load of sex-hungry mermaids – sorry, sirens – is particularly unique.'

'And yours? How exactly are you making your story unique?'

'I'm not saying I'm any better. Shit, I don't even have a story. At the moment the sum total of my work here amounts to journal entries, impressions, thoughts, feelings—'

'We could collaborate?'

'What? You and me?'

'Why not? I might be able to suggest some ways forward. I could help?'

'I don't need any help.'

'OK.'

'You don't believe me?'

'Your editor is waiting for a synopsis from you.'

'You've been reading my emails?'

'I couldn't exactly help it. It was open on the desktop when I borrowed your laptop. I wasn't snooping.'

'You're way over the line here.' I took a deep breath. 'I'm sure, in your own way, you're trying to help but I don't need it. I don't want it. OK?'

'Of course, I'm sorry. Forget I ever said anything.'

I stood up. 'It's late,' I said, carrying my plate over to the work surface. 'I've got a lot to do in the morning.'

*Saturday 8th July, late morning*

Woke up this morning feeling guilty. I shouldn't have said those things about his book being soft porn. And then his offer to collaborate. He's clumsy and blundering and almost certainly barking up the wrong tree with Rupert Wentham but who am I shatter someone else's dreams?

When I went downstairs he was making coffee, facing the window. 'Want one?' he asked without turning round.

'Later, I think. I'm going to take Beau for a walk.'

He nodded his head and began pouring.

'I've been thinking,' I started. 'You could use the table in here?' He turned around to look at me. 'For writing?'

He stirred his coffee and nodded. 'Thank you.'

I put my jacket and boots on, clipped the lead on Beau and just as I did, another line from *The Prophet* came to me: 'you give but little when you give of your possessions'.

It is a very small thing. But then, you've got to start somewhere, I suppose.

*6 p.m.*

Alex is downstairs, preparing dinner. I don't want him peering over my shoulder, asking me questions so I've come up to my bedroom to write this.

It wasn't difficult to find Chulainn's grave. Shaped like a lollipop, the face of the headstone a complex arrangement of raised and interlocking knots forming a tight circle, pierced by the points of a Celtic cross at its centre, it is the largest of all the headstones. There are no other markings, no room for anything else – the intricate pattern wards off any attempt at script.

Beau came over to see what I was doing. She walked the length of the mound, from feet to head and then, just in front of the headstone, right over where I imagine Chulainn's face would be, she squatted down on her back paws and had a big piss.

'You are one disrespectful bitch,' I said to her but she was busy sniffing and pawing the ground. I've seen her do this before, when she's had accidents in the bothy, I've seen her pawing pointlessly at the flags. But this morning, her pawing uncovered something

I lifted her off and took over myself, pushing back a thin layer of soil and grass until a flat stone about the size of a sheet of A3 paper appeared with the following inscription:

HERE LIES THE REMAINS OF THOSE
WHO PERISHED IN UAMH CHULAINN
LAID TO REST WITH GRANNY
JULY, 1912

July, 1912. The month and year Finish was abandoned. I felt moved by the sight of it. The simplicity of the message but also the urgency of it. There must have been so much to do, so many emotions to contend with as they prepared to leave this island forever and yet, retrieving the remains from the cave and burying them with 'Granny' had to be done. And it had to be done properly.

Uamh, I knew from my research in the library meant cave. Chulainn's Cave.

Chulainn. The island midwife. Here she was, buried with the bones of all the children whose births she had attended and whose deaths she had witnessed. The most important figure on Finish Island, raised up high and facing the ocean – her epitaph inked up in dog piss.

I reached into my pocket for the bone. I had taken to carrying it around with me. I didn't trust Alex not to swipe it for one of his samples.

I knelt down and dug a small hole below the headstone, about fifteen inches deep. Beau would definitely have been interested in this part of the proceedings, had she stuck around. I held up the bone, examined the small dark holes that had – once upon a time – produced marrow, housed nerves and transported cells. I placed it in the hole.

I'm not a religious person, but that afternoon, with the sound of the waves to my right and the kittiwakes calling to one another over my head, I closed my eyes and mumbled a prayer. I thought of the islanders in the cave but also, of course, I thought of Tilly. Tilly alone in the guest room of Alana's house, Tilly hiding in the wardrobe because she was afraid of the smoke. How can there ever be rest or peace when a child dies like that? How can a witness to such evil not rise up, not spend the rest of eternity raging and screaming?

Rage is part of the grieving process. Don't be afraid to say that you're angry, our grief counsellor had said. As if expressing an emotion you might feel when someone cuts you up at a roundabout or forgets to take your order in a restaurant might be applicable to the death of your child. Your only child. Anger doesn't come close. It doesn't touch the sides, I thought – literally touching the sides of the hole – as I piled earth over the bone. I felt the damp, meaty soil collect under my fingernails, around the jagged cuticles of my right hand and then . . . then something in the dirt. Cotton, triangular, like bunting. I knelt down, looked closer, pulled harder. White cotton. An elastic waist-band. My knickers. The white cotton completely dry. The wind, the breeze that had been blowing the grass sideways now lifted and buffeted my underwear so that I was able to see they were not dry everywhere.

The crotch was smeared with bright wet blood.

*2 a.m.*

I forgot to check the OS map. In my urgency to get everything written down, I forgot to check it. I've just been down now and there it is, another cross over the burial ground. They are like pock marks. A virus. Where one spot blooms, another will follow.

I need to sleep.

*Sunday 9th July, AM*

Beau woke me just before seven this morning so it's still early. Alex hasn't come in for his coffee yet. It's nice to have the peace and quiet to read through yesterday's entry.

Alex's unwillingness to accept the idea of ghosts has made me think. I was like that too. I scoffed, before. What has made me so willing to accept the things I've seen and heard as supernatural echoes? Which leads me back, always, to the same question: how did I get here?

Jamie withdrawing financial support and Tess commissioning a ghost story; the only room in Castlebay in a guesthouse owned by a direct descendant of Chulainn. And if I push myself, if I really dig deep, then I have to consider Tilly. My daughter, murdered in the same way as the children who once lived on this island. It's hard to overlook that kind of coincidence.

Perhaps it isn't so much what is being replayed but who is watching it. Am I – like Jacob – nothing more than a suitable spectator?

Lured in by money, corralled by circumstance, conveyed by nostalgia, carried down an ever-narrowing tunnel to this bothy on this island at this time. It frightens me, the thought that I have no agency. If I'm honest, it frightens me more than anything else.

I can see a boat on the horizon. It's the Spes. Thank god. Thank god for him.

*Early evening, 6.45 p.m.*

I walked down to the beach and waited for him to climb over the rocks, which he did with ease, despite the rucksack on his back. When he jumped down onto the sand, I was ready, waiting to fling my arms around him.

He didn't know what dark thoughts he was saving me from, what light he brought.

Light. The light this morning was so beautiful. It made the waves that lapped at our boots shine like footlights; made the white crests further out to sea spread wide like the smirks of a knowing group of friends. He kissed my neck, my lips and then put me back down. 'I couldn't wait until Tuesday.'

'I'm glad you didn't.'

He took my hand in his. 'Been thinking about you. Worrying about you, really.'

'Why? Because of Alex?'

'Is that his name?'

'Yes. He's a librarian I met in Edinburgh.'

'What happened? Did you forget to return your books or something?'

'No,' I laughed. 'He's doing a PhD in September on soil.'

'He's interesting too, eh?'

'But he also wants to be a writer. So his thinking was, come gather soil samples and, while here, co-author a novel with me. Kill two birds with one stone.'

'You've told him where to go?'

'Numerous times. But what can I do? As he keeps reminding me, the island isn't mine.'

'He's staying in a tent?'

'At night, yes. He'll be in the bothy now, I bet. Making his morning coffee.'

Daley nodded. 'Let's go meet this clown.'


Beau ran to Daley in a paroxysm of joy, barking and fevered jumping. Alex, who was sitting at the table with a cup of coffee and my laptop open, was also surprised when we walked in together. He stood up quickly and I saw a look of alarm cross his face. 'I wanted to check my email,' he said. 'I hope you don't mind. You weren't around to ask.'

'It's fine. Alex, this is Daley. Daley runs a boat charter company in Castlebay. I think I told you before, he's been keeping me supplied with—' I don't know why I hesit-ated. Fresh fruit? Vegetables? Multipack knickers? Down at the beach, holding one another felt easy. But up here, explaining our relationship to a bespectacled librarian felt difficult.

'So you're the reason Seren doesn't need me to fetch supplies?'

'What's that?' Daley asked.

'I have my own boat here. I offered to go and get whatever we need from Castlebay but Seren was quite clear that she had someone.'

'We have an arrangement,' Daley said.

'I'd say the islanders wouldn't have been so quick to abandon the place if they'd had a service like yours,' Alex said.

'How's that?'

'Daley's people were from Finish,' I explained. 'His grandmother was one of the last to be born here.' I hoped Alex would get the hint and drop the subject.

'They weren't quick to abandon it,' Daley said. 'It was a heartbreaking decision.'

'But it would have been a very different proposition,' Alex continued. 'Internet connection, regular gas exchange, pancetta from the Co-op—'

'You make it sound like some sort of holiday camp. This isn't easy. What Seren's doing here – it isn't easy.'

'But certainly easier. That's all I'm saying. Your distant relatives – they would have been more likely to stay had they been able to stream Netflix or order underwear from M&S.'

Daley didn't answer. He just stood there, regarding Alex – a look of curiosity on his face – and then me. Alex sat back down before the laptop. 'I'm joking of course,' he continued. 'There's no way you could stream Netflix with this bandwidth.'

Daley shook his head and walked over to the gas stove where he picked up the pot and poured himself some coffee. 'You want one?' he asked, turning to me.

'Yes. I'm out of sugar though.'

Daley lifted his rucksack on to the table, almost knocking Alex's cup over. 'I've got some in here.' He began unloading the shopping around Alex.

'Where do you want this?' he asked, hoisting up a bag of puppy food.

'Over there in the corner,' I said. And then, because the silence stretched out too thin and wide, I added: 'I'm not exactly blessed with storage here.'

'Still, it's better than a tent,' Alex mumbled.

Daley took a sip of his coffee. 'It is a one-bed. Perfect for, you know, one person.'

'True,' Alex conceded. 'Though Seren and I have shared a one-bed before.'

My face flushed. Daley looked at me. 'Is that right?'

'That's right,' Alex confirmed, not looking up, just blithely tapping away on the keyboard.

Daley stroked the stubble on his chin. I knew I should say something, some disavowal, but I had nothing. Not only had I not seen this coming, I'd also somehow managed to forget that we'd ever actually slept together. I found him so unpleasant, so unappealing that I'd buried the memory. 'I reckon, if that is right, you'd do well to keep that kind of information to yourself.'

'Seren doesn't mind. Do you?'

'It happened back in Edinburgh,' I said to Daley. 'A one-night stand. Nothing more.'

'I see,' Alex said, looking from Daley to me and then back again. 'You're delivering more than just groceries to our mutual friend here.'

'Stop being a twat.' I had finally found my voice.

He laughed. It was his defence mechanism. I saw that.

'Do you think you could finish up whatever you're doing there and give me and Seren a bit of space?'

Alex looked surprised. 'Yes, I can do that. But before I go, can I ask a question about your rod?'

'What the fuck?'

'He means the fishing rod,' I said, putting my hand on Daley's arm. 'Don't you?' I remembered that morning in Edinburgh when I'd had to try and stop Jamie from punching him.

'I do. I was wondering if you could get hold of more bamboo.'

'What?'

'I want to tie a net on the end of it.'

'You know the birds are protected? It's illegal to hunt them and their eggs?'

'Of course. No, I was planning to use it for collecting soil and fragments of eggshell from the cliffs. For my PhD.'

'Right.'

He gathered his papers together. 'I'll leave you two. It looks like you have a lot to catch up on.'

We waited for him to leave before taking our coffees over to the fireplace. I sat down in the rocking chair.

'Want me to light the fire?'

'Sure.'

He crouched down and began sweeping away the ash from last night. 'What's the deal?'

'There's no deal. He's a dick. End of.'

'You tell me he's a librarian and then, next thing I hear, he's an ex-boyfriend of yours.'

'Ex-boyfriend, no way. It was a one-night stand. One I immediately regretted, I might add. Seriously, he's nothing to me.'

'He looks mighty comfortable in here.'

'That's because he's an entitled arsehole. Not because I've welcomed him in.'

Daley blew on the flames that were just catching. 'He's sleeping outside now. How long before he's in here?'

'Seriously, what can I do? Much as I'd like to, I can't just tell him to fuck off. And I have tried.'

'September will be closing time for both of you,' Daley stood up and reached for my desk chair. He brought it close to the fire and sat down. 'Neither of you can stay much beyond that anyway.'

'I know that,' I said, miserably.

'You've got seven, maybe eight weeks.'

'I was supposed to be alone. That was the whole point of coming here.'

'Do you want me to have a word? Suggest he move on?'

'The dirty protest was no joke then?'

'If I take a shit in his tent, he'll definitely want to come in here. No, I could go and talk to him. Make him see a bit of sense.'

'No. No, I don't want you to do that. He's annoying but harmless, a massive geek really. Leave him to his soil samples and fossils. I found Chulainn's grave, by the way,' I said, keen to change the subject.

'Oh yeah? The big one?' he pulled my rocking chair closer to him. His breath smelt of coffee. Beau, left out and jealous, trotted over and sat down by his ankle.

'It's hard to miss. Did you know there's an inscription? A flat stone on the actual mound? It was buried under grass and soil. Beau here helped me find it.'

Daley reached down to pick her up. 'I didn't. But it makes sense. What was the date?'

'July, 1912.'

'That'll be it then, the interment I was telling you about. What else did it say?'

I stood up and reached over him for the notebook on my desk. 'Here lies the remains of those who perished in Uamh Chulainn. Laid to rest with Granny July, 1912. Uamh means cave, doesn't it?'

'Sure does.'

'But what does Chulainn mean? Why was she called that? Presumably she had a normal name before.'

'She was given the title later, I think. After the massacre. What's that called?'

'Posthumously.'

'Yeah. She would have been MacKinnon at the time of her death. All midwives on Finish were MacKinnon.'

'I know, you said. But Chulainn – it means dog?'

'Yeah, hound. But like, warrior really.'

'So she fought? Defended herself, the islanders?'

'I don't know. Nobody knows.'

'What about your aunt? You said she might come to Finish?'

'I could ask.'

'Do you think she might know? Or even remember what she knows if that makes sense?'

'Rosalie thinks her long-term memory is pretty good.'

I stared at the fire. The flames had turned the kindling into red-hot embers. I got up, threw a couple of peat bricks on the flames and returned to my seat.

'He's making himself useful, I see?' he motioned his head at the fire.

'He didn't even have to watch a YouTube video. Just marched off with the – what's it called?'

'Treisgeir.'

'Yeah, that. I've seen him, over by the cliffs, there's a stone platform and he's got a pile of peat blocks stacked up there. Thinks he's some kind of early man. It's only a matter of time before the loin cloth comes out.'

'Just as long as he doesn't take you for his Jane.'

'You're confusing your periods. Tarzan's early twentieth century.'

He lifted Beau gently from his lap and put her down on the floor. He leant down over me, his hands on the armrests of my rocking chair. I looked up at his face, flushed now by the fire and the blood flow. 'Why don't you talk me through the difference? Upstairs?'

*Midnight*

Can't sleep. Keep going over something Daley said a few weeks ago, about the MacNeil boy who floated back in the boat, half-dead, to Kisimul. He said, 'he'd come to the island unannounced, did something he shouldn't'. Did something he shouldn't. What if the cries I heard up at the stream were just that? Him doing something he shouldn't?

New hypothesis: The firstborn son of MacNeil came to Finish and raped a woman. His crime was discovered, somehow, and avenged by the islanders who decided he should die a slow, agonising death. Except the slope current took him north to his father's castle where he arrived, almost dead. Unable or perhaps unwilling to explain why he'd been subjected to such violence, his broken body was the catalyst for an unspeakable act of revenge.

*Tuesday 11th July*

Alex loves to show off. I saw him while I was on a walk with Beau, a small group of Daley's day-trippers gathered round while he slid the treisgeir down into the peat beds he'd dug. Daley said later he noticed all of them had been given a small block to take home.

*Wednesday 12th July*

I need to reply to Tess with my synopsis. It's been three weeks since she asked for one. But when I look at what I have, it just seems so fanciful.

*Thursday 13th July, PM*

I've spent the last couple of hours trying to cobble together a synopsis that feels horribly meta:

A writer, in search of solitude and space to grieve, goes to live on an abandoned island in the Outer Hebrides.

Who is this writer? Why am I hiding behind the third person?

Her island solitude is soon resonating with the echoes of a violent past.

I tried listing those echoes:

- a booming call from out to sea
- a desperate plea in a dark cave
- anguished cries by the stream

but itemised like this, each one attached to a bullet point like a prisoner to a ball and chain, they look random and muted. I tried writing what I thought was the story of the massacre:

a remote island community, moved to murder by an unspeakable act of sexual violence, become themselves the target for an act of revenge so abhorrent and disproportionate in its intensity that—

What? Without the supernatural echoes, it reads as an historical account. And a very partial one at that. No, I need all three elements: me, the echoes and the historical facts of the massacre. I need all three to come together but without knowing who Chulainn was or why the island is still alive with the impressions of an event that took place several centuries ago, I'm going to struggle.

Of course, I can just make it up. Give Tess what she wants for Frankfurt. That's the job after all. My contract clearly states I have to write 'an original work of fiction' but this, whatever this is, is more than fiction. It is more than writing.

*Friday 14th July*
Alex is making coffee in the kitchen. I wish I had some headphones. Or ear plugs. When I wandered round Edinburgh town centre, imagining my life here, wringing my hands over whether I should buy a potato peeler, ear plugs were the last thing on my mind.

He's just offered to make dinner tonight. I said yes. Anything to shut him up.

Thinking of Alana this morning. How stifled she felt by Johan. The memory that keeps replaying is of her sitting, her head in her hands, at the table in my kitchen in Morningside. Not quite crying but grimacing as if she were about to. Tilly was in the lounge watching something on television, some programme on CBeebies, designed to anaesthetise her while we talked.

Johan was fighting her on everything: he wanted half of her shitty salary as a lab technician and full ownership of the miserable little smallholding they'd bought the year they got married. He wanted everything because she'd stopped giving.

In their second year of marriage he'd started questioning her failure to get pregnant. She said he regularly accused her of taking contraceptive pills behind his back (she'd had the implant but the stupid fucker was so stuck in the past he didn't know you could take hormones any other way) or, even worse – even more enraging to him – that she must have been terminating his babies before he could become aware of a pregnancy.

All she wanted, in those final months of her life, was to be left alone.

I think it's having Alex here. I'm not comparing him to Johan exactly but his near-constant presence has triggered something in me, some empathy I suppose, for my little sister who just wanted to be left alone.

This is all quite new for me. Disentangling Alana from Tilly; thinking about how she might have felt, what she went through. Progress?

*5 p.m.*

Preparing bannocks in the kitchen. I was kneading and folding the dough on the table when I saw a huge grey cloud roll in. It had the look of something important, some event that attracts spectators. Watching weather on Finish is like turning on a TV. It's a drama, a spectacle, breaking news, worthy of a piece-to-camera. Or entry-to-journal.

Knock at the door. It's Alex.

*Later*

'I brought you some clams,' he said, holding up one of Daley's shopping bags. I could smell the sharp tang of salty, fishy water that dripped on to the hard standing of the doorstep. 'I can take them up to the stream and rinse them if you like?'

'OK,' I shrugged.

'Are you making bannocks?'

'Yep,' and then because he seemed to want to come in and the peace had already been disturbed, I opened the door wider.

'We could have them with some samphire? You liked that last time I made it. Some of the tomatoes are looking red enough to eat now.'

I went back to my dough. 'You're dripping all over the floor.'

He put the bag down outside and returned, closing the front door behind him. 'Listen, Seren. I want to say I'm sorry. I should never have told Daley about us – about that night. I didn't realise you were a couple.'

'We're not.'

Silence. I continued kneading while watching my cloud. 'Except, clearly you are.'

'I'm not discussing this with you, Alex.'

'No, of course. It's none of my business. I just brought it up because I wanted to explain that this is what I do: I make connections and say stupid things. Like Daley saying this is a one-bed and the fact that your flat in Edinburgh was a one-bed. It's moronic and clumsy but I made the connection and then, before I knew it, I'd said it.'

I turned my bannock over. 'Am I supposed to feel sorry for you? That you have no filter?'

'No, I just want to explain. I think I just genuinely struggle to put myself in other people's shoes. Like that stuff about streaming Netflix and deliveries from the Co-op. I was trying to make a joke but it landed badly.'

'It landed badly because you're not funny.'

He touched my forearm with the tips of his fingers and I felt a sudden chill. He must have noticed how rigid I became because he was quick to pull his hand away and apologise, again. 'Can we eat these clams together tonight?' he said. 'Break bread, or bannocks, and make peace?'

I picked the bannock up by its edges and placed it on the stone. 'I'll put this on. If you're going up to the stream you can fill that container up.'

Dinner, in the end, was quite pleasant. Alex boiled the clams in a kind of liquor of butter, wild garlic and white wine from an already-open bottle. We sat, cross-legged, on the stone flags before the fire. I felt relieved, buoyed by the thaw between us. He would stay in his tent, I'd have the bothy and we would share the island. It was not what I wanted, not at all what I'd envisioned when I made my plans for this trip, but he was here now and it would be a hell of a lot easier for both of us if we could get on.

'I'm intrigued,' he said, dipping a hunk of bannock into the sauce. 'What made you choose the island setting for your book?'

'It was kind of dictated by what my editor said she wanted. Isolated setting. Deserted location. Where else?'

He nodded his head and chewed – as if this was the answer he'd been expecting. 'It's a bit of a coincidence though, isn't it?'

'What is?'

'The fact that my book is also set on an island.'

'Like I said,' it was an effort to continue chewing, 'it was my editor's idea.'

'It's all come together quite nicely for you though, hasn't it?'

'What has?'

'Your editor asks you to write a ghost story set on an island, you come here and then, voilà, you're visited by the muse.' He reached for the bottle of wine that was rapidly losing its chill on the warm hearthstone. He held it aloft and offered to refill my glass. When I shook my head, he took it back and emptied it into his own glass.

'By muse, I assume you're referring to what I said happened to me the night you arrived?'

'When the ghost children stole your clothes,' he nodded.

'You caught me at a very vulnerable time. I never should have told you what I did.'

'It's curious though. Because I remember finding that article about the shepherds in the *Stornoway Gazette* and showing it to you. The ones who came to live here after Finish was abandoned, how they saw a band of children running around?'

'And?'

'And, I guess I'm trying to say, in my clumsy way,' he grinned as he wobbled his head, 'that I'm happy I was able to help you.'

'Help me?'

'In some small way, yes.'

'In the way of a librarian, yes.'

'I'm just expressing, badly I'll admit, that perhaps I had some small part to play in the idea for your new book?'

'Yes. Your part was showing me how to search the main catalogue at Edinburgh Library.'

He laughed.

'My book and whatever I write here has nothing to do with you. Shit, Alex, I hate how blunt I have to be with you.'

'And the troop of ghost children stealing your clothes? That's nothing to do with the article I printed out for you?'

'That happened. It literally happened to me. I know it sounds crazy but that's the truth, as I understand it. I just wish I hadn't told you. I wasn't in my right mind and unfortunately for me, you were here to witness that.'

'Look, this is coming out all wrong. I think you're a tremendous writer. I read *Indigo Lights* after we parted and I was struck by how much I believed in Indigo's powers. You made me believe something that is, frankly, unbelievable. You clearly have a very vivid imagination and that's evident in your writing.'

'After we parted?'

'It's a turn of phrase.'

'A completely inappropriate one. We had sex. Once. The only "parting" I remember was my ex-husband resisting the urge to punch you.'

'OK, but my point is that you're very good, at this,' he motioned with his hands at the edges of the room that were now in darkness.

'What is this?' I asked, mimicking him.

'Pretending. Constructing fiction, creating narratives designed to deceive and entertain.'

'OK, Alex.'

'What?'

'One minute I'm stealing your ideas, the next I'm some sort of fantasy fiction virtuoso. Make your mind up.'

He put his hands down flat on his knees. 'I can see that I've offended you and for that I apologise. I was simply trying to point out where I might have helped you and to express my pleasure that I had. But I can see that has come across as conceited, which was not my intention. I admire your writing very much.'

'Good to hear. Now, if you don't mind, I'm quite tired. I'd like to go to bed.'

*Saturday 15th July*
It's gone eight and still no Alex this morning.

I've been going over last night's argument and I think the thing that bothers me the most is that the visions, the hauntings – whatever you want to call them – have stopped with Alex's arrival. I really don't care that he doesn't believe me or that he suspects me of using his article as fodder for my ghost story. No, what I can't ignore is how his presence has stopped the flow. In my desk drawer are a pair of bloodstained knickers, on my notebook, two names – Catriona and Ruaridh – and now, now nothing.

I'll go up to the stream with Beau this morning. She might even manage a climb to the top of Cnoc fiacail.

*Sunday 16th July, early evening*
Beau and I walked up to Crois an fionnadh this afternoon. Nothing. Came back and read a book for a few hours. No sign of Alex. Think he's keeping to his tent.

Pasta and butter for dinner followed by dried apricots.

A very disappointing day.

*Monday 17th July*

Left Beau in the bothy this afternoon and climbed down from the Ceum a'Mhaide headland to Chulainn's cave. Didn't go in. The tide was too high but even if it hadn't been, there's no way I could have gone in there alone again. It's frustrating, that despite my desire to know more, I can't bring myself to cross that threshold again. I can't enter that dark – the only word that comes to mind – womb. Instead I sat on the rocky ledge across from the opening and listened to the sound of the waves repeatedly slapping the cliffs. 'Get up,' they seemed to say. 'Can't you see?'

No, I can't. And that's the problem. There's nothing to see.

*Thursday 20th July, 7.30 a.m.*

Daley coming today. I need to go up to the stream and have a wash. Alex and I have said very little to each other. He hasn't been in for coffee since our fight last Friday. Nearly a week.

I've written nothing. It's hard not to feel dejected. I've got about six weeks left and I still don't have a working synopsis.

Alex has just knocked on the door. He's in the kitchen now making coffee. Neither of us said much though he's just offered to make dinner tonight. When I said Daley's coming, he just nodded and said he'd stay out of our way.

He does a good line in playing the victim.

Heading up to the stream now.

*9 p.m.*

No noises at the stream, nothing. The island has gone quiet.

Daley and I went to bed as soon as he got here. Couldn't get our clothes off fast enough. He's a man of few words at the best of times and this afternoon really was the best of times. It felt good to get out of my head and into my body.

Afterwards, I felt a bit sick and shook my head at the post-coital rollie. 'You OK?'

'Not really. I think it's the limited diet. If Alex cooks dinner, it's bloody razor clams or a skinned rabbit roasted over the fire and if I cook for myself, it's bland and boring. Can you bring me some apples when you next come? I woke up dreaming about apples this morning.'

'Yeah, although it might be a while before I come back. Bookings have really dropped off and I've got some work on a roof over in Craigston.'

'How long are we talking?'

He shrugged and laid his cigarette down to burn on the upturned jam jar lid he used as an ashtray. 'A few weeks. Mid-August maybe? You've got Beau.' We both looked down at the floor where she was curled up at the foot of the bed. Even curled up, you could see she was growing at an alarming rate. 'You could always come back with me? Today? Stay with me if you like. I'll be out during the day. You'd have all the peace and quiet you need to write.'

It was appealing. The thought of his bungalow, the double-glazing, central heating, a short walk to the Co-op. No Alex. But my story? And the echoes and re-enactments, they would also disappear. At least, as long as I'm here, there's a chance they'll start up again. In Castlebay, there would be no chance. 'It's very tempting,' I said. 'But I want to see this out. Five more weeks. And then, if the offer still stands, Beau and I would love to come and stay with you for a while. Until I find my feet.'

'In that case, I hope you never find your feet. Where's Alex?'

'God knows. Last time I checked, he was building a bathing seat.'

'A what?'

'He was up at the stream this morning. The deepest part where you can sit and immerse yourself is very rocky and uncomfortable so he's decided to hunt out smooth stones, to build a seat. It keeps him happy.'

'And you? Are you happy?'

'I'm over asking him when he's leaving, if that's what you mean. I keep getting the same answer: I need this sample or I need to rewrite this scene.'

'And what about you? How's your writing coming along?'

'Honestly?' I ran my hands through my hair. Several strands came away in my fingers. 'I don't know. I can't even get a synopsis together for my editor.'

'Writer's block, eh?' he said, leaning away from me and calling to Beau. I put the flat of my hand against his back, felt the small bones of his spinal cord move as he lifted her on to the covers. 'What are we going to do with you?' he said, stroking her ears. I felt my stomach turn over in a sharp, acidic wave.

'You OK?'

'Yeah.'

He got up, put Beau back down on the floor. 'Do you want a bucket?'

'No, thanks. It's passing.' I took a deep breath and moved over so I was sitting on the edge of the bed. I put my head between my knees. He stroked the small of my back while I breathed through the nausea.

'Can I get you a glass of water?'

'Please.'

Beau followed him downstairs and then back up when he returned. Her face wore a puzzled look: why was my time on the bed having my ears stroked so brief? Can anyone explain that, please?

Daley crouched down before me, his hands on my knees. 'I meant to say to you, Rosalie's quite keen to get Aunty Kitty here. Thinks it would be good for her. A goodbye, kind of.'

'A goodbye? Is she dying?'

'No, but she's getting on a bit. It's unlikely we'll get her here again.'

I took another sip of water.

'And I thought, you have questions about the massacre – I've been pretty useless on that front but my Aunty Kitty, she'll know stuff the history books don't.'

'True.'

'I said to Rosie, I'll need a bit of time to think about how we're going to do it. She can't exactly scramble over the rocks. I'm not sure we could get her much beyond the beach, to be honest.'

The water had helped moisten my throat and my stomach was starting to feel more settled. I felt a little glimmer of hope. Perhaps Kitty would be able to tell me something that would break the deadlock. 'Sounds good. I'd love to talk to her.'

*Sunday 23rd July, afternoon*

He's such a dick. I cannot emphasise this point enough. He is stupid and determined. The very worst combination of character traits. But I'm worried. I'm worried his actions will have consequences for both of us.

I was on my way back down from Cnoc fiacail with Beau when I saw Alex beside the stream. He was lifting small rocks from a pile on his right to an arrangement on the bank, inches from the water. I could see a circle of round rocks around a much larger one. Further down the bank were two long logs, pieces of driftwood he'd clearly whittled down to use as rollers for the bigger, heavier stone. It took me a moment to think where he might have transported it from. Why would he need to fashion a trolley? Then I realised. There was only one place it could have come from.

'What have you done?' I shouted. It was the most I'd said to him in a week and a half. He looked up at me, I was still a few metres off but Beau had run on ahead and was standing respectfully on the edge of the arrangement.

'Hello,' he gave Beau a quick stroke. 'You complained it was uncomfortable to bathe here. I have fixed it for madame.' He picked up another small rock and placed it near the font stone. 'I'm just trying to get the arrangement right before I put them in the water.'

With its smooth base and deep lozenge depression, empty and dry, it looked strange and out of place. Like a mutilation. Like a limb that has been ripped off and then inexpertly sewn on elsewhere. I could see the tidal mark of dark earth up the sides, see the moist clods that still clung to it from the spot where it had been ripped out. I saw all these things and wanted to cry. 'You took the font stone.'

He looked confused and stood up. 'This?' he kicked it with the tip of his boot. 'I found it up in that stone circle near the headland. When I saw it, I thought: that's a perfect bath seat.'

'You took the font stone.'

'So you keep saying. What is it then? Am I to guess from your melodramatic responses that it's precious? That I've committed sacrilege?'

He is amused, I thought. He's enjoying this. 'Yes. To the people of this island, Crois an fionnadh is a sacred place—'

'I haven't touched the big stones. There's no way I could—' he motioned towards his rollers.

'But this,' I crouched down and touched it gently. I felt Beau's wet nose on my wrist. The central dip, where the Lixivium collected, was bone dry, the sides calcified and rough to the touch. 'What have you done?'

'I don't know, what have I done?'

'The people who lived here. They believed—'

'Look around you, Seren. The people who lived here. There's no one here. The people left a long time ago. Do you know why? Because it's an awful place to live. You complained that it was uncomfortable, sitting in the stream – I'm trying, very hard I might say, to fix that for you.'

'You need to put it back,' I said, trying to move it, even just a few millimetres, but it wouldn't budge.

'The only place this is going is in the water. Just as you asked.'

I stood up. 'I did not ask. I didn't tell you to do this.'

'Not in so many words but you made it clear that's what you wanted.'

'No, I didn't.'

'You know, this is so typical of you. You say you want something and when I do it for you, when I go to great lengths to do it for you, you're horrified. You ask for my help and when I give it to you, you're quick to downplay it, telling me it's what any librarian would have done. You ask me to stay the night in your flat and then, the next day, you can't get rid of me quick enough.'

'What are you talking about?'

'I'm talking about you. About women like you. Always changing your mind and expecting me to somehow guess what's going on in your head. You say you want to read my book but then I find it discarded in the kindling box. You want a bath seat but oh no, not this bath seat.' He put his hands to his face and spoke in a shriek that was supposed to resemble me. 'What have you done, Alex? Put it back, Alex.'

Stay calm, I told myself. Breathe. 'What you have done is sacrilege. It is a desecration. This stone,' I swallowed, 'was laid in the centre of the circle millennia ago – for the protection of innocents.'

He threw his head back and laughed, a great bark of derision.

I picked up Beau's leash and pulled her away.

'Oh, come on,' he shouted. 'That was funny.'

'It's not funny,' I turned around to face him again. 'You'll see.'

'I'm not afraid,' he said, returning to the stones. 'Unlike you, I'm much better at keeping my clothes on.'

*Monday 24th July*
Heavy rain this morning and no sign of Alex. I didn't think it was possible for things to deteriorate between us any further. Turns out I was wrong.

*PM*
The sky has brightened up a little. Just seen Alex walking in the direction of the stream. Off to continue his handi-work, no doubt.

Maybe I did overreact. Jamie often accused me of it, during our marriage. 'You make too much of everything,' was his standard refrain, shouted at me on more than one occasion. But then, of course, we lost Tilly, so there was nothing to make any more. You can't do much with zero.

Isn't that the job of the writer though? To make too much of something. I'm not really a writer though.

Not a mother any more either.

*Tuesday 25th July, 7.30 p.m.*
My period should have come by now. Is it possible? I'm forty-two. Certainly unlikely. There's also the fact that Tilly had no siblings because Jamie and I had not been able to conceive again.

Maybe it was a sperm issue and Daley has super-charged Aussie swimmers. I imagine them, all zinc oxide and tiny speedos racing with determination towards my last geriatric egg, hobbling its way along the fallopian tube.

It would certainly explain the nausea I felt at Alex's dinner offerings and the fact that I've been craving apples. Just the thought of an apple has made my mouth flood with saliva. Could it be? Yesterday, I was so down, so low, and today – now that I've come up with this possibility – I feel hopeful. I think I'll leave Beau here and go up to Crois an fionnadh. It's not quite dusk, there's still time. The font stone might be gone but the powers of the stone circle might remain.

*After dark*

A girl. A young woman. It was difficult to tell in the seconds she was before me. But certainly young and lithe, judging by her movements.

I was kneeling beside the hole where the stone should have been but instead, like an eye socket that had had its soft tissue ripped out, it gaped dry and sunken. I was thinking of the Lixivium, of how I'd rubbed it on my face and neck when I first arrived; how it had made me feel connected to the women who had lived here and how I could do with the gift of its protection now when I sensed movement. A darting flash that stroked, like soft pencil on paper, at the very edge of my peripheral vision. I turned my head to look, saw the stones on the western side of the circle, like long and decayed teeth in a jaw split wide. 'Who's there?' I called.

When there was no answer I stood up and walked towards the stones. I could see, between two of them, the

Ceum a'Mhaide headland. I was in the very place I'd heard the call of 'thall' when I first came here and where the smoke had risen. 'Who are you?' I said again, but this time quieter. I watched the space between the two stones for a long time, sensing the island going about its nightly business: brushing the grasses flat, wiping the stones with a sheen of moist, cool air and then, then a flash. A figure darted from one stone to the next, obscuring – briefly – the Ceum a'Mhaide headland my eyes had been trained on.

It was the figure of a young woman with long, red hair. Hair that was big and curly. It bounced up from her back as she ran. 'Wait,' I shouted, my voice betraying my fear and urgency. Walk over, I told myself. You know where she is now so just walk over.

I kept my eyes trained on the next gap, willing her to cross it. But my window of opportunity was closing. The sky had lost patience, it was keen to turn the lights off and close up for the night.

I don't know how long I stood there but when I did finally pluck up the courage to go and look behind the stone, there was no one there. Of course there wasn't. I'd left it too late. I go on about listening, tuning in, how writing this book is an exercise in sensitivity and yet, when I have an opportunity to go and look and see, I don't take it. That's the bottom line. For all my 'I'm not afraid, the worst has already happened to me,' the truth is, I am. I am afraid to really look at what is being shown to me.

Frustrated, I was about to turn around and head home when I noticed something small and cream-coloured on the earth, nestled in the grass at the base of the stone.

It was a bone. The same bone I'd buried with Chulainn.

*Later*

Another X on the map. Hardly surprising really.

*Wednesday 26th July*

He knocked on the door just after ten this morning and asked if he could come in. I was sitting at my desk, turning the bone in my fingers, trying to update my hypothesis. The bone belongs to Catriona, one of the names in my notebook. It's a leap but it's the only girl's name I have. The names I had assumed, hoped is probably a more accurate verb, belonged to a couple of teenagers in a WHSmith's in Edinburgh, trying a pen out.

If I'm right then this bone, returned to me, belongs to the girl I saw last night. The girl-not-yet-a-woman who ran from stone to stone while I stood, stupid and scared, watching her. I was turning the bone and all of this over in my mind when Alex knocked. He was wearing his waterproof jacket and his cheeks were flushed. 'I brought you some peat,' he said, laying some sacking open on the doorstep. The blocks were already turning from a moist dark to a patchy light brown and my first thought was of the hole where the font stone had been. 'Shall I carry them inside for you?'

I said nothing, just stood back while he lifted the corners of the sacking and carried the bundle inside like some sort of rough-sleeping Santa with his dark curls and North Face jacket. He lay the pile down in the middle of the floor. 'They'll need to dry out first. This is certainly the best place on the island for doing that.' Can I make some coffee?'

'I'll do it.'

He took his boots off and sat down at the table, drumming his fingers while I filled the percolator, spooned coffee into the filter and set it going on the gas stove. 'Do you want me to light the fire?' he asked.

'It's a bit early. I need to take Beau for a walk anyway.'

'The new bathing seat is ready for you to use.'

I pulled my lips between my teeth, nodded my head. 'Is that so?'

'Believe it or not, I did that for you. For your benefit.'

'I just wish you'd told me what you were planning to do.'

'OK, I take that on board. But, and I'm really not trying to start another fight here, what good would telling you have done?'

'I could have explained to you that it was a very bad idea.'

'A bad idea, why? Because of your supernatural fears? No, please, just hear me out. I want you to understand that your fears are valid, yes, but they are not founded in any objective, verifiable reality.'

'I know that.'

'So if you know that, you must also understand that it's not reasonable to expect others, i.e. me, to fall in line with those beliefs. That the island would rear up and enact some sort of hideous revenge because I moved a stone is just not logical or reasonable.'

'Yes, Alex, I know all this.'

'Is there a chance that, when this is all over, you might perhaps make an appointment to speak to someone. A professional?'

I stared at him, long and hard.

'What? It's no secret what happened to you. I've read all about it. It must have been deeply traumatising.'

'And?'

'Please, don't let's start all this again.'

'What do you want from me? You come here with peat, I make you coffee and I think, for a minute, that we might be able to establish some kind of peace but then, in no time at all, you're back to your old ways.'

'My old ways?'

'Passive-aggressive, condescending. Is it possible I provided more help than you're prepared to credit? Is there a chance you should see a professional? All of your opinions, and frankly, there are too many of them, are set forth in these gentle, enquiring tones. You act like a character from a bloody Austen novel. All polite enquiry and sitting down to tea but really you're here to stick the knife in.'

He laughed then, which just enraged me more.

'Just come out and say it, Alex. What you want to tell me is that you think I stole an idea from you and also, that I'm probably batshit crazy. That's about the extent of it, isn't it?'

'I think you're overreacting.'

'That's what crazy people do. They overreact.'

'I should leave you. Would you like me to walk Beau?'

'No.'

'OK,' he said, drinking what was left in his cup. 'The peat needs two weeks to dry out.'

*Later, after lunch*

If anything, it's the thought of sharing this place with him a moment longer than necessary that makes me want to email Daley and take him up on his offer to go and stay with him in Castlebay.

It seems Alex and I cannot get on. And the failure of every encounter is just so wearing. I'm tired. Of him, this place, a book I cannot even plan, let alone write.

*9 p.m.*

Another evening walk with Beau. Very little wind tonight, just a few thin wisps of cloud lit pink from below. Went up to Crois an fionnadh first, hoping to see the girl again but there was no sign of her. As there was still an hour before sunset and the evening was so calm, I decided to walk along the headland of the western cliffs.

At the highest point, some two hundred metres above the cave, there is a stone platform with an iron ring. The islanders would have used it for their peat pyramids or as an anchor point while hunting down the cliff-face for wildfowl and their eggs. In Edinburgh library, I read about the children whose small, lithe bodies were ideally suited to this pursuit, regularly jumping down from the headland, hanging perilously above the two hundred-metre drop, searching for guillemots, razorbills, puffins and cormorants.

As I got closer, I saw there was a carabiner and rope attached to the iron ring. The rope didn't look particularly taut. When I peered over, I saw the top of Alex's head. He was crouching down on a ledge about twenty metres below, in the process of sealing up a small plastic bag. More soil samples. Could this be a last-ditch effort to gather what he needed before returning to Edinburgh? Had the PhD option won out? The thought made me hopeful.

He didn't see me and I didn't wave or do anything to attract his attention. No, better to keep my distance. Perhaps it's the hostility between us that has prompted the exit planning.

The sun was very low and Beau was starting to shiver. Time to go home.

*Thursday 27th July*
Early morning, inside Alex's tent

I need to get the events of last night down. I've slept a little – perhaps two or three hours – not nearly enough, but there's no chance I'll go back to sleep now. Alex, completely unaffected by what happened, is snoring quietly in his sleeping bag beside me.

I went to bed as usual, around midnight, and woke to the smell of smoke. At first I thought I was dreaming, experiencing for myself the terror that Tilly and Alana must have felt that night. But the air was heavy with the smell of peat, it was filling the tiny cavity of my attic bedroom, spreading, shuffling up into the corners of the sloping roof like passengers on a busy bus. In my confusion I looked around for Tilly, reached around my blankets and felt, instead, Beau come to life beneath my hand.

The stairwell, at the opposite end of the room, was lit up. A flickering glow that revealed the clouds of smoke in the room. My second thought, after Tilly and Beau, was Alex. Had he done this? Was he Johan, trying to burn me alive in the bothy? The thought made my heart beat harder, like I'd seen something – something that had remained below the surface of consciousness – and it made me gasp so that I started coughing. I rolled from my bed to the floor, searching for something to use as a mask. I found the T-shirt I'd been wearing last night and soaked it with water.

Beau overtook me as I crawled down the stairs to the ground floor, where I saw – right in the middle of the room – a perfect circle of flames, exactly where Alex had deposited the peat earlier. The fire was throwing out intense heat and smoke. I'd never seen the inside of the bothy lit up like that. So bright. The flames, the smoke, the fire – they felt – they felt theatrical.

I was so terrified I couldn't move.

I couldn't move because something about this fire was not right.

It was licking at the ceiling and it would – if it continued – weaken the rafters but none of it was spreading beyond its immediate perimeter. It went up but not out. How could that be? Why had it not engulfed my desk or the rocking chair?

It was too close to the front door. Any attempt to get out that way would result in me or Beau being caught by the flames.

I should have climbed out of the window, but there was something about that fire. I felt the same hesitation I had when I saw the girl move from one stone to another at Crois an fionnadh the other night.

I need to be braver, I told myself. I took a few steps towards it. As I moved closer to the flames I saw they were surrounded by a circle of small stones, all a similar size and shape to the ones Alex had been collecting and arranging around the font stone at the stream. These stones marked the boundary of the fire, so thick and orange at its base; thinner, more yellow at the tip. Through these flames, on the side nearest the fireplace, I saw something move.

A figure in the chair. Rocking back and forth. I tried to get closer but the heat was too intense, it was like a flat palm held out to me. I saw a head, covered with a black scarf, rocking. I trained my eyes on one particular spot and when it came back into view, I could see it looked like an old woman. Definitely not the young, lithe girl I'd seen darting between the stones.

I heard a whine from Beau behind me but I stayed where I was. Now was the time. Be bold, I told myself. I took another step forward, into the hand of the heat. And then, through the flames, I saw the figure rise to stand. The room was raging with heat but I felt cold and frightened. I wanted this, I'd searched for it, but now that the figure – was it Chulainn? – was turning to face me, I wished I'd run.

Her irises were coloured orange by the flames and her mouth hung open – slack and toothless – her throat all the time moving in a gagging motion, as if she was trying to bring something up. Instinctively, without thinking, I took another step forward. She opened her mouth wider so I was able to see. I see it now as I write. I will always see it.

A bloodied stump where her tongue should have been. The wound was wet and still clotting, like it had just happened.

A bark from behind me. Beau was up on the kitchen work surface, her nose against the window handle. Her bark broke the deadlock, freed me from my paralysis. I ran to her, terrified the woman with no tongue would follow me. In my mind, I saw her stride through the flames, follow me to the window and reach for my leg, my foot, any part of my body that would keep me in the burning bothy with her.

But there was no grasping. The only thing that followed me as I left the bothy was smoke. Great choking clouds of it. Beau, who was too impatient to wait for me to fall out of the window, ran around to the back of the bothy, her barks coming in short, shallow bursts.

I heard Alex shout my name. He appeared just as I jumped from the window. He was in his underpants and nothing more. His body, lean and shivering, struck me as too young to deal with what was inside the bothy. 'Shit,' he said and began kicking at the front door.

'It's locked from the inside,' I shouted. 'Go in through the window,' I pointed.

'Give us a leg-up.'

I held my hands together for his foot. It took all of my remaining energy to hold his weight. 'But Alex—' I said. He was busy hauling himself over the sill. Either he didn't hear me or didn't care to hear me. 'There's someone—'

'What?' he called. He was already clambering forward over the sill.

'Never mind,' I said, giving his foot a final, useless push.

He emptied the water containers over the fire, dousing the worst of it quickly, and then handed them back to me through the window, told me to fill them up again. 'Not fully,' he shouted to my back. 'You won't be able to run with them.'

I ran as fast as I could, across the dunes and down to the water. Beau kept pace with me, happy to finally play and splash in the waves while I frantically filled the containers. The horizon was just cracking open, I was aware of it as I would be of a fly landing on my forehead or damp seeping through my clothes. But then, a ray of light so bright, so sharp it sliced through my vision. Sunrise – it was later than I had first thought.

When I returned to the bothy, I could see all the windows and the front door were wide open, the spent smoke drifting up into the early-morning clouds. Inside, the fire was out but the peat blocks and stone flags were still smouldering. Alex took my containers of water and poured them over the circle of embers, each one emitting a steamy hiss. I watched him do this, silencing the urge to say, did you see her? Did you see the old woman?

He crouched down at the edge of the burn circle and turned to me. 'What on earth were you thinking?'

'What was I thinking?'

'You must have left the fire burning. A spark or an ember, that's all it would have taken.'

'The fire was dead, it was no more than ashes when I went to bed.'

'Don't you know the story of the Great Fire of London? That was all it took, one spark from a fire in the middle of the night.'

'The fire was dead, I'm telling you.'

'You cannot take responsibility for anything, can you?'

'Me? You're the one who put a pile of bloody peat in the middle of the room! How about you take some responsibility?'

'I put it there to dry out. For you, I might add.'

'It's a bit strange though, isn't it?'

'What? Doing something for you?'

'No, the peat going up like that. You said it needed to dry out and it went up like an inferno.'

He shook his head and stood up.

'What?'

'Not this again.'

'Alex, I saw someone. A woman. She was in here.'

'You saw her where?'

I pointed to the fireplace and the rocking chair. It was completely untouched by the fire.

'Well, I didn't. And I was the one who put out the flames. I can say, with absolute certainty, there was no woman in here.'

I felt tears rising. The thought of crying in front of him embarrassed me more than any claims I might make about an old woman in a rocking chair.

'I think you need some rest.' He said it gently, taking a step towards me. I think he knew not to try and touch me. 'I don't think you should sleep in here. The smoke isn't good for your lungs. Do you have a sleeping bag?'

I followed him out to his tent. He offered me his thermarest but I shook my head. Comfort didn't matter to me. I was pretty sure I wouldn't fall asleep anyway. How could I, after staring into that woman's bloodied, mutilated mouth?

But then I thought of that sunrise down at the beach. It was so beautiful, so peaceful, I could have almost forgotten the bothy burning behind me. Almost.

This is an island of contrasts: like the tides that withdraw and make a treacherous crossing benign again; the cries of pain that quickly turn to laughter; or the darkness that gives way to the most beautiful light. This is a place you can never get a handle on. Never say you truly know.

But the thought that swirled round and round in my mind most, as I lay under the canvas of Alex's tent was this: Chulainn has finally shown herself to me.

*2 p.m.*

Alex and I have spent most of the morning sweeping out the ash, wiping down the walls and floors and just airing the place out. By one o'clock we were both exhausted. I cooked us a lunch of boiled rice and tuna and then, because I felt somehow obligated by his efforts to restore a place he doesn't live in, I said he could go and take a nap on my bed upstairs. He seemed pleased by the offer.

It was not entirely selfless. I want some time alone at my desk. I want to look at the OS map without attracting Alex's attention or his questions. He is altogether too interested in my work, this journal, all my notes. I've caught him watching me as I write in the mornings, walking up behind me and peering over my shoulder on his way back to the kitchen.

Another cross. Over the bothy. There are so many now. Join the dots? I better email Daley.

From: Seren Doughty
To: Daley MacKinnon
Date: 27 July 2023 at 14:23
Subject: hello

We had some unexpected excitement here last night. A small fire broke out. Please don't worry: Beau and I are fine. So's Alex. He helped me put it out actually. I don't know what I would have done had he not been here.

We were drying out some peat in the bothy and Alex thinks a spark from the fireplace set it going.

The good news is no one was hurt and there's very little damage, apart from a few scorch marks on the stone flags. We've spent the morning cleaning and airing the place out.

I know you said mid-August before your next visit but I wondered if you might be able to come any sooner? Beau and I are missing you.

S x

From: Daley MacKinnon
To: Seren Doughty
Date: 27 July 2023 at 14:31
Subject: hello

What is he playing at? Peat inside? Please tell me you've moved it outside now. There's a stone platform up on the headland, opposite Finamuil. You can dry it out there. Stick a tarpaulin over it – there's one in the lean-to.

I'll try and come soon. Still working on this roof and the manager's keen for us to get it done while this dry spell lasts. I'll let you know how I go.

D

No kisses, no I miss you too. Hard not to feel deflated. But then, another email.

From: Daley MacKinnon
To: Seren Doughty
Date: 27 July 2023 at 14:44
Subject: hello

Sorry I went off on you like that. Just annoyed he put you in danger like that.

I miss you too. Won't be long now. I'll see what I can do. Xx

I closed my laptop, poured myself a glass of red wine and sat in the rocking chair. I went back and forth, looking at the scorch marks on the floor. A perfect circle. And then I remembered something Daley had said when that family had visited the island and the man had asked to come into the bothy. He'd said the old cottages, built on this site, hadn't had chimneys. 'The islanders used to light a peat fire, right in the middle of the floor, and it would vent through a hole in the thatch.'

Chulainn. She had wanted me to see her, in the place she feels comfortable, beside her home fire. She wanted me to know that this had once been her home. And the missing tongue? No dictionary or reference book required to solve that puzzle.

*Saturday 29th July*
Still no period. Four days late.

*Monday 31st July*
Alex and I harvested a load of carrots from the vegetable patch this afternoon. He's offered to make vegetable soup for dinner tonight (we have a glut of courgettes and runner beans). I'll make bannocks.

It's nice actually that we're getting on. I guess I have the fire to thank for that.

*3 a.m.*
Woken up feeling nauseous. No sign of my period though.

*Tuesday 1st August*
Taking it very easy today. Just water and crackers. Alex has been in to check on me a few times, offered to cook lunch but I don't want anything complicated. He always makes everything so complicated.

I can hear him downstairs, crashing around in the kitchen. I wish he'd leave me alone so I can sleep.

*Wednesday 2nd August*
Much better today. Already been for a short walk with Beau and going to warm some water on the fire for a flannel wash. Can't face a dip in the stream – not strong enough.

Still no period.

*Wednesday 9th August*

It's been a week since I last wrote. There is nothing to write, I have nothing to note down. The weather has been fairly good, not especially warm though today is the warmest at seventeen degrees. Alex has gone for a swim so I thought I should take the opportunity to sit down with a cup of coffee and write something.

I keep thinking about Chulainn, or the figure across the fire, showing me her mutilated mouth. The message: I can't speak so you need to speak for me? Or is there a more obvious, immediate parallel: your stupid companion dug out the font stone, which is the same as doing this to me?

Daley emailed earlier to say he's going to come this weekend. He said he'll stay the night too. It could not have come at a better time.

I really need to get out of my head.

Still no period. Also late: my synopsis.

*Thursday 10th August*

Fog. In the distance, sandwiched like raw dough between sky and sea, it rolls and spreads towards us.

I'm up at the top of Cnoc fiacail with Beau. It's the first time she's managed a climb unaided. She's sitting beside me, up against my boots, and panting while I write this. Normally, the wind will whip against you up here but not this afternoon. This afternoon everything is calm and still.

It doesn't feel good, the way it's rolling in – slow and certain – preparing to blanket us. I'm worried it's going to put the kibosh on my weekend plans with

Daley. Should I email him? Check the weather forecast? There won't be any power to the battery once this fog settles. Perhaps I'd better use whatever remaining charge there is in the laptop to see how long it's going to last. Is there time to get off the island before it does?

The thought makes me afraid. Running or preparing to leave has always made me more afraid of the thing I'm up against. I felt it the other night, in front of the fire. The moment I turned my back and tried to climb out of the window was – for me – the most terrifying. It was when my heart rate shot up and my mind began imagining a hand reaching for my ankle.

It frightens me, the thought of being held back, held against my will when I want to leave.

The fog is in the bay now. Beau and I have come down from Cnoc fiacail to the walls of the abandoned village to watch its progress. It's like thin wool, like the fibres of a fleece pulled apart, and it floats, harmless, gentle even, through the walls and up to the bothy.

That's the thing with fog. You watch it close up for long enough and before you know it, everything else has gone. The sea, the sky, the mountains – they've all disappeared from view, obscured by the heavy layers of white vapour.

The fog reminds me of huge, drapey blankets thrown over the props on a stage just before the play begins. Am I the audience? The thought unnerves me. Because it begs the next question: what, exactly, am I about to see?

*Later, sometime after 4 p.m.*

Alex was agitated when I got home. He'd been using my laptop to do something when the power had cut out.

'What did you expect?' I asked him. 'There's no sunlight. Or wind for that matter.'

'But I'd pressed send. I'd literally just pressed send when it cut out.'

'OK,' I shrugged. 'So, we wait it out.'

'You don't seem too bothered by it.'

'Bothered? Alex, it's fog. There's nothing I can do about it.'

'Daley isn't coming.'

'Well, I gathered as much. How do you know? Did he send an email?'

'I saw a little notification flash up,' he said dismissively.

'What did he say?'

'Nothing. Just that he won't be coming. We should probably do an inventory of food.'

We had plenty of dried stuff: pasta, lentils, rice but the fresh fruit and veg was already in short supply. It had been nearly three weeks since his last visit. In the kitchen we counted out the tins of tuna, peered into the packet of flour, weighed the butter and baking soda by hand. We had enough to keep us in bannocks and tinned protein, plus there was the veg from the garden. It was far from perilous, I assured him. We could last for weeks and it wouldn't be that long anyway. But still, unusually for him, he seemed on edge. His eyes kept darting around the room, taking in one thing and then another: peat – should he cut some more? Did we have enough kindling, and then, strangely, sugar. 'Do we have any?' he asked.

'Yes, loads. Why?'

'I could make us some of that meadowsweet cordial?'

'I'm fine with water.'

'Do we have enough tablets?'

'Enough to purify the sea.'

'OK,' he nodded but still, I could see he was rattled.

'I'm actually feeling better,' I said.

'That's good,' he agreed, not looking at me.

'I think crackers help. Just plain, dry foods.'

If he suspected, as I did, the reason for the nausea, he kept it to himself. 'I can make up a jug easily? I only need about fifty grams.'

'Forget the cordial. It doesn't matter. Anyway, it's not sensible to go foraging in this. You can't see where you're going.'

'Is that your way of saying you wouldn't want me to fall off the headland?' he said it kindly, with a smile I felt I should return. It had been nice actually, having someone else in the kitchen – taking stock, counting the tins.

'I don't think I ever said thank you. For putting out the fire.'

'I don't think I said sorry for that comment up at the stream. About you not keeping your clothes on.'

'Forget it.'

He stepped a little closer and instinctively, I stepped back. 'Can we?' He held his arms out.

His chest was lean and muscly beneath his T-shirt and he smelt sour. Not bad exactly, just the kind of organic odour that comes from a complete absence of perfumed toiletries. 'I've got some meadowsweet already picked in the lean-to,' he said to the crown of my head. I pulled back. 'Are you sure I can't make you some?'

In the end I said yes. It was easier than continuing to refuse.

*Night-time, early hours*
My guts feel like they've been run through with acid. It's difficult to move and every time I do, I feel a wash of burning, corrosive liquid move around in my stomach. I don't know what to do. It could be an early miscarriage but there's still no blood. Plus, the pain feels intestinal. Like I need to shit or vomit.

No internet, no Daley. What the fuck am I going to do?

*Friday 11th August, afternoon sometime*
I can't do it. I can't bring myself to write it down. Too soon.

*11.30 p.m.*
I fall asleep but then I wake again, twenty or thirty minutes later. Always with that same cry echoing in my head.

*Saturday 12th August, 5 a.m.*
Fog. Still here. Still thick and blanketing everything. The silence outside the bothy is as eerie as the silence inside. If you walk towards the beach – which is difficult, the torch light does very little but illuminate the soup – you can hear the wash of the waves on the sand. Life goes on, it says. Look at me. I'm not letting it get me down.

I have to write what happened. I wanted more and that's exactly what I got. Time to record it now.

In the early hours of Friday morning, I woke up, clutching my stomach in pain. Beau, beside me, was whining her concern, nosing my arm, my side, hoping to be reassured. I pushed her away – oh, god, I pushed her away – and fell out of bed onto the floor.

It wasn't far and the fall was calculated: I couldn't contract my abdominals enough to sit up and swing my legs over the side.

I crawled towards the top of the stairs, Beau's claws clacking on the floorboards following me as I moved. I bobbed down on my sacrum, trying to keep myself as straight and flat as I could, but the cramps, coming in waves, made me cry out.

Beau started barking then. She really was afraid and anxious and, perhaps remembering the fire, skittered down past me to the kitchen area and then back up to where I lay, as straight and still as I could. 'Shut up,' I hissed. 'Shut up, Beau.' I was afraid Alex would hear and come in. I didn't want him in the bothy.

I managed to get the front door open and then, as if my body had been waiting for the cool air, a wave of pain brought the burning vomit up. I knelt on all fours and emptied my stomach. The sound was strangely deadened by the fog. I saw the bits of bannock, the chewed-up courgette, the small fizzing tendrils of mead-owsweet. I saw it all, on the doorstep of the bothy.

I sat back, let my head fall against the door jamb, let the fog roll in to the bothy and I fell asleep. The pain was not gone but it was, like me, taking a little breather.

Did I question it? Did I sit there and think back to the early weeks of my first pregnancy with Tilly? The answer is no, I didn't. I was so exhausted, so scraped out, so comforted by the cool moist air that caressed my face and hair that I closed my eyes and let sleep take me.

Tilly. She came to me then in another dream. She sat beside me as I slept on the doorstep. And even though I was tired and still feeling sick, I knew to keep my eyes closed and my body still. 'Wake up,' she said. Her voice was older, a little deeper.

I didn't answer. I didn't want to move a single muscle in my body, for fear she'd leave me again. 'Wake up, Mummy.'

Again, I said nothing.

'Beau's gone.'

It was like breaking water, coming up from that dream. I woke with a deep, painful intake of breath and before anything else, before the answering exhale, before even a cursory glance for the Tilly of my dream, I looked for Beau.

I called her, searched inside the bothy, laboured up the stairs but there was no sign. Outside it was dark, the fog close. I called, then cried, then shouted at the top of my voice for her, each time trying my best to allow a few seconds for her answering bark. At first nothing. Then I heard footsteps to my left.

His voice, like his torch, cut through the soup. 'What is it? What's wrong?' And it felt like a re-run of the fire except this time the smoke had been replaced by some other opaque substance designed to disorientate me.

'Beau,' I said and turned to walk back into the bothy.

'What the fuck?'

'What?' I walked back to him.

He lifted his foot, shone his light on the wet, viscous strands that tried to hold him to the concrete of the doorstep.

'It's sick.'

'She was sick?'

'I was sick.'

'But where's Beau?'

'I don't know.'

Knowing something is wrong but not what. That's the worst feeling. Worst. Such an inadequate word. Driving to Alana's house that night, watching the sky absorb the smoke and flames and fumes of a new build on fire, not knowing if Tilly had been pulled from it – it was the worst I've ever felt but it was also a moment of calculation. Of bargaining. If this is what I think it is, if the thing I fear most has happened, then I won't need this phone in my hand, these slippers on my feet, the car that we have not yet finished paying off. None of it will matter. Everything will become irrelevant in the face of this.

The feeling I had on Thursday night was similar. Not the same but similar. It was a shot of déjà vu, a frenzied punch of adrenaline: you know this. You've been here before.

I took my torch and walked out into the fog.

Alex came with me. He had the good sense to keep quiet, apart from the odd, 'watch the ground here' or 'we're rising up now – it's a bit rocky. Careful you don't slip'. We went to Crois an fionnadh first, our torches skimming the tall, silent stones and calling Beau in high-pitched, friendly voices – as if this were all just a game.

Backstage, like an actor impatient for his cue, the sea roared loud and deep. I called Beau again and again, until my voice was hoarse. I hoped and prayed out loud: 'Please don't let her have gone into the water.' Even then, even when I knew something awful was underway, I thought I could hope and pray. That anything from my lips might save her.

From Crois an fionnadh, it was a short walk to the Ceum a'Mhaide headland. I could tell Alex was nervous. 'Really small steps now. Keep your torch trained at least a metre ahead. The fall will be upon you before you know it.'

The fall will be upon you before you know it. That sentence has stuck with me. A curious, strangely archaic thing to say and yet it made sense. It did then and it does now. A fall was coming and all we could do, in order to save ourselves, was take tentative, cautious steps towards it.

'Do you want me to go down?' he offered. 'I can check the cave.'

'The tide is in. You won't be able to get across.'

'Do you want me to try?'

'I don't know.' I was finding it very difficult to think. I couldn't see Beau making her way down the steps, but then I hadn't thought she would wander off like she did.

'Try to think. Where does she love to go?'

'The stream? Or we climbed Cnoc fiacail ... yesterday. Christ, was it only yesterday? We saw the fog come in.'

We walked in silence along the western edge of the island. I looked right, in the direction of the bothy, which should have been a beacon, lit up by the oil lamps

Alex had lit before we left, but the fog blanketed everything.

'Do you think one of us should wait in the bothy? In case she returns?'

'If she returns, she'll wait there,' I said.

'But would she?'

'I'm not sitting around in the bothy, Alex. I need to find her.'

We continued walking. I thought of the stream, the rocks, the cries I'd heard, the bastard kids who'd stolen my clothes – I couldn't help it, I couldn't stop myself from recalling all the malevolence, all the sinister echoes I'd been witness to – and I lost my balance, stumbling on a hummock. 'Lean on me,' he said, threading my hand through his arm and pulling me forward. Our steps took on a rhythm as we walked together, calling for my lost dog.

At the base of Cnoc fiacail, the ground rises gently to the cut of the stream and then, beyond the collar of rocks, more sharply. It's the kind of gradient that can only be understood with perspective, with an unobstructed view of the top. But in the dense fog, placing one boot perpendicular to the other with no idea of how far away we were, I felt disorientated and hopeless. 'What are we going to do, Alex?'

'We'll find her.'

'Will we?'

'It's important we stay positive.'

'We've called and called.'

And then, from above us, a bark. An answering bark. 'What did I tell you?' he said, letting go of my arm and moving ahead.

I tried to follow but it was so hard. My stomach was empty, worse than empty; it was swilling with rank, sour bile. I had used up all my energy and couldn't seem to draw enough oxygen into my lungs. 'Are you OK?' he asked from above.

'Yes, go on. Go and get her.'

'I don't want to leave you.'

'I'm fine. Beau!' I shouted and again, her answering bark. 'Please, Alex. Go. You're faster than me.'

He continued. I watched his boots pound the wet grass as he powered up and away.

How long was he gone? More than seconds, it was minutes. Maybe three or four.

'No!' Alex's voice from above. He was screaming. 'No! Don't! Please, no!'

I got up and started running. I heard a scream. Was it his? Or mine even? The blinding spotlight of his torch dazzled me. I closed my eyes but still my vision swam with light that blurred and merged beneath my eyelids. I thought I was going to pass out. Pass out and fall backwards, down to the rocks, the stream and beyond. I clung on, dug my nails into the earth and then, like a sharp knife, the air was cut through by an agonised cry I knew was Beau's. High-pitched, frightened, it pierced the blanket of fog.

I knew. Oh god, I knew.

I continued up, my boots a dead weight, my stomach sore and empty. With my torch, I searched right and left until eventually I picked out a paw. It rested on Alex's bent knee, who was, I realised, sitting cross-legged on the ground. I saw that Beau's body, soaking wet, was in his lap. Her face was turned away from me, it was somewhere in the crease of Alex's hip. All I could see was the back of her head, so soft to touch, her ears and inert spine.

Alex looked up at me, squinting, as I passed the torch-light over his eyes. There were tears on his face. I couldn't bring myself to say the words. To ask the question. It seemed obvious.

She'd been barking and now she wasn't.

I knelt down beside them. 'What happened? Why is she all wet?' I said, reaching out.

'No – Seren—'

No, Seren. What covered her body was not water.

'What happened?' I asked again.

'Children,' he stammered. 'Three or four of them, I don't know how many but they were here, they were up here with her.' His eyes were unfocused, looking past me like the blank light of a projector. 'I saw a knife. A big, shiny blade. One of them held her head and the other, he had dark, black hair – he looked at me, Seren, he looked at me before he—' He dropped his head and shoulders to Beau and sobbed.

I put my hand out to comfort him but found Beau's back paw instead. It didn't matter who I touched. It didn't matter what I did from now on. The fall would be upon us before we knew it.

*Sunday 13th August, afternoon*

We buried her this morning. Alex dug the hole, fashioned a cross out of the bamboo Daley had brought for him and then came to call for me at the bothy. Like a shy suitor, he offered me his arm and together we walked over the gentle rise of rocks and grass to the burial ground.

The fog makes a surprise out of everything, unveiling objects at the last minute: a mound of dug earth, a small cross made out of bamboo, a small bundle of flesh and fur that you loved and prayed for, wrapped in some sacking.

I was supposed to look after her.

I tried not to think about Chulainn's grave behind me as Alex filled in Beau's. I tried not to think of how I'd been hoping for more visions, searching for more material for my ghost story as Alex mumbled a prayer about peace. You wanted more, Chulainn's giant mound seemed to shout at my back. Well, here's more.

*Early evening*

Just got my period. Very late and heavy, with thick clots on the sanitary towel.

*Monday 14th August*

Another morning of fog. That's four days now. I wish I could message Daley. But what would I say?

*PM*

I'm sitting in the rocking chair, Alex is making dinner. For himself. I've told him I have no appetite for anything.

He's been very kind to me these past few days. Lots of thoughtful offerings: tea with too much sugar, feeding up the fire with peat, picking the prettiest verbena flowers and arranging them in a cup on the shelf above the fireplace. Earlier, he left a dog-eared collection of Philip Larkin poems on my desk. I haven't picked it up but still, it's a nice gesture.

I think, the truth is, I feel – in a strange, unhealthy way – closer to him now. He's the only other person who has shared my experience on this island, who now understands exactly what forces are at work. But then, even I didn't really know what I was up against, what lengths they'd go to – slaughtering Beau like that. It was so barbarous. So brutal.

He is clearly very shaken by the whole thing. I had at least known there was something supernatural here. Aside from my own incoherent ravings after my clothes were stolen at the stream or the night of the fire in the bothy, he hadn't really understood or witnessed for himself what was happening. 'Why don't you sleep here tonight?'

I heard a heavy object placed down on the table behind me. 'What's that?' he asked, walking over to stand between me and the fire.

'If you want to, you can sleep here. On the floor,' I said lowering my eyes.

'Are you sure?'

I nodded.

'Thank you.' And then, 'It's hard to be alone. After that.'

'I know.'

'I understand now. Why you didn't want to talk about it before.' When I didn't reply, he went on, 'it's impossible to explain—'

'—without someone thinking you've lost your mind,' I finished for him.

'I'm sorry if I made you feel like that.'

'It's OK.'

'I just thought you'd been on the island too long.'

'You're not the only person to think that.'

'Daley too?'

'Daley too.'

'You haven't told him any of this then? About the things you've seen?'

'No. I knew if I did, he'd just try to get me to go back with him.'

'You didn't want to leave?'

'Not then.'

'You do now?'

I nodded, tears rising. 'Seren,' he said, crouching down before me, his hand on my knee. 'I know we haven't always got on but right now, we need each other. We need to be strong for one another.'

'I need a glass of water.'

'I'll get it for you.'

'Thanks.'

'You think it was a message?' he asked as he handed it to me.

'Maybe,' I took several small sips. 'Can you stick it up there on the shelf?'

'Tell me.'

'I don't know. All I know is that the island was raided by some men back in the sixteenth century – one of the men was the firstborn son of MacNeil, the clan chief – and, while here, they did something they shouldn't.'

'As in?'

'As in, raped a woman. I don't know, I'm reading between the lines – a lot of euphemisms handed down from generation to generation. But now I'm starting to think they may have also slaughtered an animal, cattle grazing nearby perhaps. I don't know. I'm tired of trying to work it out.'

'Perhaps the best way to work it out is to write it down.'

'I've been doing that.'

'Have you though? I haven't seen you at your desk very much.'

'That's because my dog died, Alex.'

'I know, I know. I'm just saying – it might help you work through what's happened. The trauma of it.'

'Maybe.'

'There's no time like the present. I'll get on with dinner and leave you in peace.'

So that's where he's left me. Writing this. But, with the best will in the world, no amount of looking back at my hypotheses and previous failed attempts at a synopsis can help answer the big question that now absorbs me completely: how on earth am I going to tell Daley about Beau?

*Tuesday 15th August*
The fog has gone. It has finally gone. I woke to blue skies and sunshine through my bedroom window this morning but still, not trusting it, I went downstairs and out the front door to check. Full, bright daylight. I walked around to the southern end of the bothy and looked out to sea. In the middle-distance the stones at Crois an fionnadh were visible. So much light, it's intoxicating. I feel a little drunk with it.

Daley will come today. I'm certain he'll come.

*Later*

'Why weren't you watching her?'

'It was foggy. It was the fog. She wandered off. Seren and I searched for her. We were both out with our torches, in the middle of the night, calling for her.'

He was walking back and forth across the stone flags. 'She was a baby,' he said to me. 'How could you let her get out like that? In thick fog?'

I was leaning against the kitchen table, the shopping bags he'd brought behind me, like ballast.

'It's not Seren's fault. She was feeling unwell. She was vomiting.'

'You were vomiting?'

'And the door was open.'

'Why are you doing all the talking? In fact, why are you even here?'

'I'm supporting Seren.'

'Do you need his support?'

'It's been—' Alex began.

'Seriously, mate. Take a breath. 'Cause I'm losing my patience here. You were feeling sick again?' he asked, turning back to me.

I nodded.

'Is there something you want to say to me? Something away from this clown?'

'Alex, I think you better leave us.'

'Are you sure?'

'Yeah, she's fucking sure.'

'Alex, please.'

Daley walked over to the fireplace, both hands on the headrest of the rocking chair, and waited for Alex to leave. He seemed to take all the urgency with him because neither of us said anything for a while. And then: 'Is there something you want to say to me?'

Alex's yellow sleeping bag was rolled up on top of the logs. I'd forgotten to move it. 'I said he could sleep down here. The whole thing, it's difficult for you to understand, but we had no contact with the outside world—'

'The sickness, Seren.'

I walked over to my desk, pulled my chair out but then I remembered it had been a while since I changed my towel. What did it matter anyway? Regardless of whether it was saturated with a late period or an early miscarriage, it was still the answer to his question. I thought of the warm blood I'd felt on Beau's fur. It's always an end; always a wet and painful no. 'I'm not. Not any more, anyway.'

'So you were?' he looked alert, suddenly distracted. Like he'd just picked up the strain of a long-forgotten song playing in another room.

'Possibly. I don't know. But then Beau—'

'Was that what did it, do you think? The stress?'

'I woke with terrible cramps so it's possible that was the start of it but I can't be sure.'

'Where was Beau? When you woke with the cramps?'

'She was beside me, on the bed. She followed me down to the doorstep.'

'And then what?'

'Then, you know what. She must have wandered off.'

'You didn't see her?'

'Daley, I was vomiting. And then—'

'What?'

'I fell asleep.'

'For how long?'

'I have no idea. A while.'

'Did you see what direction she went in?'

'Daley, stop.'

'I'm just trying to work out what headland she might have fallen from.'

How could I tell him? She didn't fall. She was slaughtered. Her throat cut, her body sacrificed in order to tell me something, to relay some crucial component of a story I thought I wanted to write. There was just no way I could say those words to him. 'I'm sorry,' I said, instead.

He shook his head, walked around to the front of the rocking chair and sat down. Then he lowered his face to his hands and started to cry.

I crossed the room to stand beside him. 'I should have taken better care of her.'

Did he know? How painful it was for me to say those words? Obviously not. He leant away from me, digging his elbows into his knees as he wept.

*Later, after dinner*

He left just before three. We managed a kiss down at the beach but things were strained, anyone could see that. When I returned, I could see Alex in the distance, cutting his peat rows. It would keep him busy for a while yet so I let myself back in, made a cup of coffee with the fresh milk Daley had brought and sat down at my desk to write this.

I can't stop thinking about all I didn't tell him. How the things that have happened on this island have made me ashamed, afraid to tell him the truth. I came here bullish, dismissing people like Linda and Elspeth as alarmist or even just having an especially low IQ, so perhaps it's that that's stopping me. A strange, residual pride. Pride comes before a fall. Christ, there's that word again.

No, there's no way I could have told him the truth. Alex and I both agreed it would be impossible to explain what happened without also forcing Daley to make the difficult decision to raise the alarm. I hadn't shared any of my suspicions about the island with him so to suddenly present him with the story of how Beau had her throat cut by a band of malevolent ghost children was too much of a stretch. The only conclusion he could possibly come to is that we'd lost our minds – that we'd gone the same way as the shepherds. What had Alex called it back in Edinburgh? Folie à deux.

But there's no denying the fact that I've somehow – blindly, stupidly perhaps – walked into an alliance with Alex; one that keeps the truth from Daley.

*1 a.m.*

I can't sleep. Every time I feel myself go, I snap back into consciousness. Into thoughts of Daley but then also my neglected vegetable patch; the courgettes piled up in the lean-to; the mouldering squash and then, of course, Beau in her cold grave.

I need to get out for some fresh air.

*3.47 a.m.*

Your character needs to get on top of internal pain, Tess had said. In order to tackle forces at play outside, she must conquer the terror within. It's the kind of shit that sounds good in a Soho restaurant with a forkful of risotto in your hand but not here. Not when those forces are reconstructing a trauma that closely – too closely – mirrors your own; not when you're subject to screams that are exactly what you imagine your own child and sister produced in their final moments. No. Fuck this.

Stealing my clothes, Beau – oh god, what they did to Beau. But this, this play, these fucking theatrics. I need to go home before I lose my mind. I'll ask Jamie for a loan. I'll pay back the first chunk of my advance to Tess, I'll extricate myself from the whole horrible thing. It's the only way forward. I'll give notice to my agent, look for a job, a new flat and move on. I cannot do this any more.

But first, I should record what happened.

I decided to go to Crois an fionnadh, for my walk. I left the bothy as quietly as I could, picking up my boots and jacket from the kitchen and tiptoeing out the front door. Alex, I noticed, slept naked. His long, lean thigh was thrown over the unzipped side of his sleeping bag, the material snaked under him like a pregnancy pillow. He didn't stir.

I had a torch in my hand but the moon was full and it lit my way. It was a cool night with a light breeze. The stars were bright and hard in the dark sky and I was glad of my jacket. I tucked my pyjama bottoms into my boots so they wouldn't get wet on the dewy grass. At Crois an fionnadh, I knelt down beside the font stone hole and put my hand on the earth and exposed roots. The sides had fallen in a little more and grass was starting to grow over the wound. I couldn't think of it as anything else.

I closed my eyes and pictured Tilly. Font stone or no font stone, this was where I pictured her: in my memories, my dreams. In my first dream on the island, this is where she'd been: pulled along joyfully by other children. And then the night of Beau's death, she'd come to me again. She'd been the one to whisper in my ear: 'Beau's gone.'

'Mummy, can we live here?' That's what she'd asked me on our only visit here as a family. 'We can drink the sea,' she'd said in answer to Jamie's laying forth of all the reasons why it was not possible. I stood up and unzipped my jacket. I let the wind get at me: felt the cotton fibres of my pyjama top turn cold, my nipples rise and gather the surrounding tissue so that my chest felt hard and impermeable.

And then, as if on cue, a thin ribbon of smoke rose up in the distance. It was thin, tendril-like. I walked across to the other side of the circle and saw it was coming from the Ceum a'Mhaide headland. It dispersed, fanned out once it got past the top of the headland, and, no longer protected by the rock face, it was blown towards me. I could smell it was green, organic – the burning of fresh vegetation.

What could I do but walk towards it? I didn't want to go back to Alex and the bothy. Whatever was being shown to me was for me, this time. Standing on the edge of the headland, I shone my torch down on the top of the Finamuil sea stack. I could see the smoke was thicker down there and, if I was not mistaken, it was coming from the opening of the cave.

I clipped my torch to my jacket and started climbing down. The ledges and footholds that are fine in the day were more slippery at night and slick with birdshit. I could taste the salt of the water sucking and gushing against the rocky platform below. As I got closer, the smoke started billowing towards me, waving me away, making my eyes water. You can't handle this, it said. This is too much for you.

I made my way carefully along the ledge and round to the bottom of the cliff that faced the cave. The tide was still high, the water just below the level of my boots. It would be another hour at least before the rocky beach between the island and sea stack was passable. But the bigger problem, the problem that made me stop in my tracks, was the thick, creamy smoke that billowed between them. The entrance to Chulainn's cave, from where I stood, was a mass of burning gorse, marram grass and exploding driftwood. I had no option but to retreat. The fire was taking hold, the smoke suffocating and—

A scream. High and pure, it cut through the wind, the waves, the smoke – all the elements that tried to muffle it. I felt my blood run cold as the first scream was quickly followed by another. And another.

Voices from inside the cave.

A chorus. An ensemble of voices hitting the high notes of panic. Their straining sounds joined and merged and reached out for me.

I did nothing. I stood there and did nothing. Until it stopped. I stayed long enough for the voices to fade away one by one; to watch the fiery thicket across the entrance to the cave eventually burn itself out, leaving only ash and embers. The smoke continued to trickle out, rising up from the top of the opening like a ribbon suspended above something frivolous and inconsequential – a bauble, perhaps – before being dispersed and carried away by the wind.

The tide continued its slow, imperceptible retreat. Almost. After some time, I saw I was able to sit down on the ledge and dangle my feet over the now-shallow waters. I sat there for a long time and heard nothing. No sound from within the cave, no rustling or sign of movement. Eventually, I pulled myself up and walked back along the ledge that skirted the cliff to the Ceum a'Mhaide steps. The climb up was easier than the climb down; no smoke or sea spray – all urgency past. Like the journey from Alana's house to the hospital in the back of a police car. No sirens, stopping at red lights, the police officer adjusting his rear view mirror once or twice. Normal things, mundane things. This way, please, past the doors on the right, here. Can I get you a cup of tea or coffee, Mrs Doughty?

At the top of the headland, some feeling of things not being finished made me stop. I turned around, peered over the edge and saw the top of the sea stack. To the right, bobbing under the shelter of the natural arch was the blue hull of Alex's boat. And there, on the newly-exposed beach to the right, a figure. I got down on my hands and knees, felt my pyjama bottoms soak through as I pulled myself as far over the edge as I could. A dark head glinting in the moonlight. It was a little boy whose black hair matched the description given by Jacob, the child who visited with his parents back in June.

I watched him climb the rocks and stand under the arch and there, just as he was leaning out to sea, I heard it. 'Thall!' boomed from somewhere in the distance, shaking the ground beneath me and the rocks he stood upon.

He almost toppled from his perch but he caught himself in time.

I watched him for a long time. No longer afraid, just curious. Eventually he climbed down from the rocks and walked back along the shingle beach, close to the still-smoking cave entrance.

He turned, craned his neck and looked directly up at me. And with one hand across his stomach and the other extended towards the burnt-out cave, he took a long, deep bow.

I can't take this any more. This re-enactment. I know what happened. I know that many innocent people died in that cave. I also know that the little boy, dispatched as look-out, inadvertently gave the game away. Why stay and see it endlessly repeated?

I have my laptop up here in my room with me. We had plenty of sunlight and wind during the day so there should be enough power to send Daley an email. I'm going to tell him I want to leave Finish as soon as possible.

I open a browser, click on the email shortcut and begin composing a message. It takes me a few seconds to realise the font and background are different and that it isn't my account. And then I remember: Alex had been in the middle of something when the battery gave out – the day the fog rolled in.

I am about to sign out, when I see there is a message still pending in the outbox. It is an email exchange of five messages. I read from oldest to newest.

From: Alex Jennings
To: Rupert Wentham
Date: 24 March 2023 at 16:03
Subject: The Siren Calls by Alex Jennings

Dear Rupert,

I'm writing to seek representation for my literary novel, The Siren Calls.

The novel centres around the relationship of a young boy, Arturo, and his father, a village fisherman, who goes out to sea early one morning and never returns. Arturo, who feels he must leave his elderly mother to look for his father, soon finds himself lost at sea. During this time, he hears the sound of female voices calling him from a nearby island. The island is inhabited by highly sexed, aggressive sirens who take him in and use him as their plaything. Despite several attempts to leave, the call of the sirens proves too powerful and compelling a force for Arturo. The island becomes a battleground between lust and loyalty, sex and survival, fornication and fealty. Until, that is, he discovers his father is no stranger to this island and that he too has fallen victim to the lure of the sirens.

I attach a synopsis as well as the full manuscript. I hope you enjoy my story and should you wish to discuss it further, please do not hesitate to get in touch.

I look forward to hearing from you.

Best wishes,
Alex Jennings

From: Rupert Wentham
To: Alex Jennings
Date: 2 May 2023 at 12:33
Subject: The Siren Calls by Alex Jennings

Dear Alex,

Thank you for submitting your novel but I'm afraid this is not for me. I do, however, have a few thoughts.

- The novel doesn't 'centre' around the relationship of a young boy with his father. It is mostly a sex festival with mermaids.
- Avoid alliteration in a synopsis. Agents are interested in story, not gimmicky flourishes.
- It is not literary fiction.
- The island setting is interesting, stick with that.

Best,
Rupert

From: Alex Jennings
To: Rupert Wentham
Date: 10 August 2023 at 15:07
Subject: The Siren Calls by Alex Jennings

Dear Rupert,

Please forgive the impromptu email after so many months but your remarks on the island setting have got me thinking. I have an idea for another novel. Please may I send it to you?

Best wishes,
Alex

From: Rupert Wentham
To: Alex Jennings
Date: 10 August 2023 at 15:53
Subject: The Siren Calls by Alex Jennings

Why not?

R

From: Alex Jennings
To: Rupert Wentham
Date: 10 August 2023 at 16:17
Subject: The Siren Calls by Alex Jennings
Dear Rupert,

Please see below.

An unsuccessful and sexually promiscuous writer with a history of mental illness decamps to an abandoned island in the Outer Hebrides with the manuscript of a promising young writer in her possession. She settles upon plagiarising the work, hoping that this will be her big break. Soon after her arrival, she realises the island is haunted, the place resonating with the echoes of a massacre that took place hundreds of years ago.

The spirits humiliate, terrify and abuse her until she starts to lose her mind. Forgetful, tired and weak, she hides away in a cave, where she seeks shelter. It is in this cave that she is given a simple instruction: stay and write the story of what happened here. At first, she refuses to do the spirit's bidding and continues with her own project but when her beloved dog is slaughtered right before her eyes, she realises she has no choice. She knows that she must get on and write the story of the island before it's too late.

I would appreciate your thoughts.
Best wishes,
Alex

This last email was written hours before Beau's death.

*Wednesday 16th August, early*
I've just checked the OS map. There is no cross over Cnoc fiacail. Every single vision, echo, sighting has been accompanied by a cross on the map but not this one.

I need to keep it together. I cannot let on that I know.

From: Seren Doughty
To: Daley MacKinnon
Date: 16 August 2023 at 06:13
Subject:

Daley,

I've decided it's time to leave. Would you be able to come and get me? I can't really explain now but I will when we're together. I just can't stay on this island any more. I don't mean to panic you (I'm fine), but could you have a think about when you might come?

Thanks,
S x

From: Daley MacKinnon
To: Seren Doughty
Date: 16 August 2023 at 08:47
Subject:

Are you OK? What's happened?

I'm coming out on Sunday with Rosalie and Aunty Kitty. I was going to email you to say we'll bring lunch. Can you wait until then? If not, just say and I'll come get you sooner.

D x

From: Seren Doughty
To: Daley MacKinnon
Date: 16 August 2023 at 09:56
Subject:

I can wait until Sunday. Looking forward to seeing Rosalie and her mum again.

Please don't worry about me. I'm fine.

S xx

*Thursday 17th August*
Quiet day. Long walk this morning and now I'm up in my room. I told Alex I have a headache. Keeping my journal with me at all times.

*Friday 18th August*
Just told him Daley's coming on Sunday with his aunt and cousin. Haven't mentioned my plan to leave with him. Don't want to arouse any suspicion that I've worked out what he did.

*Sunday 20th August, 10 a.m.*
It looked a little touch-and-go when I woke up this morning but the heavy cloud has lifted and though it isn't warm, it's quite still. Still enough to land.

The *Spes Secunda* has just rounded the rocks. I mustn't forget to put the bannock dough outside on the windowsill to rest. My boots are by the front door. Alex has no idea I'm leaving today. It won't take me long to pack. Plus, I'll feel happier doing it while Daley and the others are here.

I better get down to the beach to meet them. It's just occurred to me that this is the last entry I'll write on Finish.

*Evening*
What is it they say? The best laid plans of mice and men oft go awry?

Down at the beach this morning I could see Kathleen MacKinnon sitting in one of the fold-down red plastic seats at the stern, wrapped up in a coat, a headscarf and a life jacket beside Rosalie, who was similarly protected from the elements.

Daley had the rubber dinghy tethered to the back of the *Spes Secunda*. I had wondered how he'd do it, deposit a woman in her eighties on an island with no landing place. I watched him untie it, pull it to the side of the Spes and open a small door in the gunwale. He jumped down into the dinghy and tied it tight to the hull. At this, Rosalie stood to help her mother up from her seat and guide her slowly to the opening where Daley's hands reached up, waiting for her. I watched all this from the beach, this careful transfer of fragile age and experience into younger, stronger hands. The trust it must have taken for Kathleen to lift her foot into the air and allow her nephew's arms to guide her down. Clearly, she longed to be back here.

When they were all inside the dinghy he motored as close to the beach as possible, then jumped out and pulled the dinghy up on the sand. He smiled when he saw me, a big beaming smile that, I could tell in spite of his sunglasses, lit up his face. It was a relief to see – after Beau, after that terrible afternoon when he'd sobbed for her – that there was still something between us, some connection that might get us through this. 'You OK?' he asked.

I nodded. 'Much better now you're here.'

He slid a metal ramp that extended in sections towards me. 'Hold that steady, will you?'

He turned to his aunt and cousin on the bench. 'Ready? Time to disembark.'

'Mam?' Rosalie stood and took her mother's hands. 'Hello Seren,' she said, glancing my way before turning back to Kathleen. 'That's it,' she said, lifting her to a standing position before guiding her towards the rubber edge that would allow access to the ramp. 'Whoever said taking a visually impaired woman to an island with no landing pier was a bad idea?' she laughed.

'The weather's been kind to you,' I said.

'The weather's always kind to Mam.'

Daley reached up to grab Kathleen's arm, guiding his aunt down the ramp to where I stood.

I held my hand out to her. She didn't just take it, she gripped it – warm and strong – her eyes once again searching for me. The thought crossed my mind that they had never stopped searching, these past months.

Rosalie and Daley took an arm each and led her away up the beach. She said something I couldn't catch to Rosalie, who stopped, reached a hand to her throat and unfastened the silk headscarf. Her thin hair, long and white, so white it merged with the cloud-lit day, flew behind her in the breeze. There was the ghost of a smile on her lips. They led her up to the bothy slowly, very slowly, but not before she stopped at the sand-blown walls of the abandoned village. I hung back.

She put her hand – the skin so thin it was blue in places – down on top of the wall, resting it on the very spot where Tilly had stood as a four-year-old in her red wellington boots, and told me and Jamie she wanted to live here and drink the sea. Kathleen took a deep, sudden breath in and I saw a small, imperceptible shake of her head. 'Come on, Mam,' Rosalie said. 'Let's get you in the warm.'

'Where's David Attenborough?' Daley asked as we followed them up to the bothy.

'I asked him to give us a bit of space this afternoon.'

'Is he behaving himself?'

'Kind of.'

'Kind of?'

'I'll tell you later.'

'Tell me what?'

'It's difficult . . .'

'Has he done something? To you?'

'No, not to me. Let's talk later, OK?'

In the bothy, Rosalie seated her mother in the rocking chair. I'd already lit the fire earlier that morning – for Kathleen who I knew would be cold and damp from the crossing and also for the bannocks I was making for lunch. The room felt warm and dry, the rich aroma of the peat, like a solicitous host, relieving them of their heavy damp.

I took my boots off and went straight to the kitchen where I set about rolling out my dough. 'I'm impressed,' Rosalie said, coming to stand beside me.

'Daley showed me how to do it. Using the bannock stone.'

'Our granny used to finish them on the fire. Always. Even when she had a gas oven.' I felt her press against my arm as she leant across me and then, with the joint of her right thumb, she pressed a little dimple into the centre of the dough. 'Now, did Daley not show you that?'

'That being?'

'To keep the fairies from your house. It's a tradition from way back, before there were chimneys. If the fairies spied an undimpled bannock through the smoke-hole in your roof, they'd swarm in and set up chaos.'

'I can't believe Daley failed to mention this.'

She laughed. 'It's mad, I know. But do you think I can make a bannock without dimpling? And Mam is exactly the same.'

'I don't know what I would have done without Daley.' I said, keen to move on from the bannock chat.

'Oh, he's been helpful to you all right.'

I turned to her, looking for a smile, but she was looking down at the flattened dough, her incisors pulling her lower lip in as if she were about to say something difficult. 'I hear you have a house guest.'

'Uh-huh.'

'Is that the fella who wrote to me?'

I nodded.

'And he sleeps here now?'

'On the floor,' I said, looking over at the stone flags before the fire, where Daley, crouching down before Kathleen, was saying something. 'He sleeps on the floor.'

'What's the plan?'

'The plan? With him? No plan. My plan is to leave today.'

'You don't look as though you're packed,' she said, turning around to take in all the packets of food and papers on the table.

'It won't take me long. Most of that stuff is Alex's,' I said. 'He uses the table and I use the desk.'

'What's he doing?' she said, picking up one of his papers. 'What's the electrometric determination of pH?'

'God knows. He's doing a PhD on soil. Starting next month so he won't be here much longer either.'

'What's he been doing then?' Daley joined us, offering an open packet of peanuts.

'I'm just going to get this on,' I said, carrying the bannock stone over to the fire.

I heard him say, 'the guy's a wank stain,' as I knelt down. 'Thinks his shit smells sweeter. You know the type.'

'I've got a guesthouse full of them,' Rosalie laughed.

'Hey Seren,' he called, his mouth still full of peanuts, 'I'm just going to show Rosalie your garden.'

'It's very overgrown. I haven't been tending it much lately.'

'You sit and chat to Aunty Kitty. Come on,' he opened the door and waited for Rosalie to step outside before following her.

The silence in the room after he closed the door behind him was absolute. Kathleen sat with her eyes closed and her head leaning back against the wooden rest. The thought came to me that she was like a big battery, plugged into the chair, her forehead lit up like a progress bar.

I thought of the fog, the power going just before Alex could send his email. I had deleted it in the end. The unsent email. If he asked to use my laptop again, I reasoned, he might just assume it was lost in the power outage of that afternoon.

It was a numbers game for me now: be here to welcome Kathleen, extract as much information as I could from her and then return with everyone to Castlebay. I would have plenty of time, on the other side of all this – in

Daley's bungalow far from Finish – to try and explain what would be very difficult for him to understand. Namely, why I had been so willing to accept Alex's explanation for how Beau died.

These were the thoughts going through my mind as the smell of burning punctured the air. 'Shit.' I ran to the kitchen, found a spatula, and returned to the fire. As I slid it under and prepared to flip the bannock, I felt Kathleen's eyes on me. The bread hit the stone with a slap and then I turned to face her.

Her eyes were no longer roving or milky. The irises were blue, so blue I could squint and still see their sapphire lustre, staring back at me with focus and precision. 'Your child was taken from you,' she said.

Some instinct told me this was not a conversation.

'She has found her way here. To the other children who know. You need not worry. Chulainn is watching over her. Chulainn watches over all innocents.'

I said nothing.

'But you must do what she asks. It's very important. You must stay and finish.'

'Finish what?'

'You know what.'

'And if I do? What then?'

'Then she will be returned to you.'

'Tilly will? Do you mean my daughter?'

But just at that moment the door opened and Daley walked in, shouting something about a mighty courgette – a comment Rosalie seemed to find immensely funny. I turned back to Kathleen but her eyes had clouded over again.

They had brought scallops with them, purchased in Castlebay that morning. We had them with lemon, cracked black pepper, salad and the charred bannock. I'm sure it would have been delicious if I had been able to eat any of it, but I found it difficult to chew and swallow. I was too absorbed by Kathleen and the way she regressed before my eyes. Rosalie pinned a large bib to her woollen cardigan, cut up her food and proceeded to spoon it into her mouth. I don't need to add: like a baby but that's what she was. For all to see. A big baby who had just told me my daughter was here, on this strange island and that, provided I stay and write, I would be reunited with her.

It's not as if I didn't know there was some connection. The dreams, the strange parallels between what happened to the children on this island and what happened to my own child. I returned to the thoughts I'd had last month – how much of this venture had been of my own choosing. It seems the question had now been answered. I was supposed to come here. I am the writer destined to give shape to the events of five hundred years ago. But that does not answer the bigger, overriding question: what is it about this story that needs to be retold? The raiders came, they did something they shouldn't, they were punished – brutally – by the wronged islanders who were in turn subject to an unspeakable act of revenge. I'm guessing from the cries I heard up at the stream and the knickers I found buried in Chulainn's grave that a girl was raped. That would make the islanders' rage more understandable but what I don't know is why does it need to be written down and why am I the only one who can do it? There must be some-thing, something in the finer detail that she, Chulainn, wants everyone to know.

After lunch Kathleen wanted to go to the burial ground. As we walked over there I thought about what she'd said to me and how I was going to tell Daley that I'd changed my mind. That despite my urgent email earlier in the week, I was now resolved to stay a bit longer and finish what I came out here to do.

As we walked away from the bothy in an easterly direction, I saw, to my left, what looked like Alex's head bobbing up and down near the cliff edge. He was right above the steepest drop on the island. He was busy doing something, climbing up, fiddling with something on the peat platform and then back down again.

Ten days. A week and a half. That's what we're talking about here. It's not so long.


Rosalie followed her mother's slow, careful steps to the northern-most edge of the burial ground, not far, I noticed, from Beau's little grave. We stopped at a collec-tion of small stones and crosses, weathered and green-tinged, some of them facing the sea, others Cnoc fiacail.

'Mam's people,' Rosalie said. The marker stones were sunken, lopsided, pushed back by the winds that had careered off the mountain for centuries, generations. These bodies, these perished MacKinnons, had lain here, under the soil of Finish, while descendants like Kathleen's mother had departed, had their babies elsewhere, in hospitals, tended by doctors and nurses wearing starched uniforms, who used sterilised equipment and wrapped the newborn babies in boil-washed towels.

They had made their choice; they had shut up their cottages, loaded their few belongings into the boats bobbing in the bay. They had sailed away from the hills and rocks, the hummocks and standing stones, past cliffs that cried their useless, salty tears at them.

I felt something of their exhaustion. The dead MacKinnons and every other islander who had been lain down beneath the earth, grown over by pink clover and ferns. It was hard, too hard, living so far from others; exposed to the elements, beyond the steadying reach of the mainland. I remember my dad telling me that when the world started to open up in the nineteenth century, when the fishermen from Finish started travelling to Barra and Stornoway to sell their catch and saw what life was like for everyone else, the rot of dissatisfaction set in.

Thinking of my dad brings me back to those childhood visits to Finish. Alana and I on the boat, gazing over the side as he grew wistful. And then on land, clambering over the rocks, leaving our life jackets in the sun and then down to the beach ... all the time thinking if I could only lift it up. If I could lift the whole island clear, like a big heavy stone, I might peer at what lay beneath.

'Chulainn,' Kathleen said. It came out like a cough and sure enough she brought a handkerchief to her mouth to wipe the spray of saliva away. Rosalie led the way to the biggest mound. The last time I had stood beside Chulainn's grave was when Beau had urinated on the inscription. 'Here,' she said to Rosalie and Daley, who seemed to understand she wanted to be lowered to her knees. With both hands flat to the grassy mound, she closed her eyes and began mumbling what I assumed was a prayer. I leant in, as close as was respectfully possible, but given her garbled speech and the easterly breeze that whipped us, all I caught was the word 'knee'. I thought she was asking to be adjusted but then, out of nowhere, a phrase that struck me as familiar: 'it can't be helped.'

It can't be helped. And I remembered, in the guesthouse on my last night in Castlebay, I had stood just outside their private apartment and heard – amidst the crying and brushing of hair – Kathleen say the very same words.

Back at the bothy, Rosalie sat her mother down in the rocking chair while she made a cup of tea for everyone before their return journey to Castlebay. I knelt down on the hearthstone and revived the fire but really, I wanted to be closer to Kathleen who, unprompted and uninter-rupted, began telling us about life on Finish, as it had been relayed to her by her own mother.

She told us about the school and the effort that went into building a home that would attract a teacher to the island. Rosalie brought our teas over and Daley took my desk chair and brought it closer to the fire, motioned for Rosalie to sit. But before she did, she draped a woollen scarf over her mother's shoulders. 'Seren,' Rosalie whispered, 'ask her whatever you like,' she motioned towards her mother, 'she's in the mood to talk.'

I looked around, at Daley sitting on my desk, his fingers lightly resting in the handle of his mug; at Rosalie's eager, encouraging face. 'There was a massacre here – on this island,' I swallowed.

'Keep it light,' Daley said.

'Shut up, Daley,' Rosalie said. 'Carry on, Seren.'

'Many people died,' I said as if explaining something difficult to a child. Kathleen's eyes roved. I looked at Daley again and took a deep breath. 'They were burnt alive in the cave. The cave in the Finamuil sea stack.'

'Chulainn's cave,' the words came from her lips, like a reflex. And again, the sound was akin to mucus being cleared from the wind pipe. That night in the guest-house, her crying had sounded like she was being suffocated.

'Yes, Chulainn's cave. Can you tell me what you know? Why the people of this island were murdered like that?'

'Cousins,' she said and reached out. Without thinking, I took her hand, looking at Rosalie as I did so. 'Catriona and Mairi. Born of two brothers. Delivered, as they all were, by Muirnīn MacKinnon.'

## CRIOCH

She told her granddaughters to go on ahead. Their fathers – her sons – were among the men fishing just off the coast, where the Ceum a'Mhaide steps led down to the south-western tip of the island. 'Take Mairi,' she said to the eldest of the two cousins. 'See to the cows and move them on.'

'Will we take victuals?' Mairi asked.

Muirnīn Chulainn was sitting on a stool outside the front door of her cottage, twining wool on the *fearsaid*. A cloud of fleece rested on the back of her left hand while, with her right, she maintained the rotation of the spindle. It was a fine April morning – bright, sunny, still – but cold when the sun went behind the clouds. She knew what her granddaughter was asking: how long will I be over there, tending the cows? It was a boring job and Mairi hated it.

'Take yourself and let that be enough,' her grandmother said, winding a length of newly spun yarn onto the spindle.

Muirnīn watched them walk away towards Cnoc fiacail. She pulled her shawl – knitted by her sister, now dead – closer round her shoulders and calculated how Catriona, at seventeen, was now a head taller than Mairi, who came only to her shoulder. Catriona's hair, red and given to curl, had been plaited into a long braid but Mairi, who never gave a thought to her appearance, had short, chestnut brown hair that hadn't so much as seen the brush this morning.

The men would soon be back with the morning's catch. Catriona's father, Muirnīn's eldest son, would follow the girls up to the stream when he could. The island, she knew, gave them a false sense of security. Muirnīn, like everyone else, had heard stories of raiders; men who breached the shores and helped themselves to whatever they could lay their hands on. No, Muirnīn was taking no chances: the girls had to go in pairs.

Catriona and Mairi moved the cows along; Catriona leading her favourite, Bo, by a rope she'd watched her grandmother make with her long, slender fingers. She loved her grandmother's hands, loved holding them, tracing the individual joints from knuckle to tip and thinking how every woman on the island trusted them, wanted them near when her time came.

As they walked, Mairi took the opportunity to ask Catriona about Ruaridh. They were the same age, they had played together as children: down at the beach, up at Crois an fionnadh – hide and seek among the tall stones. They'd played together whether they liked one another or not. Island life was like that. But Ruaridh had always liked Catriona the most. He favoured her, just as Catriona favoured her precious Bo. 'Angus says Ruaridh will soon lie on top of you.'

'For shame, Mairi! That's dirty talk.'

'It wasn't me that said it,' she said, reddened by her cousin's reproach. 'It was your own brother.'

They continued in this way – chatting and walking the cows to new grass – when the two men appeared; slowly at first, a head, then torso, then arms as they climbed over the headland. One of them was tall, stocky, his face yellow with illness and his eyes an angry green. The other – younger but slower – was short with a long, ugly nose. Despite his youth, his hair was already falling back, retreating to the crown.

Catriona and Mairi stood still, frozen by the sight of these men who were no relation to their fathers, uncles, brothers or cousins. Everyone on Finish was connected or related in some way; their names bore that relation. Neil, son of John or Sarah, daughter of Roderick. Prefixes like *Ni* and *Mac* were links in a chain, anchoring the islanders to each other and the land they lived on. But these men? They had crawled into this world on their bellies, like snakes.

The taller one approached first. He looked hungry, desperate. And when he locked eyes with Catriona, his hunger seemed only to intensify.

'Come away,' Mairi said, pulling on her cousin's arm.

But Catriona would not let go. She could not let go of Bo. The younger man joined his partner, he reached for the rope, his dirty fingers closing around the twine spun and made by her grandmother's own hand. Where were those capable fingers now? He pulled the animal away from her and with his other hand he pushed Catriona backwards. She fell. Mairi bent down to help her up but she was yanked back by the hair she'd neglected to brush that morning and dragged backwards, her heels digging and scraping in the earth as she was pulled away from Catriona.

The men forced them down to the rocks near the stream, made them strip naked and then raped them. In an effort to keep them at the stream for as long as possible, they took their clothes and went back to where Bo was grazing as if nothing had happened. They hacked up the animal and set about carrying her, in pieces, down to the waiting boat.

*Monday 21st August, AM*

He was on me first thing this morning, as soon as I came down the stairs. 'Do you want coffee? I've just made some. It's still hot.'

'OK.'

'I saw you had the light on very late last night – were you up writing?'

'Yes,' I said, putting my journal down on my desk and pulling out the chair.

'It was helpful then? Having the old lady visit?'

'Yes. It was helpful.'

I had been too exhausted last night to finish yesterday's entry. So desperate to get everything that Kathleen had told me down, I stayed up until two this morning writing the first part of *Croich*.

'Let me get your coffee,' Alex said, walking back into the kitchen. I waited until he'd gone before picking up my pen.

'You need help packing?' Daley had asked, once we'd finished our tea.

Rosalie appeared uncomfortable as she looked from me to Daley.

'I'm going to stay a bit longer. I'm sorry – I know I said I'd come with you today but I think I'm close.'

'Close to what?'

'To a plan. A working outline for this book. Once I have that, it doesn't matter where I write it. I can come back to Castlebay—' I didn't add 'and stay at yours' because that offer had not been reiterated since Beau's death.

'I thought Aunty Kitty here would have given you more than enough to be getting on with.'

'She has, it's been brilliant—' I said, looking down at Kathleen, who was sitting, slumped, in the rocking chair. She was clearly exhausted by all she'd said and seen and done since arriving on Finish just a few hours earlier. She watched the fire, apparently oblivious to the conversation going on around her. 'I think I just need to be here to finish. And we're talking about nine or ten days, at the most.'

He nodded his head but both Rosalie and I could see he was disappointed.

Alex has just put my cup of coffee down on my desk, all mock servile. 'If that will be all, I think I'll head out to the cliffs.'

It's hard, resisting the urge to throw the coffee in his face. But I want him out while I write this next bit. 'Yes, I saw you there yesterday. What are you doing?'

'I'm attaching a hook to the rock face – so that I can get down lower.'

'Why? I thought you'd have plenty of soil samples by now.'

'I do. But I need waterlogged samples too. Molluscs, insect exoskeletons, that kind of thing.'

'Sounds fascinating. Let's hope you don't slip in the pursuit of such treasures.'

He looked at me for a moment, puzzled by my tone, but then reverted to type, giving me a shallow bow with his arms tight to his side. Like a courtier to a queen. 'Very good, madam.'

Once it became clear I wasn't going back to Castlebay with them, Rosalie was keen to get going. She stood behind Kathleen and tried to lever her forward while Daley gripped her forearms but her body became rigid and she shook her head.

'What's she doing?' Daley asked Rosalie.

'Mam?' Rosalie said, leaning over so her face was near Kathleen's. Kathleen reacted by clamping her lips and eyes shut and began making a strange, humming sound. 'Mam? What's going on?'

Kathleen threw her weight back in the chair and set it going on its rockers. 'Mam?' Rosalie asked, a little pale now. 'Talk to me. What's happening?'

The answer came in a voice that sounded nothing like hers, nothing like the one we'd just been listening to. It was deeper, more husky and strangely melodic.

'If it comes through my knee, it can't be helped but it shall not come through my mouth.' The words were not hers, no more than the voice was hers but they were crystal clear. And getting louder. 'If it comes through my knee, it can't be helped but it shall not come through my mouth,' she repeated, now shouting.

These were the words that I'd heard as she bent over Chulainn's grave earlier in the day. Repeated over and over, I had thought they were the mumblings of an uncomfortable woman. But watching Kathleen MacKinnon rock back and forth in the chair, her eyes fixed by some distant memory, they sounded much more like an invocation. A lost but not forgotten war cry.


*Friday 25th August, evening*

This is the first chance I've had to write in my journal all week. *Crioch* has been taking up all my time and energy. I've never written like this before, writing with a frenzy that generates actual heat. Several times I've found myself sweaty and damp at the desk.

At such moments, when I come to, I can also see that the intensity of my work has released some kind of pheromone that Alex is picking up on, observing me all the time, nosing at me like a dog near a bitch. He'll often take a slow walk past my desk but like a child conscious her classmate might copy her, I do my best to hide it from him. He makes regular offers of tea, coffee, lunch or dinner in his stupid way but I say no to everything. I want nothing to do with him but also, I'm not at all hungry. What was it Hemingway said? Hunger makes good discipline, or something like that. I don't know, I just know I have to get this story written.

## CRIOCH: 11

It was left to Catriona and Mairi to walk back to the village – naked and shamed – to their grandmother's door. When Muirnīn saw them and heard their account of what happened, she set up a scream so loud and piercing, it brought all the men of the island to her cottage.

They took their knives, scythes and cudgels and ran to the stream, where they found the butchered remains of Bo and a bloody trail that led all the way to the top of Ceum a'Mhaide. The wind blew in a westerly direction and brought with it the sound of a rock falling. The men ran to the headland and began climbing down. They knew the depth and gradient of each ledge, they knew the quickest route, they had grown up hunting for wildfowl and their eggs along the slippery ledges of the western cliffs.

The raiders stood no chance.

Within minutes they had surrounded the two men on the rock face, the men above kicking them down to those waiting below. And there, on the platform where the dark gneiss of Finish comes within kissing distance of the Finamuil sea stack, the older of the two with the green eyes was forced to his knees, his head pulled back and his throat cut. The younger man, anticipating the same fate, was momentarily relieved when the blood-soaked knife was set aside on the rocky ledge. His relief quickly turned to terror as he was set upon, his limbs bent and snapped, the air ringing with his screams. They threw his body into the bottom of his boat, removed the oars and pushed him out to sea. A fitting death, they all agreed. This is what happens when you pillage Finish.

The boat tossed on the waves of the Finish sound and floated towards a current of warm water that immediately drew it northwards, towards Kisimul Castle. Some fishermen, trawling their nets, recognised it, pulled it in to shore and discovered the chief's firstborn son, as close to death as any fish they'd ever pulled from the water. He was taken to his father's castle, nursed by his mother and her waiting women in the castle keep, but it was to no end. He died a week later but not before he whispered in his mother's ear what had happened to him on Finish Island.

*Monday 28th August*

From: Seren Doughty
To: Daley MacKinnon
Date: 28 August 2023 at 12:13
Subject: Inbound

There's good news and bad news. The good news is, I think I've finally got momentum on this book. The bad news is that I'll need a place to stay where I can continue writing it up. Do you think you might be able to help me out with the latter? Hope so.

S x

From: Daley MacKinnon
To: Seren Doughty
Date: 28 August 2023 at 12:37
Subject: Inbound

I'm confused, your email is all good news as far as I can see. Of course you can stay. I can come out for you on Friday (1st September). Is that any good?'

What about Alex?

D x

From: Seren Doughty
To: Daley MacKinnon
Date: 28 August 2023 at 13:01
Subject: Inbound

He has his own boat so he can stay or go, I really couldn't care less.

Friday 1st sounds perfect. X

*Tuesday 29th August, evening*

Just had an argument with Alex. It's so difficult not to react, not to get angry when I'm around him. And bursting his self-satisfied bubble was too tempting.

I was at my desk, writing the third part of *Crioch* when he came in to make dinner. He drained the pasta, tipped the last of the Co-op pasta sauces on top and announced: 'We need to ask Daley to bring more of these.'

'No need,' I said, not looking up. I was reading through what I'd just written and I was irritated by the interruption.

'What's that?'

'There's no need. I'm leaving,' I said, putting my pen down.

'You're leaving?'

'That's what I said.'

'When?'

'Friday.'

'This Friday?'

'Yes.'

'Were you going to tell me?'

'I'm telling you now.'

He shook his head as he poured the pasta from the pot into two waiting bowls. His hair was long, too long. The length made his curls look thin and straggly.

He placed my bowl and a fork on the desk and took his own over to the rocking chair. I shouldn't have said anything. I should have turned to my own dinner and eaten it. But I didn't. I was too pissed off by his hurt. 'What?'

He speared a tube of pasta and stuck it in his mouth, chewing slowly and thoughtfully. 'Nothing,' he said.

I turned back to my desk, closed my notebook. The twisted, red morsels of pasta appeared to me as something gruesome, like entrails – slippery and live. I felt my stomach turn.

'I just thought, after all this time, I might have merited a bit more than a casual goodbye.'

I shouldn't have laughed.

'That's funny, is it?'

'Yes, that's funny.'

'And why's that?'

'I just find it amusing that someone who's supposed to be intelligent could so consistently and catastrophically misunderstand a situation.'

'And?'

'And I don't want you here. I've never wanted you here.'

'I'm confused.'

'Why are you confused?'

'Because you seem to want me here when there's no one else. When you need someone to cook your meals or collect peat or find your dog.'

'Oh, you found my dog?'

'What's that supposed to mean?'

'Nothing.'

'It's not nothing. That was pretty loaded. What did you mean by that?'

'Tell me about the kids again, Alex.'

He nodded his head and leant down to place his bowl on the floor. 'I thought this would happen.'

'What?'

'That you would accuse me.'

'Accuse you? Now, why would I think it was you? It was clearly the ghost children. Those supernatural little shits. Pretty convenient though, don't you think? I mean, let's say – hypothetically – you wanted to kill a dog, you wanted to suggest a plot twist you're not talented enough to write yourself. It would be useful to have some ghost kids in the wings, some malicious spirits you could pin it on.'

'Can I just remind you that I'm not the only one who claims to have seen supernatural visions on this island?'

'No, but you are the only one to use it for your own naked ambition.'

'And you're not? What do you call the pantomime of last Sunday? Welcoming a decrepit old woman who can barely see or walk just so you could squeeze her for spurious details of a massacre you didn't have the staying power to actually sit and read about yourself. Yes, that's right, I remember. I brought you all those books, pinpointed particular chapters in my efforts to help you but you were bored, you were more interested in sitting in the café 'people watching'. As if that pursuit makes you interesting.'

'For a librarian, you seem to require a lot of gratitude. Do you know that's not reasonable? I don't get down on my hands and knees and thank the supermarket staff because I've eaten food purchased from the shelves they stacked.'

'I'm trying to point out that your primary focus is always selfish but you like to delude yourself that you're embarked on a worthier mission. You've just said it yourself, you don't want to be here really, you're longing to return to your Australian bit-of-rough in Castlebay. The only reason you've stayed so long is some last-ditch, desperate attempt to rescue your name from obscurity.'

'That's not it at all. I couldn't care less about my name—'

'So what is it then? Some moral duty you feel to the ghosts who took your clothes? Or perhaps it's a misguided belief that your dead daughter is among them? Because if it is – and judging by your face, it looks as though I've hit the nail on the head – then I would strongly advise the first thing you do, when you get back to the mainland, is see a doctor.'

'I'm not about to start taking advice from you.'

'Suit yourself,' he shrugged.

'I think I'll eat this upstairs.'

'Fine. Goodnight, Seren.'

'Go fuck yourself, Alex.'

*Friday 1st September, 6.30 a.m.*

I'm writing this on the beach. I've come down here to enjoy my last sunrise on Finish. It's a still, cool morning but I would have been here had it been raining and windy. I feel nervous, a little scared of leaving, given Kathleen (or should that be Chulainn's?) instruction to stay and finish. But what she told me, the details she gave me, are enough, I think, to finish the book somewhere else. Besides, it was never going to be possible to stay any longer than September. And then there's the fact that I really can't bear to spend another day in Alex's company.

The island was supposed to be mine. From May to September: the bothy, the beach, the stones – they were supposed to be mine. A place of retreat where I could write my book, tend my garden and perhaps, maybe, start to chip away at the huge, heavy lump of grief I carry everywhere. A lump that feels, somehow, indigestible.

Indigestible. Funny word. My nausea, stomach pain and fatigue disappeared – briefly – with my last period. I had assumed, at the time, that it was a very early miscarriage. The blood that collected in my sanitary towels had contained the kind of clots that made me think it was more than the lining of my womb shedding.

But now I'm not so sure. On Wednesday this week, the day after my argument with Alex, I began to feel unwell again. At first it was a bout of diarrhoea that woke me in the middle of the night and felt so urgent and explosive, I had to run down the stairs and out the front door.

I've thought back to all the times I've felt sick or tired or just unwell; I've tried to remember if Alex had prepared the meal that preceded those symptoms. I've looked back through this journal but it's difficult because at the time I didn't suspect a link so I wasn't particularly careful about noting down the two events. The only one that sticks out, loud and clear, is the meadowsweet cordial the night the fog rolled in. He was so keen to make it and kept, despite my refusals, offering it to me. The night Beau was led to her death.

I feel lost. It's so difficult to disentangle it all: the horrifying visions; a phantom pregnancy; my fears about Alex – some justified, some perhaps the result of paranoia and all the mad things that have happened to me on this island. I know I can't blame it all on him.

The sun is rising, the light so pure and blinding I feel momentarily reassured. It's like a doctor entering a treatment room before any questions or answers can be exchanged.

I need to leave this island. As soon as possible.

*Afternoon*

When I got back, there was no sign of Alex. I began packing. I'm leaving the little gas stove, the coffee pot, oil lamps, peeler, knife, anything that will be of use to the island's next resident and, in the short term, Alex. I bagged up my rubbish, gathered my laptop, pens, papers, the OS map and then, because there were still a few hours to kill before Daley was due, I decided to sit down in the rocking chair with one of the novels I never got round to reading.

I heard the front door open. It was Alex, he looked soaked – which confused me because it wasn't raining. He was wearing jeans, boots and his waterproof jacket, the hood still pulled up and circling his flushed face. 'You're back,' he said, sounding a little out of breath. We hadn't spoken since our argument on Tuesday night.

'Yes.'

'I need to ask a favour.'

'Right.' I put my book down on my lap.

He took his jacket off and hung it on the back of the front door. It began dripping in sporadic, atonal beats on the floor beneath. 'You're all packed up?'

'Yes. Daley's coming in a few hours.'

'OK,' he nodded. 'I'm leaving too.'

'OK,' I said, picking up my book. 'Happy for you.'

'But—'

'What?'

'My boat. I've just been down to the arch. The engine won't start. I can't get it to turn over.'

'OK.'

'It's dead. No surprise, really. I haven't tried it in weeks.'

'Sorry to hear that.'

'Jesus, Seren, can we not put our petty differences aside and discuss this rather pressing problem like adults?'

Petty. You killed my dog. I'm pretty sure you've been trying to poison me. You want to steal my story and pass it off as your own. I said none of this, of course. I still had to get through a few more hours. I opted for a shoulder shrug instead.

'Could you message Daley? Ask him to bring a jump pack when he comes?'

'I can do that.'

'I would offer to do it myself, except I can't seem to log in to your computer any more.'

'Funny that.'

A few minutes passed before I heard the door slam.

From: Seren Doughty
To: Daley MacKinnon
Date: 1 September 2023 at 10:32
Subject: Alex

It would appear the only way to get rid of him is to leave myself. Can you bring a jump pack for his boat when you come? Can't wait to see him disappear into the distance.

Come as soon as you can.

S x

Daley and I held one another for a long time, the waves, messenger of the seals, lapping at our feet and trying to move us on. He smelt good, freshly showered, and I felt a little pinch of arousal for indoor plumbing, shower gel in squeezy bottles, clean, dry towels. It would be OK, I told myself. I would write my book, start running again, eat normal meals and sleep in a proper bed. I had Daley now, my first real relationship since Jamie, and even if it wasn't exactly love, it was good sex with someone I really liked. It's no small step forward.

'So, his engine's fucked?' Daley asked as we walked up to the bothy.

'That's what he says.'

'Who leaves a boat untouched for weeks and weeks?'

'A long-haired narcissist.'

'I've bought some pizzas and a bottle of wine for tonight. I thought we could watch a film or something?'

'Well, that depends.'

'On what?'

'On what film you had in mind.'

'*Castaway*? It'll help with the homesickness.'

'A hot shower and clean sheets will help with the homesickness.'

'So that's a yes then?'

'It's a yes.'

'Awesome. Now we've got that sorted, let's get rid of this dozy prick.'

When we got back to the bothy, Alex had pushed the rocking chair to one side and put the other chair, my writing chair, upturned on the desk. In the space he cleared, he'd laid out what looked like the entire contents of his tent: thermarest, the yellow sleeping bag that made him look like a caterpillar, water bottle, folders, notebooks, transparent bags full of what looked like birdshit, several torches. He was on his knees, sifting through the detritus, when we walked in. 'Hi,' he said, barely looking up.

'You all right?' Daley asked.

'Yes, I'm fine.'

'Your boat's down at the arch?'

'Hmm?' he was completely distracted, barely listening.

'Where's your boat, mate?' Daley said, louder, like you would to someone hard of hearing. Or stupid. 'Seren said your boat needs a jump start.'

'Oh, yes. Down by the arch, yes.' He turned to me: 'Have you seen my rope?'

'The last time I saw it you were tying it to the peat platform. That was on Sunday – when Kathleen and Rosalie were here,' I said, more to Daley than to him.

Alex got to his feet, mumbled an 'excuse me' and shouldered past us towards the door.

'I'll bring my boat round, shall I?' Daley shouted after him.

'No,' Alex stopped and turned back to us. 'I was thinking ... I need to collect a few more soil samples before I go. That's why I need my rope.'

'You've had two months,' I said. I couldn't help myself.

'I know,' he patted down his pockets. 'The end has come quite suddenly and my supervisor thinks it would be good to get some gannet droppings and feathers, if at all possible. If I don't do it now, I won't be able to get back here until what, end of April, early May next year?'

'At the earliest,' Daley agreed.

'OK, I'm going to go down there now,' he said, turning to Daley. 'Would you mind helping me? I need someone to bag up the samples while I climb. It won't take long.' There was something helpless and pitiful about the way he looked at us. Like a little boy who'd wet himself. 'Please?'

Daley looked at his watch. 'I'll go get the leads,' he said, kissing me on the forehead and then, pointing to Alex, 'Meet you at the headland.'

'Great, thanks. Thanks, Daley,' he said, a massive molar-revealing smile on his face. I had never seen him look so happy.

I watched Daley walk down to the beach, watched his shoulder blades move under his light blue T-shirt as he walked past the abandoned village. I thought about how they'd feel later, in his bed. I felt a little shiver of excitement at the thought of running my fingertips along their edges as he moved on top of me.

I needed to distract myself with jobs in the bothy; I wiped down the table, shook out my mattress and wrote this entry. I'm up-to-date. Nothing to do now but wait.

From my rucksack near the door I hear the flat, shapeless sound of a new mail notification.

I could ignore it. Daley and Alex have been gone forty minutes or so. He'll be back soon, without Alex hopefully, and then we can leave together. I'll be able to check email to my heart's content once I'm back in Castlebay.

Fuck it. I've got nothing better to do.

From: Rosalie MacKinnon
To: Seren Doughty
Date: 1 September 2023 at 14:59
Subject: Mam

Hi Seren,

I just wanted to send you a little message to say how lovely it was to see you a couple of weeks ago and to thank you for your patience with Mam. It's so hard sometimes, dealing with the outbursts and then managing the fallout from those outbursts. I've met plenty of people (guests mainly) who don't or won't understand that Mam can't help it.

She has certain intuitions, shall we say. It's always been the case – long before the dementia took hold. That said, please forgive me if this tries your patience even further but Mam asked me to get in touch with you. As mad as it sounds, she wanted me to tell you that she had another one of her spells last night. Crying like she did when you were with us. It's awful to watch – she brushes her hair so violently – but anyway, that's what she did and this morning, the first thing she said to me was: 'Tell Seren'.

So I have. What good it will do you, I don't know.

Looking forward to seeing you later. Daley had a bit of a spring in his step this morning!

Love,
Rosalie

Couldn't she have waited? And what even is this message? There's no actual information aside from Rosalie telling me her mother was crying – something I've already witnessed once, on my last night in the guesthouse, when she woke us all with it.

But then, the next day, Cameron died. Cameron with his great greats. So proud of his Finish ancestry.

Linda. What was it she said? When the banshee cries, someone dies.

When the banshee cries, someone dies.

# Part III

# Seven

I SAT DOWN HEAVILY on the doorstep, Rosalie's email lit up on the screen before me and Linda's words ringing in my head. I needed time to think. I looked out to sea, my view of the water framed, reduced, crowded – what was the right verb? – by the rocky inlet to the south.

I stood up and somewhere, far away from the panic gathering in my stomach, I was aware that my laptop had fallen hard against the ground. I ran as fast as I could towards the headland, jumped dips and hummocks and then climbed, climbed to the headland. I replayed Alex's actions in the bothy earlier: his frustration at the missing rope, the sudden and unaccountable urgency he felt to collect more samples from the cliff but above all, that beaming smile. The happiness I saw writ large on his face when Daley agreed to help him.

I am destined, it seems, to run headlong towards catastrophe. It is the colour, the marker of my life. I imagine it now as a strange kind of biofilm, a creamy coating that covered my skin as I was pulled from my mother's womb.

That day at the beginning of September, in the middle of the day, just when I had decided to put the island behind me, to enjoy a quiet night in Castlebay, I knew – I just knew – that I was racing towards a giant full stop. But still I ran, my chest heaving, my lungs straining to draw in as much oxygen as they could from the moist air I tumbled through.

I made it to the headland, my chest screaming and my heart at a dangerous tipping point. I was bent double, clutching my stomach and looking down to the rocky pit where the waves crashed.

There was nothing. No sign of Alex or Daley.

To my right, I could see the light blue hull of Alex's boat bobbing in the waters under the natural arch. Directly behind it, sticking out with its stern into the sound, was the *Spes Secunda*.

I searched along the edge of the cliffs from left to right until I came to the sea stack and the cave. I realised I was standing in the exact spot I'd been in two weeks ago when the air was full of smoke and human cries and the dark-haired boy had bowed to me.

I screamed Daley's name into the wind.

'Over here!' A voice further along the headland. I moved towards it; I was now above the steepest, most treacherous drop of the western cliff.

Just below me, a few feet down, was a narrow platform where Daley was kneeling. In front of him was a pile of what looked like freezer bags, weighed down by small rocks. He had a pen in his hand. 'What's up? Has something happened?' He wasn't hurt. He wasn't dead.

'Where's Alex?'

'Further down,' he pointed. 'Don't worry, he's on a rope.'

Beside me, on the stone platform, the iron ring creaked with the strain of Alex's weight.

'We're nearly finished. I'll come up now.'

'Be careful,' I shouted as Daley got to his knees.

'Are you sure you're OK?'

'I will be. When you're up here and he's in his boat.'
I held out my hand and he passed me the freezer
bags – filled, as far as I could see, with a few feathers
and droppings.

'Have you managed to get his engine going?'

'Not yet,' he climbed onto the headland and stood
beside me, rubbing the palms of his hands on his shorts.
'He's too busy collecting all this birdshit.'

I sat down on the grass, my legs dangling off the headland, and peered right over so I could see the top of Alex's
head about fifty metres below us. With Daley beside me,
I felt myself relax. 'He's losing his hair, you know.'

'That's the least of his troubles.'

Below me Alex was brushing at something with his
fingers. 'What's he doing?'

'Christ knows. Something about loamy scree.'

'You didn't ask any questions?'

'Too worried he'd answer them.'

I reached out a hand and stroked the back of his calf.
I felt his muscles flex as I did so. He raised his hands to
his mouth and shouted, 'Alex!'

Below us, Alex shifted over to a large overhang on his
left. I saw the rope scrape across the grassy edge as he
did so. He leant back into thin air, confident and certain
that no harm would come to him, and raised a hand. He
was agile, good at climbing – anyone could see that.
'Coming,' he shouted up.

Daley sat down beside me and we watched Alex scale
the remaining distance between us. He was skilled and

swift on his feet, testing each foothold before he'd commit, locking the rope each time so it remained taut.

I thought back to our conversations in the library café. Had he told me about this? I remembered that his father had been a GP, that they had a small boat and would go fishing in Culloden or Cromarty – somewhere beginning with a C. But this? His evident skill at mountain climbing. I couldn't recall any mention of it. Which was strange because he wasn't one for modesty. We waited for him to come back up.

But at the platform, the same one Daley had just left, he ran into trouble.

'What's wrong?' Daley asked, getting to his knees.

Alex's face was running with sweat. He looked like he was in a lot of pain. 'I've turned my ankle.'

'When?' I asked, getting to my feet.

'Just now,' he grimaced.

'I didn't see it.'

Daley looked at me, confused. 'Can you get up another metre? I can pull you from there.'

My heart started racing once again. 'He's lying,' I said. My pulse was rasping and insistent in my ear, like the scraping of hard bristles through fine hair.

I watched Alex cry out as he tried to put weight on it. 'I can't,' he shook his head.

'All right, hang tight,' Daley said and leant further over, reaching his hand down.

'Don't,' I cried. 'Don't help him.' I put my hands on his shoulders, tried to hold him back. 'It's too far. You'll fall.'

'I'm not going to fall, OK?'

He didn't know the truth about Beau. He didn't know what Alex was capable of. I'd kept it from him. One of many mistakes I'd made.

'It's a trap. I know it.'

Ignoring me, Daley dug the fingertips of his left hand into the edge of the soft soil of the headland and, with his other hand, reached as far as he could down to Alex.

Late, too late, I saw the metal ring – this one new, shiny, held fast to the rock face with bolts recently screwed in. Alex gripped it with his left hand and then, standing tall on perfectly healthy ankles, he took Daley's hand with the other and pulled. I watched, in horror, as the muscles in Alex's neck became long and livid with strain. I screamed, dug my fingertips into Daley's shoulders as I felt him try to rear back to safety. But he was too far forward. In his precarious, trusting position, he was no match for Alex's strength and determination to tug, heave and finally pull him clear off the headland.

# Eight

WHAT DID HE THINK as he plummeted two hundred metres, the rocks coming quickly – too quickly – to meet him?

Did he look for me?

The fall will be upon you before you know it.

I have no memory of what happened after that split-second of horror. I did not see him hit the rocks. I did not hear him scream through my own screams.

I need whoever reads this to understand something. I was not thinking. I was not in any position to consider my new and desperate situation. Had I been, I might have connected the movement of the iron ring beside me with Alex's climb back up to the top. I didn't have a knife or anything sharp enough to cut the rope. Perhaps I should have attempted to disconnect the carabiner but, in the same way I had no knife, I had no capacity to think like that, at all.

The rest is difficult. For so many reasons, it's difficult for me to write what happened next.

I knew what Daley's death meant. I knew what a light he'd been for me and what darkness was now to come.

I knew it and the island knew it. Kathleen MacKinnon, howling her banshee cry in a guesthouse in Castlebay, knew it. The only person who didn't know what darkness had arrived was Alex.

He is absent from any recollection I have of those hours, or perhaps days is more accurate . . . I'm not sure how long it was between what happened on the headland and waking up in the attic room of the bothy. All I know is that I was in a dark, warm place that was not unpleasant but then, neither was it welcome. A rope, some chemical tie, held me – inert, stunned – in mid-air, where I hung, somewhere between dark and light; rocks and sky. From time to time a helicopter hovered above me, its frantic blades too concerned with staying high in the sky to come down and meet me in the darkness.

I got it. I understood. I was unreachable now. But surely they could try a bit harder? Come a bit closer?

I came to consciousness more frequently. I glimpsed things: a bright light, strands of hair, clouds through glass. I heard movements around me: furniture being repositioned, the clang of mugs collected by their handles, cold water poured from a height. I'd been drugged into submission and, as futile and ineffective as an injured climber scrabbling the final few metres of an ascent, I tried to make sense of what these small sights and sounds meant. It's daytime again, he's made tea, the three-legged stool is being brought closer to the bed. But then, even as I grabbed hold of these things, these facts, I would lose my foothold, I'd slip and fall back down, to oblivion and rocks and darkness.

*Thy drugs are quick.* This line from *Romeo and Juliet*, played in a loop in my head. I'd studied the play once, in my first or second year of high school. I remember finding it difficult and boring. We watched an old adaptation, by Zeffirelli, I think, but it never got under my skin, never stayed in my memory and yet this line, read in a Welsh classroom over thirty years ago, crawled out of some inert, sedated coil of my hippocampus. It crawled out and presented itself as the only viable option. Here, say this.

'You were hysterical. I had to give you something,' came the answer.

There should be no answer. Romeo says these words and dies. He fucking dies. Beside the woman he loves. But Alex didn't understand any of that. He was younger than me, no doubt went to a different school. Perhaps he didn't do *Romeo and Juliet*.

A cracking sound and then cold air on my face. It was fragrant, fresh.

'That's better,' he said and I opened my eyes. The Velux windows, two of them sunk in the grey of the corrugated roof, were open to the sky.

The sky. Helicopter.

'That was the coastguard, based in Barra, I think he said.'

Had I said the words out loud? Why couldn't I keep my thoughts to myself?

'Pretty efficient, I must say. Daley's cousin must have raised the alarm.'

I tried to push myself up and realised I couldn't. Something was wrong with my hands. I looked down and saw the rope, his climbing rope, bound around my wrists.

I felt his fingers snake under my armpits and then I was hauled up into a sitting position. It hurt me to be handled in this way. My skin felt tender, especially under the arms. My lymph nodes were giant tender eggs that Alex pressed on too hard. I cried out.

'What is it?' he asked, as he leant me back against the wall.

I shook my head.

'Seren?' he leant in close and lifted my left eyelid, shone a light in.

I blinked my eyes closed, recoiled.

'Sorry,' he said, his face still too close. 'I just want to check your pupil response.' His breath stank. His lips and tongue made a sticky, tacky sound as he spoke and it produced – all that thick saliva – a foul, sour stench that made me heave.

I clamped my lips shut – anything to keep my thoughts inside.

'You haven't eaten since yesterday, you must be hungry. I'll go make some lunch.'

Later – I don't know if it was minutes or hours – I heard the clanging of a pot on the stove downstairs and cutlery being gathered together. And then, in no time at all, he was in the room and I was sitting upright again. He tried to spoon some mush between my lips but I kept them clamped shut, just as I had with my eyelids before. 'Come on, Seren, you need to eat something.'

I shook my head, pursed my lips tighter. I felt the saliva build, because – despite myself – it was food and I was hungry. But I wouldn't relent. I was determined not to open any part of my body to him. I kicked the bowl out from his hands and heard it land with a heavy thud on the floorboards below us.

He was left holding the half-filled spoon in mid-air. I watched him, wondering if he'd persist with the feeding, but he just smiled and shook his head. 'I'm trying to help you.'

It was difficult to speak. My tongue kept sticking to the roof of my mouth. 'Fuck you,' I managed.

'Still hysterical, I see. Perhaps you need a little more rest. I'll get you something to help you sleep.'

'No,' I shook my head as he moved towards the stairs.

'You're not well,' he concluded, before descending.

And then? I don't know. He returned with a syringe and then it went dark.

It came while I slept. A boat in the bay. Daley, I thought. He's back.

Daley. Daley was dead. The thought, like a chemical solution shot straight into the vein, circulated and chilled me.

Downstairs, Alex also heard it. He dropped something heavy and then footsteps, the sound of a jacket being zipped up, the front door being pulled hard against the frame. The key in the lock. He must be going down to the bay.

It must be another visit from the coastguard. A boat this time.

There was nothing in the room aside from the three-legged stool and the upended bowl, from which – splayed like a fan – lay the streaks of the now fetid, yellow mush he'd tried to feed me. I needed to cut the rope.

I could scoot across the room on my bum, get myself down the stairs. I could find something sharp in the kitchen or even use the gas stove to burn through the rope. I didn't care if I injured myself in the process. All I wanted was the use of my hands again. Once I managed that, I'd be able to open one of the windows and escape, just as I had the night of the fire.

I was at the top of the stairs when I heard the front door close.

'Where do you think you're going?' he asked from the kitchen, his hands on his hips like some pantomime dame. 'Let me guess,' he said, coming up about halfway. 'You heard a boat and thought you'd run down to the beach and wave your arms.' He stepped over me, crouched down behind and threaded his arms through mine, fluid and free: 'Allow me to save you the trouble.'

'They're going to keep coming,' I warned as he dragged me backwards to the bed, narrowly avoiding the upturned, yellow mush.

'Is that right?' He lifted me, like a sack of potatoes, onto the bed.

'This was the last place he visited. His boat is still here. They're going to keep coming until they find out what happened.'

'I've told them what happened.'

He was beaming, desperate for me to ask the next question.

'I told them you and Daley planned a stop on Pabbay on your way back. You'd never been and were keen to see it.'

Thinking was hard. I tried to sift through the dates, work out how many days had elapsed since that Friday. 'What day is it?'

'Tuesday.'

'The 5th?'

'I believe so.'

'I was due to return the key to National Trust Scotland yesterday.'

'And?'

'And my failure to do so will trigger a search. My ex-husband will want to know why I haven't returned. You're never going to be free of this.'

'As soon as Daley's body washes up, which – fingers crossed – will be any day now, they'll step down the search. Given what I told them about you and Daley's planned stop on Pabbay, it's likely you will be assigned a missing person, presumed dead.'

Daley's body. I hadn't seen him hit the rocks but hearing Alex say those words was like a punch in the chest. It did happen. There was a mass of broken bones and smashed tissue that used to be him, floating in the Finish Sound somewhere. Waiting for a hook, a search light, a positive identification.

I felt the pad of his thumb on my cheekbone.

'Don't touch me.'

'I think someone needs a drink,' he said, dumping a bunch of keys on the stool beside me before disappearing downstairs to the kitchen.

He returned with a jug of water and poured some into a mug. I had no choice but to take a few urgent sips from the cup he pressed to my lips. It made me choke at first but the water, even as I coughed it up, felt good and after a few seconds I indicated I wanted more.

It was the same enamel jug he'd used for the meadow-sweet cordial the night of the fog. 'You've been poisoning me,' I said.

'I gave you a sedative because you were hysterical.'

'Before that. I've been sick, a lot. Since you got here. And always after you prepared food.'

'I believe they call that paranoia.'

I lifted my bound wrists. 'I'd say my doubts about you were justified, wouldn't you?'

He shook his head. 'This whole situation, it was never meant to come to this. Believe it or not, I didn't come here to hurt you.'

'I don't believe it. You have hurt me many times in many ways. Of course, you meant it.'

'Everything I've done has been – has been in retaliation.'

'Retaliation? For what?'

'You stole from me. You've *been* stealing from me.'

'What are you talking about?'

'I was the one who gave you the idea.'

'The idea?'

'The idea for your story. The island setting?'

'But – Alex – you must know that that is not original to you. I can think of at least five, six – no, seven – authors you'd need to put on your hit list.'

'Not just that. Also the massacre, the testimony of the shepherds who came to live here after the island was abandoned?'

'So? That was a matter of historical record. You *found* it. You're a librarian. That is literally your job.'

'But you didn't. You didn't find it. That's the point.'

'Hang on a minute. You think the idea of this island being haunted is yours because I couldn't look something up?'

'Isn't it?'

'No.'

'And I suppose it's a coincidence, is it, that you read my manuscript and decided to set your story on an island?'

'Yes.'

'Even then, even when I knew you'd stolen my idea and setting, I was generous. I offered to collaborate. I gave you material when you were stalling.'

'What material?'

'Beau.'

'Beau.'

'It worked, didn't it?' The raiders who came to the island, they only ever raided for cattle – animals. Anyone with a modicum of common sense would understand that. You started writing again after Beau.'

'I started writing because Kathleen told me what happened to those girls.'

'Except your story has a slaughtered cow named Bo in it?'

'You've been reading my journal.'

'Conducting due diligence. I've been auditing the extent of your theft.'

'My theft?'

'Yes, theft. It's called intellectual property for a reason. You have stolen from me. I'm sorry to be so blunt, but you have.'

'Oh my god.'

'I just want some credit, Seren. Is that too much to ask?'

'You are – you're crazy.'

'And you're a user. You invited me out to dinner that night in Edinburgh, took me back to your place, asked to read my manuscript—'

'I didn't! It was shit. I never wanted it.'

He put a hand to his chest, his mouth turned down, mock-wounded by my words. 'You took what you wanted from me and you know it. And then, when all I wanted was to share some of this place, when I needed space to try writing something new, you got territorial and entitled, relegating me to the garden, only allowing me to use the kitchen table for a few hours when it suited you. Anything to keep me from writing a book when you couldn't. And all the while still feeding off me, allowing me to wait on you hand and foot, sucking ideas and inspiration from me. These are the kind of things that try a person's patience, Seren. You must agree, I've been very patient.'

I tried to lick my lips. What to say? So much of my life has been cyclical, repetitive; a strange, endless replaying of the same event – just with characters and background changed. Alex, sitting on the end of my bed, working himself up, recalling his injuries was just like Johan at my front door, picking off on his fingers all the ways Alana had wronged him. 'She doesn't want to see you,' I had said slowly and calmly to a man who was already beyond all reasoning.

'I did not use you,' I insisted. 'I never wanted you in the first place.'

'But the book you're writing. Just admit it, to me at least. You stole the idea from me.'

'The island *is* haunted. It's not an idea that can be stolen. It's the truth.'

'And you call me a lunatic,' he laughed.

'I'm not making it up. The things I've written – the things you've read. They have happened. They're real.'

He laughed. 'So real you had to plot every sighting on an OS map?'

'I didn't do that.'

'You're deluded. Just like the shepherds before you. Too much time alone here. Cabin fever, I believe they call it.'

'And you decided to use my *delusions*, as you call them, against me by slaughtering my dog and blaming it on a black-haired phantom child you'd read about in my journal?'

He sighed and dropped his shoulders. 'I was trying to help you.'

'You're a psychopath. Do you know that?'

He shook his head with a rueful smile. 'I'm simply trying to explain to you that the idea of a haunted island with children spirits running amok, that idea, those ideas, were given to you by me. You must at least accept that.'

'There's no point trying to reason with you.'

'I came here with nothing but good intentions. I have supported and inspired you to keep going, provided valuable material to keep up the momentum even when your story was clearly stalling. I did all that for you.'

'And murdering my boyfriend? How does that fit with this narrative?'

'We're talking about the book.'

'We're talking about you.'

'Please stop. You push me, Seren. You push me to the limit of what I can endure and then act surprised when I'm forced to retaliate.'

'Take the book. Take it all: my journal, notebooks, my laptop, the fucking map if you think that's so important. Take it all and pass it off as your own. I don't care. I don't want it. Just untie me and let me have,' I had to think, 'one of the boats. I promise you, on my life, I will never lay claim to any of it.'

'I can't do that.'

'Why not? You are the only person who cares about this. Literally, you're nuts for it. Have the story, do what you want with it. I couldn't care less.'

'Oh, Seren,' he laughed. 'You're not very bright, are you?'

'What?'

'It's actually quite endearing.'

'What are you talking about?'

'You think I'd leave the *Spes Secunda* moored where it was? Right behind my boat?'

'Where is it then?'

'Pabbay, of course,' he looked at the keys he'd dumped on the stool. 'They're Daley's keys, right there.'

'But how – how did you get back?'

He smiled at me: 'I towed mine, of course.'

'There was never anything wrong with it, was there?'

He laughed and shook his head – like he'd just delivered the punchline to a long-awaited joke.

# Nine

THE WEATHER WAS TURNING from damp chill to hard cold. I felt it in my bones and in my thin, wasted muscles.

Alex had left a plastic bucket for me to use as a toilet. It was close, too close, to the splayed yellow mush and it stank. The whole attic stank. His policy, I'm sure he had one – Alex was a planner – was to wait for me to ask for food. He was pushing me to the limits of what I could endure and I had to decide if I was going to push back. I counted two sunsets since he last told me the date, so by my calculation it was almost a week since Daley had died. I hadn't heard any more helicopters or boats in the bay. Perhaps they'd found him, at last. I didn't like to think of his body floating unclaimed but, at the same time, I knew its absence meant the search would continue.

I thought of Kathleen MacKinnon often during those days of hunger and loneliness. I thought of her milky blue eyes unclouding as she spoke to me. I remembered how she had looked at me with focus and precision and told me Tilly was with the other children on the island. 'You need not worry,' she had said. 'Chulainn is watching over her. Chulainn watches over all innocents.'

I thought of the knickers I'd found in Chulainn's grave, the cries I'd heard at the stream, the little finger bone that had been returned to me up at Crois an fionnadh. I thought of my own wounds: the discomfort of being so hungry and dirty all the time. But also, the huge heavy mass of grief that had been Tilly but was now Beau and Daley and really, it was too much – too much for one person to possibly live with. But it begged the question, what about me? Why wasn't someone watching over me?

I cried a lot during those days. Often without even registering it was happening. Hunger does that. Take any toddler or young child before lunch and introduce some unforeseen impediment, that's what you get. Tears. This was just a darker, more fucked-up scenario: I wanted to go home, I wanted Daley back, I wanted Alex to die a painful death and none of that was going to happen.

The crying often led to sleep and that was my only refuge in those terrible days. But, one afternoon, just as I was drifting off, I remembered something Kathleen had said to me that day she came to the island. 'You must do what she asks. It's very important. You must stay and finish.'

I opened my eyes and sat up, suddenly very awake.

'There is nowhere for me to go. Even if I made it down to your boat, there's no way I could operate it or navigate my way around the rocks.'

He held the bucket of shit and piss in his right hand, a kitchen knife in his left. The same 20cm one I'd bought in Castlebay. The same blade, I'm sure, that he used to slice Beau's throat.

'If you untie me, let me eat something and maybe write—'

'You want to write?'

'I think it might be the way through this. You want this book. Or the outline – is that right?'

'It's at least fifty per cent mine.'

'OK, whatever. I don't want to get into that again. How about I write it, finish it,' I swallowed heavily on that word, 'and then send it off to my editor? To Tess.'

'And watch you get all the credit? I don't think so,' he said, turning away from me. The contents of the bucket washed up more of its stench as he did so.

'With a forwarding note,' I said, my voice becoming more shrill. He turned back to me. 'To say the idea came from you and that I relinquish all claim to its intellectual property.'

He sucked his thin lips together as he thought it through. He put the bucket back down on the floor.

'And then, then you let me go,' I continued. 'You'll have it recorded then, time-stamped from my own inbox, that it was your idea. I'll never breathe a word.'

He looked me up and down, weighing my words carefully.

I knew it didn't matter to him, my promises of silence or relinquishing of IP. I knew that, ultimately, his plan was to ensure my silence with the knife he held in his hand. But the freedom to go downstairs, I reasoned, and have my wrists untied was all I could think about. That, and the opportunity to escape.

CRÍOCH: III

Muirnín MacKinnon raised the alarm. She sensed the blood-thirst coming from Kisimul Castle as she sat on the font stone of Crois an fionnadh. It reached the back of her neck, lifted the white strands of her hair and whispered in her ear. Once the islanders had taken their places in the stone circle, she told them that none of them were safe. The raiders were dead but their vengeful fathers were coming.

For three days and three nights, Muirnín MacKinnon remained on the font stone, listening. Her sons, Catriona and Mairi's fathers, as well as their own sons, kept vigil on the highest hill, Cnoc fiacail.

It was Catriona's youngest brother, a little boy with black hair called Angus, who saw the boat. Small, fast, intelligent, he was the perfect look-out. And just as he'd been instructed, on sight of a boat, he blew the horn.

Everybody – man, woman and child – on hearing the call, ran to the cave. They pulled gorse and heather across the entrance to conceal it. And there they waited.

# Ten

ALEX STOOD OVER ME as I wrote, questioning everything. 'Three days and three nights is ridiculous. She's supposed to be an old woman.'

'She is an old woman.'

'So how could she do that? It's completely implausible.'

'Says the man who wrote a novel about nymphomaniac mermaids.'

'They were sirens. But this is supposed to be a true story.'

I put my pen down. Everything had to be done by longhand. He wouldn't allow me any access to the laptop, wherever it was. 'She was the island midwife. She frequently had to stay up days and nights with labouring women. That's the job.'

'Change it. One day, one night.'

I picked up my pen and made the change.

'OK, so they all go to the cave—'

'Do they?' He was making the same assumption everybody, including me, had made – that Muirnīn MacKinnon had gone into the cave with all the others. But what about Kathleen's repetitive prayer, *'if it comes through my knee, it can't be helped but it shall not come through my mouth'*? What was that if not a woman under pressure to keep a secret?

'Of course, they did. Their remains were found. That is a matter of historical record.'

'I don't know that Muirnīn did.'

'You think they left an old, lame woman alone in her cottage to die?'

'I don't know. Do you know for sure?'

'Get up,' he said, pulling me roughly by my arm. 'I'll do it.'

I stepped back, relieved to be out of that chair and able to stretch my legs. It was ridiculous really, his attempt to get the story factually accurate. 'Why does it matter to you?'

He shook his head as he wrote and I understood I was to wait. He was sitting on the knife. The handle pressed between thigh and chair so that the blade was pointing in a forty-five-degree angle towards the door. 'If you can get the autobiographical details right, or as factually accurate as possible, you gain the reader's trust. Enough to hang an implausible ghost story on.'

'You should teach creative writing.' I couldn't get at the knife without closing my hand around the blade and it was so wedged, I doubted I'd come away with anything more than a sliced palm and fingers. I stepped backwards and tried to get a look at the closed door. 'And you know, if you find yourself stuck with a difficult student, you could always hold a knife to their throat. That can be very motivating.'

'Very funny,' he mumbled.

'Forced sedation if their tenses don't agree. You could really break some new ground.'

It was the first day of our truce, our new collaboration. I was trying to act as normal as possible but my eyes were hungry, searching for a potential weapon. The bottles I'd used as candle holders were gone, along with every knife or sharp instrument. Even the poker that was usually upright in the alcove beside the fireplace had disappeared. I was searching for something heavy, like the cast-iron bannock stone, when I heard it.

Alex did as well. He half-stood from the chair and the knife clattered down to the flags.

I became very still, my eyes on the knife.

And then it came again. Unmistakable. A boat's engine, nearing the bay.

He picked up the knife and knocked over the chair in his rush for the door. 'Stay here,' he said, holding the tip of the knife towards me. But it was shaking a little and for the first time, he looked rattled.

He opened the door and leant out. I thought about pushing him, slamming the door behind him, but even if I were successful – and it was a very big if – how would that help me get down to the bay? I needed to get out of the bothy.

Another blast of the horn from the boat.

Alex stood on the doorstep for several more seconds, turning the handle of the knife in his hand, thinking. And then, without warning, he stepped outside and walked around to the back of the bothy. I stood absolutely still, the only movement a small area of flesh between my breasts that visibly vibrated with the now-rapid beat of my heart.

I heard rustling from the lean-to. This was my opportunity. I knew, as soon as the rustling stopped, he'd be on his way back to the bothy. If I didn't go now, while the door was open and a boat was waiting in the bay, I never would.

I ran. My bare feet pounding the prickly grass. I didn't consciously look for the boat, my goal was short-term. Get to the abandoned village, then the beach, throw myself in the sea. He'd have a difficult job pulling me out or stabbing me with the knife in churning water. I could wait there, wave my arms, shout for help.

It was the run of dreams. When you can't get your legs to move fast enough. I was still weak: malnourished and recovering from the drugs he'd given me. I imagined him behind me: the fast, frenzied footfall of a much younger, stronger person. I ran down the hummocky slopes, praying one of my ankles wouldn't turn in a rabbit hole. Just get to the water, Seren. If I could get to the water, I had a chance.

I saw the abandoned village rise up before me and the proximity of the sand and the sea made me run faster. I was almost there, I was just about to pass the first stone wall when I caught sight of a figure just beyond it. Small, hunched, it looked like an old woman with a dark woollen scarf covering her head.

I felt a huge weight slam into the back of me. I hit the ground and felt a searing pain in my ribs, and a hard, irrevocable loosening of an incisor. My nose felt hot and wet. I tried turning my head to look for the boat, the sea, but Alex was shoving me into the sand, tying my hands behind my back. And then his voice in my ear: 'If you scream, I'll cut your throat. Right here, right now. Do you understand?'

Did I understand? My mouth was full of blood and sand, I'd probably broken a rib or two and my one chance at escape was gone. Yes, I understood.

There was no point mentioning the figure I'd seen, I knew that. Besides, he had a roll of gaffer tape in his right hand. There would be no more speaking once he got to grips with that.

Every time I breathed, my ribcage pleaded with me to stop. That wasn't the only issue with breathing. He had taped my mouth shut and my nose was still bleeding; I had to stay calm if I didn't want to drown in my own blood.

He dumped me in the lean-to, threw me down on the ground, his knee on my stomach while he bound my ankles with the same tape he'd used on my hands and mouth. He unzipped his sleeping bag and covered me over with it, leaving me there on the cold stone flags like so much rubbish while, presumably, he went to deal with whoever had motored into the bay.

Once he was gone, I made small, incremental movements back and forth with my head. It was the same motion Kathleen had made in the rocking chair. I felt a strength gather in the back and forth motion, in the up-and-down – like the build-up to an orgasm. It starts something, the rocking. It generates energy – in this case, anger.

But anger was not going to help me. I needed logic. I needed to think. There was a key to this.

I stared long and hard at the wall of the lean-to, just below the shelf where I'd positioned my tomato plants back in May. In his rush to get down to the boat in the bay, he had neglected to clear out the tools. The same tools

Daley had pointed out to me that first afternoon we came to Finish, recounting their names in effortless, perfect Gaelic. In front of me were a dibble, peat cutter, foot plough, rake and an axe. Naturally my attention was drawn towards the axe and the bloody big blade it presented. But I quickly discounted it as too heavy and unwieldy. I couldn't see how I would find the opportunity or strength to lift it high enough to inflict any kind of lethal injury.

I continued my inspection. Behind all the tools, circumspect in its thin, spindly appearance, was the bamboo fishing rod. It brought back memories of that afternoon on the beach with Daley when I caught my first flounder; how happy and exhilarated I'd felt with Daley's hands on mine, his chest pressing into my shoulder blades. He'd shown me how to yank a fish from the water and what to do with it once you had it in your hands.

I stared at that fishing rod for a long time.

It was getting dark by the time Alex opened the door of the lean-to. A quick glance at his watch told me it was just after eight, which – by my reckoning – meant we were somewhere around the middle of September.

He looked busy, harassed and something about me clearly bothered him. He reached down and pulled the tape from my mouth and then stepped back, his hands on his hips with a *what-have-we-here* expression on his face. He looked around the small space and then spotted the tools.

He gathered them one by one, leaning over me each time. I heard them land with a thud in the overgrown vegetable patch.

'You brought drugs with you.'

He said nothing. He had the peat cutter in his hand.

'And the gaffer tape.'

Again, he said nothing. Just reached for the last tool, which happened to be the rake, with grim determination. All that remained in the corner was the fishing rod.

'I've got to hand it to you, you came prepared.'

He paused, albeit briefly.

'I underestimated you.'

The corners of his mouth turned down. It was very subtle, an almost imperceptible, involuntary movement of his facial muscles but I saw it. I saw it land.

*Indigo Lights*. A novel about a little girl who could read and identify the intensity of a particular emotion. 'Where did the idea come from?' I'd been asked that question countless times, in various ways: in interviews, at festivals, by readers on Twitter. I'd always replied with a variation of the same deflection: I don't know, or sometimes, more cryptically, that it had just come to me.

I did know. It hadn't just come to me. It was in me. I had, after a long time – too long – finally got a read on Alex.

Pride. Someone expressing approval of his actions. He liked to feel important. It mattered to him that someone listened. What didn't matter was the condition of the listener. A captive woman soaked in her own blood and urine? Not a problem. To him, I was a willing spectator. A paid-up member of an audience. I was someone conveniently placed to applaud and enjoy his genius.

Yesterday I was a problem to him. Yesterday I was something to be caught, clipped, contained. But today,

today I was the only person on the island who could listen to him. There was some advantage to be gained from this. I didn't know what exactly, but I knew getting him to talk was the key.

'Are you not worried they saw?' I asked as he untied me the next morning. On the hard standing just outside the door, a bowl of something steaming.

'Saw what?' He pulled the sleeping bag from my body and motioned for me to sit up.

'The coastguard. I was pretty close to the beach when you rugby-tackled me.'

He bent down to pick up the bowl and placed it in my lap. Boiled rice and lentils. From his back pocket, he produced a spoon.

It was the definition of bland, boiled to fuck without a grain of salt, but to me, that morning, it was the tenderest sirloin; a perfectly cooked poached egg; it was manna come straight from heaven. I felt my blood cells bounce in anticipation of the incoming nutrients. I was giddy, pissed-up on one mouthful. 'Well?' I persisted, flirting like this was a cocktail party.

He smiled and leant up against the door frame. 'I'm always the subject with you, aren't I?'

I paused in my eating, my mouth still full. 'What do you mean?'

'The subject of your sentences. Have you noticed that? *I rugby-tackled you.* You're always the object.'

'But you did?'

'Or, or—' he held up his index finger, 'you could say: *when I ran away you* . . . You could assign a verb to yourself occasionally.'

It was hard, swallowing.

'But to answer your question, they didn't see. We were hidden behind the wall. Also, it was a different team to last time.'

'What did they say?'

'They wanted to double-check the date and time you and Daley left for Pabbay, that kind of thing.'

'That's it?'

'Well, no. They asked a couple of questions about me and what I was doing here, how long I plan on staying.'

'What did you tell them?'

'That I'm doing some last-minute research for my PhD. They wanted to know if the boat under the natural arch was mine. Just fact checking really.'

He wanted my approval. I cultivated this evident need in him as much as possible in the days that followed, when I was not permitted back inside the bothy. When he came to see me, to untie me briefly so I could go to the toilet, I made sure to ask him open-ended questions and feign interest in his answers. He responded to my curiosity like flounder to a bait hook, bringing the three-legged stool around to the lean-to so he could sit more comfortably while I squatted down to shit or piss, depending on how much I'd had to eat. It was worse, way more humiliating than the bucket-in-the-attic situation, but he didn't seem to notice or register my discomfort.

In the afternoon he'd permit me to do seven turns of the bothy garden. Seven times past the verbena, now dead and brown like everything else that had been planted in this wind-blown space, seven times past the wall where

Daley and I had sat and smoked and I'd told him I had a daughter.

Aside from the evening, the post-lunch walk was the best time to talk to him. He became drowsy and dull, the urge to sleep making him softer and less calculating.

'What are your plans? When all this is over?' Never mind the loaded significance of *over* or what that would mean for me, talking about what he'd do in the future was, hands down, his favourite subject.

'It's time I was published,' he said. It was an unseasonably sunny autumn day. Not warm exactly but the sky was cloudless and no barrier to the sun's rays. He sat on his stool, his eyes closed and his head leaning back against the stone wall of the bothy. Now, I thought. Now would be the right time to wield the axe if I still had it near. I would walk, soundlessly, towards him, lift it high above my head and wait for his eyes to open. Then – and only then – would I bring it down and cleave his curly haired cranium in two. They would fall, the two halves, revealing, like a split coconut, the soft, wet innards of his narcissistic, malign, cruel—

'You must know what that's like.'

A different way, I reminded myself. Read him, study him and then hurt him like he's hurt me.

'Wanting to open people's eyes to something only you understand.'

'Yes,' I agreed. 'It's important.'

He opened his eyes and looked at me. Too much? We'd been nothing but adversaries since he arrived on this island and now I was like a presenter on *This Morning,* all nods and simpering smiles in my attempt to understand him.

'But sometimes things happen. People get in your way. They take things.'

I continued walking. Third time past the dead verbena. He watched as my circuit brought me closer. When I was in front of him, I made myself stop and turn around. 'I'm sorry,' I said. 'For what it's worth and I know you don't believe or trust me, but for what it's worth, I am sorry.'

He said nothing and I continued on my way.


We were running out of food. Lunch and dinner were boiled pasta and, when it ran out, rice. And then just crackers. He disappeared off to the burial ground or the rocks around Cnoc fiacail in search of rabbits but pickings were slim. I took his disclosures of failure as a sign of him thawing towards me and, one afternoon, I went too far with it: suggesting he go to Castlebay for food supplies.

'I'd be gone for hours,' he said.

'I'm not going to run. What would I do? I can't go anywhere if you're using the only boat.'

'You could run down to the beach and flag a passing boat.'

'You could tie me up. Tie my wrists and ankles?'

'You would try and wear them down on something sharp.' He said these things dispassionately, listing reasonable objections. He didn't care that my actions would break his trust or that I might plan to hurt him – it didn't upset him or touch his emotions in any way. My predicted betrayals were merely weights placed carefully in a suspended pan; on one side, at equal distance from the fulcrum, the benefit of a trip to the Co-op in Castlebay, on the other, the very real possibility that I would try and escape. The scales were never going to balance.

Why had I never seen it before? I'd even called him a psychopath. I'd spat it out like an insult – like twat or wanker – but, as mad as it sounds, being held captive allowed me to observe certain traits that led me to believe he really was a psychopath. His narcissism, yes. But also his complete lack of empathy and now, this absence of feeling. It didn't matter that I'd betrayed him. I was nothing more than an object in a sentence, no greater significance than a grammatical construction. All that mattered was that my inclination to run must now be managed.

We began to starve.

I used the cold to plead my case to come back inside. He liked it when I used the word please. Please can I wash myself? Please can I go to the toilet? He stood taller, thrust his chest out further as he considered my appeal.

Benevolent. That's the word. He liked to view himself as benevolent. And honestly, the night I returned to the bothy, my gratitude was real. The space and comfort inside was overwhelming. I was tearfully thankful. My promises to 'not let you down again' were genuine, or they certainly felt it as I sat down in the rocking chair before the fire. I will never cross you again, I thought, if you'll just let me stay here. In this comfort.

I said and thought these things even as I fingered and turned the one object I made sure to bring with me from the lean-to.

# Eleven

THERE IS A DIFFERENCE between deciding not to eat and having nothing to eat. Refusing the yellow mush in those first few days of being held captive was one of the few acts of rebellion available to me. But as the weeks passed and we heard no more engines in the distance; when it was clear the sea was becoming choppy and unmanageable for any vessel; that the coastguard – apparently content with Alex's explanation – was staying away, that was when I began to lose hope.

And time. I was also losing track of time. I tried, whenever possible, to get a look at Alex's watch when the sun went down. By my reckoning we were somewhere around the first or second week of October. The steel grey cold of the Finish Sound packed itself around the island and that, for me, was when the panic set in. We are going to die here, I thought. And the worst of it was that we would die together.

We had water and we had peat. Which, to my mind, meant dying would be slower. Alex, though I never saw him eat anything but the crackers he broke up and parcelled out between us, did not appear to suffer from any physical or mental difficulty. I suspected he had a secret stash of food somewhere. He spent hours at the desk that used to be mine, going through my notebooks, opening the OS map and then attempting to re-fold it – simple tasks like this seemed to frustrate him but nothing frustrated him as much as when he tried to write something himself. Then he would call me up, like a teacher summoning a wayward pupil to their desk, and ask me questions: 'How did you get these names?' he said, pointing to the lone page in my notebook where Catriona and Ruaridh were scrawled in capital letters. But my answers were always frustrating to him: 'I found them there,' I said. 'After I spent the night in the cave.' He'd sigh then and drop his shoulders in disappointment and dismiss me.

I slept a lot in those days. Either in the rocking chair or in a sleeping bag on the stone flags. I was not allowed to go upstairs on my own any more. I dreamt of Daley on Pabbay, saw him wandering back and forth across the white sands of its beach, looking out to sea like a lost Robinson Crusoe. This image, of Daley marooned but alive, came to replace the horrible tumble of his death and it gave me strength. The division between consciousness and unconsciousness, strung like a washing line, was beginning to sag under the weight of all that I'd pegged to it: real memories and imagined outcomes. I was no longer quite sure what was truth and what wasn't. What was dry and what still damp.

Paranoia set in so sharply it pierced my lungs like a painful stitch. It was difficult to breathe, and not just because of my injured ribs. What was he waiting for? I was no help with his book. What was his plan for me?

I dreamt of Chulainn, of the children in the cave, of Tilly. I dreamt of them and felt the tears run down my face. Where were they? Why had the island gone quiet while this – this outrage – occurred? Was it so saturated with blood that a bit more, my own, wouldn't make much difference?

'You said something.'

He was sitting in the desk chair, his neck and spine twisted in my direction. He looked annoyed, frustrated by the interruption.

'Did I?' I pulled myself up so I wasn't so slumped in the rocking chair. Everything hurt. My bum, along with the rest of me, was skin and bone. I had his unzipped sleeping bag over me for warmth.

'Just now, you were crying in your sleep and you said something. What was it?'

'I have no idea.'

'Don't lie to me.'

'Alex, please.' It was the standard refrain: Alex, please. Please, Alex.

'You want me to trust you but you keep things from me.'

'I don't know what's in my head any more. I'm so hungry. And tired.'

He turned away from me, back to the desk. I closed my eyes, was imagining the ecstasy of having a cup of coffee placed in my hands, when I heard something being thrown across the room. I opened my eyes and saw it was the notebook – once mine but now, objectively, his. He had hurled it at the fire in an apparent fit of rage and it landed, spiral spine down on the cast-iron fire front. Half its pages were in the lick of the flames and the other half hanging over the hearth stone.

'What are you doing?' I asked, looking at him. It felt to me, in that moment, that if the book burnt, we were done for. All pretence at waiting for something would be over. But he just sat there and watched the pages burn and, powerless as I was, I did the same. He turned back to the desk and dropped his head into his hands.

A draft, a disturbance whispered past the left side of my body, the side furthest from Alex. I felt it, this eddying of the air; I felt it lift my hair, brush my shoulder and then shadow the fireplace. It covered the chimney breast, darkened the stonework and, like a heavy hand on especially thin hair, it flattened the flames and parted them either side of the burning pages. I watched it as I would watch a spider crawl towards a fly caught in its web.

The burning pages were lifted, deftly by some invisible hand, clean out of the fire, and the notebook was thrown on to the hearthstone.

Alex startled at the sound. He stood up and stared at the smouldering, blackened notebook and then at me. His mouth was slightly open, his arms hung stupidly by his side. 'How did you do that?'

'Do what?'

'Get it out of the fire?'

'You think I did that?'

'I think you did something. Something I didn't see.'

'It wasn't me.'

'You think I'm stupid. You continue to peddle this fiction because – why? Do you think if you hold fast for long enough I'll fall in and lose my mind too?'

'It's not a fiction.'

'So what is it then?'

'It doesn't matter.'

'It's a ghost, is it? A ghost just came into this bothy and pulled that notebook out?' He laughed but it was an empty, dry sound.

'Don't believe me, then.'

'You wafted the sleeping bag. Created a draft.'

'OK, Alex.'

'You're fucking with me,' he said, raising his voice and I became frightened. 'It's not the first time.'

'Perhaps it's a sign,' I said, quietly.

'A sign of what?'

'That this story – *Crioch* – needs to be finished? It needs to be completed.'

I watched him, looking for a nod perhaps or some movement of his eyebrows. But there was nothing. Instead, he sat down heavily in his chair.

'The name you heard me say, in my sleep. Chulainn. She was the island midwife at the time of the massacre. She is the one I saw when the fire happened. She's the one who just—'

He lifted his hand. He didn't need to say stop. In those days of hunger and privation, I did what I was told.

'I think it's time to end this. I need to get away. This book is a non-starter and you've been no help. It's time I started something new.'

'No, please, Alex. I'll be better. I'll help you,' I said, tears bubbling up in my throat. 'We have to finish it.'

'No, I have to finish it.'

'What do you mean?'

'You know what I mean.'

'But why keep me here? Why have you prolonged this – this hideous situation – if all the time you were planning to kill me?'

'Well, for one thing, I had to wait for the search and rescue to be called off.'

'And has it?'

'His body was recovered a mile off the coast of Vatersay. Late last week.'

It was still a shock. Even though I knew he was dead, of course I did, there was a part of me that hoped an injured Daley would reappear – an implausible plot twist in a film with only ten minutes left to go – to rescue me. I closed my eyes and tried not to cry.

He knelt down beside me. 'Plus, I had thought you might be able to help me get a working synopsis together. Obviously I was wrong about that.'

I began weeping properly then. As I cried, I felt him come closer, felt his arm snake along my heaving shoulders. Lifting his armpit like that, so close to me, released a waft of fungal air so revolting it made me gag. I tried to conceal it with a coughing sob but it was difficult, difficult to be that close to him and not vomit.

But it gave me an idea.

'Can we go to the stream?' I asked, turning to look at him. 'I'd like to wash first. I'd like to be clean.'

He smoothed my matted, greasy hair from my face and sighed, like I was asking for the impossible. And then I remembered the magic word. 'Please?'

He packed his rucksack: clothes, soil samples, carabiners, ropes, the map and the charred, burnt notebook. He carried the knife in his hand.

It was late afternoon. The time of day I used to think of as 'after lunch' though of course, there'd been no lunch. But hunger, I thought, is no bad thing in a situation like this. For all its ravages and discomfort, it also lends a sharpness, an acuity of mind borne of adrenaline and the all-consuming need to catch something.

It wasn't so much the thought of dying that frightened me. I knew now that there was *something* beyond death, even if it was a half-life of repeating and replaying the events of your former life – I had seen it with my own eyes. No, it was the thought of dying *with him*. By him. My revulsion was absolute, and if I was going to pass from this life into the next, I wanted him gone, despatched. And hurt. It was important to me that he feel tremendous pain while he still could.

Revulsion. That's what I felt and that's what made it difficult to imagine how this next part would work.

We walked up to the stream in silence. I was in the same clothes I'd been wearing the morning I packed my bags to leave the island. By my rough count, five or six weeks had passed.

He walked beside me, a horrifying companion with his long hair, grim expression and knife in hand. The clouds were stirred up, curled and foamy in their darkness, like someone had drawn a spoon through froth. On our left, the Ceum a'Mhaide headland and the peat platform he'd used to anchor himself for climbing, collecting soil samples and pulling a good man to his death. We had become timeless, ageless, ancient somehow in our dirty clothes and sombre facial expressions, surrounded on all sides by the inexhaustible, unstoppable, oblivious spring to life. The breeze that whipped our hair, the gulls that continued to fly above our heads and the waves, the waves that crashed against the beach to the east and the cliffs to the west. These things did not stop, they did not care for the petty concerns of our short lives: the fungal infections that had bloomed on my body or the acid churning in my empty stomach. Everything: all life, all wind and water continued to fly and gust and flow despite the fact that this man and this woman, walking solemnly in the direction of the stream at the base of Cnoc fiacail, wished violence on one another.

At the stream, he stood and waited while I undressed. I didn't feel shy and I didn't hesitate – the impulse to remove the filthy, fetid clothes from my body was too strong. I didn't care what he saw, what parts of me he glimpsed. The first thing, the only thing was to enter the water and find the font stone.

It was cold. The goose bumps, the tightening of my thighs, the hardening of my nipples. I knew all this as observable fact but I didn't feel it as something uncomfortable or to shrink from. I didn't gasp. I just sat down, in the deepest part of the stream, and opened myself to the sharp, clear-edged flow of water that took with it – like an efficient midwife – all the bacteria, sweat and dirt that had no place there. I must have made a noise. Some sound of pleasure, perhaps.

'You look like you're enjoying that.'

I opened my eyes. Saw the strange half-smile on his face and felt, in the pit of my stomach, disappointment that things were going according to plan. The black-haired boy who bowed to me beside the smoking cave. The booming voice from out to sea. The laughter after my clothes were taken. Performance, I told myself. All of it performance. And here was my cue.

'It's amazing,' I said, arching my back and thrusting my breasts up and out of the water. 'Why don't you come in?'

He hopped on one leg as he pulled a boot off. It made him look desperate, ridiculous. The first one landed on top of my bra; the other, flung a metre or so away. My instinct was to close my eyes but I knew that would be a mistake. I needed to see how and where his clothes fell, what he picked up and what he left on the grassy bank.

'Fuck!' he gasped, stepping down the stony side, his penis growing smaller and more shrivelled with each step into the cold water. He gripped the knife tighter so that it rose up, pointing directly at me.

'Come on in,' I said, running my hands over my hair and smoothing it back behind my ears.

'Sorry,' he said, lifting the knife. 'I can't risk it.'

'At least get your shoulders in,' I said, dipping my head back, wetting my hair up to the hairline. When I returned to face him, I saw the smile had gone. 'What's wrong?'

'What are you doing?'

'I'm washing my hair. I mean, I haven't got any soap but, you know, it's better than nothing.'

'And—?'

'And what?'

'And clearly, you're trying to seduce me.'

'I just wanted to wash. I told you that.'

'This is how you wash, is it? Rubbing yourself like some slutty siren. Is this intended as some pornographic reconstruction of my book? Are you trying to arouse me beyond reason and then, what, you'll—' he looked around him, 'pick up one of these rocks and smash my skull in with it?'

'No,' I said, standing up.

He motioned back to the font stone with the knife. 'Sit down.'

I did as I was told, my bum finding and sinking into the dip of the stone, where the Lixivium had once collected.

'You know what your problem is?' he asked.

'No, tell me.'

'You think you're clever. You think you're better than me, more subtle and strategic. But you're not. You're actually quite stupid. Do you know that?'

He took a step towards me. Instinctively I reached out, put my hand up.

'Go to Castlebay, Alex, I won't run away,' he said in a whining, high-pitched voice. 'Come and bathe with me, Alex.'

I watched him. He was enjoying himself, becoming hard with his insults and coming closer with every word. 'I won't hurt you, Alex,' he continued. 'I actually really want to fuck you. Yes, despite everything I've said and done for months . . . I think – hang on – I think I might be in love with you.'

'Fuck you,' I said, slipping off the font stone so I was on the rocky bed beside it. The water covered more of me now, only my head and shoulders were visible above the surface. It took all of my energy and concentration to breathe despite the shivering that had begun to vibrate through my bones.

'There she is. There's the old Seren we know and love.'

Under the water, I reached for the font stone. 'You're sadistic. And a psychopath. You enjoy hurting people, I can see how much you're enjoying it right now and it's disgusting.'

My fingers crawled towards the dip.

'Perhaps. But at least I'm not stupid,' he laughed. 'I'll take any insult you throw at me over stupidity. I'm sorry but it's the truth. You've put so much effort into seducing me up here when, really, what you've failed to understand is that I don't need your permission. When you came up with your little plan to lure me here, to watch you washing yourself, your breasts on display, when that particular light bulb went on in your dim little head, did you ever stop to think about the fact that I don't need to be enticed? Take a look around you. There's no one else here.'

I took a deep breath and waited. I knew it wouldn't be long now.

'Get up,' he said. 'Go over there and lie down,' he motioned towards the grassy bank on the other side of the stream. I did as I was told. The water fell from me like unfastened armour, inviting the cold wind to have at my skin. I felt myself stumble with the shock of it.

He continued on at me as I climbed up the stony bank, my back to him. 'Let's not forget little Matilda.'

I turned. I was out of the water now, standing – shivering – near the rocks at the base of Cnoc fiacail. 'What did you say?'

'Your daughter?'

'Take her name out of your mouth. You do not speak her name to me.'

He shook his head and smiled, as if this was so typical of me. He took another step up the bank. 'You let her spend the night in the house of a woman you *knew* was being stalked. Your only daughter. If that's not the definition of stupidity, I don't know what is.'

I took a step back, shifted my weight over my right foot.

'You sit before parliamentary committees and talk about changes to the law but, in the end, your daughter died because of your own stupidity. You know it and I know it.'

He was halfway up the bank, his head and shoulders down, his toes clinging to the slippery rocks for purchase. 'She died because of you.'

Now.

I ran at him. I charged. I slammed into his head and knocked him backwards into the deepest part of the stream. I felt him, soft tissue and bone and muscle beneath me, hit the stone bed. His face went under briefly but then it was up and full of surprise and fury; his mouth and eyes and nostrils wide and gushing water. I felt him grab my hair and yank my head back.

With my right hand I reached for the font stone, the same stone that had held the promise of protection to girls and women on this island for centuries, the same dip that collected Lixivium for anyone who needed it, now offered the sharp edge of a fish hook to my frantic fingers.

He still had a firm grip on my hair; I felt the strands come loose from my scalp as I righted my face so it was above his. I reached for his right eyelid, pulled it back and then – just as Daley had told me when he held that writhing flounder ('hold him tight and do what you've got to do') – I stuck the hook hard into the soft jelly of his eyeball.

The noise. It was primitive, bellowing. It was disbelief from the diaphragm. I have never heard anything like it. A kind of guttural submission, a deep call of capitulation. It was from him and yet nothing to do with him. I'd taken much more than his eye. I'd taken his understanding, his bearing and orientation in the world.

He let go of my hair, he let go of everything and turned – as if falling – onto his side, his hands to his face, his fingers a kind of dam to the blood that streamed from his macerated eye socket.

He was crying, saying something I couldn't understand, all the while curled up like a newborn baby, as the waters washed the blood and mucus from him.

I didn't feel anything but curiosity as I stood there, shivering in the cold. Certainly no remorse. I felt, and this feeling has never left me – it stays with me now even as I write these final chapters – that events were playing out exactly as they should. I had sensed how settled our actions had become; how part of a pattern they seemed as we walked up to the stream; the painful things he said to me; the upsurge of rage they provoked at just the right moment . . . and then, then that final fall. We were characters in a story; actors on a stage; talking heads relaying our grievances to an island that had seen and heard it all before.

I picked up the knife where it lay under the water and turned it over in my trembling hands. Taking it with me,

I crossed the water upstream of him. Once on the other side, I dried and dressed myself, put on my boots and, picking up his bag, set off for the Ceum a'Mhaide headland.

I didn't know what exactly I was leaving him to or what he'd do next but I was no longer worried about Alex. I knew, as I climbed down from the headland to the rocky platform below, that there was only one place left for me to go now.

# Twelve

HE'D CALLED IT A giant map of Tasmania. When I
didn't understand, he'd translated: it looks like a huge
vagina. 'If you ever get caught on this side of the island
and need shelter,' he'd said, one boot resting on a rock,
his khaki shorts riding up over his knee, sunglasses strung
around his neck – all the while ignoring Cameron and
Linda who'd grown tired of taking photographs of the
natural arch – 'now you know where it is.' I had nodded,
I think. I certainly agreed with the gynaecological compar-
ison, probably laughed. I never thought, could never have
imagined I would one day crawl along this same ledge,
gripping on with my hands and knees as huge, freezing
waves washed over me, weak with fatigue and intense
hunger, replaying his words, again and again.

In the distance I saw the blue hull of Alex's boat
bobbing under the natural arch. I could have tried to
untie it, allowed myself to drift out into the choppy waters.
I could have searched through his bag for the keys but
the truth was, I was too exhausted. I knew death was
near and I wanted nothing more than to wait for it in
the dark warmth of Chulainn's cave.

I didn't feel any of the fear I'd felt when I'd last been
inside. I didn't worry about something reaching out or
coming near. I longed for company. The company of

ghosts, yes. The company of ghosts who showed me things, made me feel things but did not hurt me.

He had hurt me so much.

The tide was only partially in. I was able to wade across to the sea stack and then climb up the rocky slope to the entrance. On my hands and knees with his rucksack on my back – a human insect seeking shelter – I crawled inside.

Dry, gritty. My hands were still wrinkled from the stream and the dampness of the rocks I'd crawled across but inside the cave floor was generous, giving of its loose, baked surface freely. Most of all, the cave was quiet and warm. All the noise, the rushing wind that whipped the sea into a frenzy of spiteful wet slaps, that was all gone. I'd been removed. Pulled away. Leave her, the cave seemed to say. Leave her to me.

He had hurt me. That thing he said about Tilly. He had given voice to something I could never bring to the surface, never say, never write. Perhaps it was precisely this, this fierce blocking or choking of the truth, always pushing it back and down, that had prevented me from dreaming of her until I came to Finish. Perhaps it was only here, it was only ever going to be this place, where I could open up enough to reflect on the guilt I felt at my own child's death.

Yes, Alex had hurt me. He'd opened a wound that had festered too long. The night of the sleepover, when Tilly had asked me to go home and leave her at Aunty Alana's. Her hands together in a pleading prayer, protesting she was a big girl. I had felt embarrassed by my worry; I hadn't wanted to offend my sister with my niggling concern. I had thought I was being silly.

When I got home that night, Jamie was drinking a can of lager while he reclined in an armchair in front of the football, a pizza menu on the arm. 'I thought you were going to stay?' he said, sitting up.

'She didn't want me to,' I said, as nonchalantly as I could manage. 'She told me she's a big girl.'

'Is that wise?' he'd said.

Was it wise? What I did? Of course it wasn't. Alex, with his uncanny instinct for weakness, had seen the wound, saw that it had never healed, that it had never been attended to. He understood that it was the kind of thing that might overwhelm a person. In his hatred of me, he'd felt no compulsion at pulling the scab off. But in doing so, he'd also allowed for this – this deep, almost pleasurable, letting go.

No, it was not wise. But it was done and there was nothing I could do to undo it.

I was so tired. So unbearably, unbelievably tired. It was nothing to me that as I curled up to go to sleep, I felt a hard, cold thing come down to rest on my head. I didn't know if it was a hand or an arm or some other body part that belonged to one of the many innocent souls that still haunted this cave.

I knew only this. It felt cool and soothing on my sore scalp.

I must have fallen asleep and that sleep – in the pitch black with the complete absence of noise – was deep. It felt as though I was woken at intervals and each time I fluttered to consciousness, a separate part of a film played. It was for me and yet it was nothing to do with me. Like an attendant in a busy cinema who might wander in and out of an auditorium, I rose up through the stages of sleep and saw sections of a longer piece: a young woman with wavy, strawberry-blonde hair that bounced on her back as she ran; a boy, just become a man, of similar age. His skin was pale, his face a battleground of spots and new hair growth. In another clip they sat together, anxious and not speaking, their little fingers intertwined on the bench that had been carved from the cave wall. Later on, I saw the boy who'd bowed to me that night beside the smoking cave. He was black-haired and restless: leaning between his mother's legs, beside the strawberry-blonde woman.

I saw men, women, children and babies. The cave was full of them as they sat and waited. Always waiting.

'Is she here?' I wanted to ask, but I couldn't speak. Every muscle in my body was paralysed by this deep and necessary sleep. There were old women in the cave, they sat with their heads covered, thick woollen skirts billowed round their ankles. I didn't know if Chulainn was among them or what I should be looking for in my search. Whenever I tried to speak, I felt a finger press down on my lips.

But then someone was speaking to me. They were speaking directly to me and it made the film stop playing and cut to black. It was time to get up, go to the toilet, go home. I had slept too long. 'Seren?'

It was him.

I reached around for the knife but before I could find the blade, before I could remember I'd positioned it under my body just before I fell asleep, he placed the sole of his boot down on my searching hand. My cry coincided with a sudden, blistering shower of light. I closed my eyes, recoiled, but still his boot held my hand to the dirt.

He shone his torch along the wall behind me and then up to the stalactites that dripped water sporadically. The movement of the light, the fact that it was no longer angled on my face, allowed my eyes time to adapt, to see how he had tied what looked like a hiking sock around his head, covering his injured eye. I couldn't distinguish colour but I could see the material that passed over the socket glistened darker than the rest of it.

'I came for my bag,' he said, simply. He lifted his boot and I immediately rolled backwards, tumbling the knife beneath me.

He got to it before I did. Picked it up and placed it on the ground behind him. 'I'm not here for that.' He touched the skin below his eye tenderly, pressing along the cheekbone. 'I'm leaving now. I just want my bag.'

I felt confused. His bag? I had picked it up. Why had I done that? I hadn't so much as looked inside it since I got to the cave. I had no interest in its contents.

'You're going to die in here anyway,' he continued, as blithely as if he were giving instructions for locking up. 'I don't need to kill you. Just give it to me.'

What was in the bag? It had felt quite heavy. I struggled to recall. Clothes, ropes, a water bottle and then, then I remembered. The burnt notebook and OS map. Of course, he wanted the bag.

'I don't know where it is,' I said, truthfully. I had no idea. I must have dropped it the minute I crawled inside.

'Don't, Seren.'

'Don't what?'

'Don't make this harder than it needs to be.'

'Or what? You'll stab me with that knife? I don't care, Alex. It's over. The whole thing is over. I don't care what you do to me.'

'Tell me where my bag is.'

'Find it yourself.'

He stepped back, picked up the knife and then shone his torch in every corner, along every wall, ledge, nook and cranny. It was nowhere to be seen. 'What have you done with it?' he asked. His voice was low, rasping and – I realised –desperate.

'I haven't done anything with it.'

'Is it in the water?'

'I don't know,' I whispered.

'If it's in the water,' he said, walking towards me and grabbing me by the scruff of the neck, 'if it's in the water, you're going in after it.' He began pulling me, pulling me hard. I was half-up, half-down, not quite on my feet but not off them either, cycling backwards in the grainy dirt. The neckline of my top cut into my throat as he dragged me towards the opening. And that's when I began to feel afraid. In the cave I was safe. In the cave I was not alone. I began screaming, calling for help. 'There's no one here, Seren,' he said grimly, still hauling me hard. And then, at the opening, he suddenly dropped me.

A cold, sharp moon lit up the stones of the rocky shore that connected the sea stack to the island. It was completely passable, open – welcoming even. And right in the middle, resting on the glistening stones, as though it had just been placed there, was his bag.

He turned to look at me, lying on my side where he'd dropped me. 'You left it there?'

'No,' I attempted to swallow. 'How could I?'

'You wanted it to get washed away,' he said, crouching low to exit the cave. He jumped down from the ledge and stood over the bag. 'You wanted the tide to wash it away, didn't you?'

'I came here hours ago. The tide was in. I couldn't have left it there.'

Alex picked up the bag and walked across the stony shore to the island, where he climbed the rocks to the ledge on the other side. He flicked his long hair from his shoulders as he walked and he looked tall, muscular and, notwithstanding the bleeding sock tied around his head, like a healthy, strong young man. He walked with purpose towards the boat, the rucksack slung over his right shoulder, the keys in his left hand. He looked, to me, like a stranger, a graduate student heading to a lecture. Like someone I'd never met before.

He threw the bag down into the boat and then climbed in himself. I was mesmerised by this image of Alex as a normal person. Someone who had spent time on an island but was now leaving. As simply and easily as that. I was watching him so intently, my eyes on him so entirely that I didn't, at first, notice the shadow that must have crossed the cave entrance. I didn't hear the sound of footsteps on the wet slippery stones.

But then I did. Then I saw her.

A dark, hooded figure wearing heavy skirts and shawls followed in Alex's footsteps with similar ease and purpose. But faster, much faster. She glided along the ledge soundlessly as the engine kicked on. The mechanical sound shook the moonlit darkness, it rocked the boat so that Alex was jolted too and, as he righted himself, he become aware of a cloaked figure that stood, waiting on the rocky ledge. Late, too late, he saw Chulainn step onto the gunwale of his boat, saw her arms spread wide and – like a sparrow hawk above a field mouse – cover him in her shade.

She swooped and fell on him. Both figures disappeared from view but the boat, the boat that had been bobbing gently, now rocked and tossed in the water. I heard Alex scream, cry out, and then a snap, a dry, baked sound followed by another and then another.

I couldn't listen. For all that I hated him and wanted him to suffer, I couldn't listen to the sound of those screams or the snapping that preceded each one. It was methodical and determined. It was, I knew, unstoppable.

I shuffled backwards into the cave, into silence, into a darkness where I knew I was not alone.

I woke with the morning sun. I must have fallen asleep near the entrance because the light sliced the cave from the east, carving an easy oblong into the dry dirt. I saw now, through the lens of strong daylight, that what I'd taken to be dirt, mud and stones was in fact a blend of gneiss rock. The particles were grey and pink and they sparkled a little in the sun.

Samples. He had wanted soil samples. This would have been a good place to come. I lifted grains of the mixture and let them fall between my fingers.

It came back to me. The shadow figure in her skirts falling on him. Somehow disappearing him. His cries and screams from the bottom of the boat. The rocking motion that accompanied it all.

I crawled out of the cave, shielding my eyes from the intensity of the morning sun. It was too bright. Too horribly bright.

The first thing I saw, as my eyes adjusted, was Alex's boat. It was still there, moving gently from side to side. From where I stood, in the shallow waters that filled the gap between sea stack and island, it looked like no one was on board.

The water, in league with the garish sunlight, was too much for my bare feet, too much like wading through vinegar. I did not want to go and look in the boat. I wanted only to stay in the cave, the long slit of the entrance a welcome barrier between me and the fierce liquid light of the outside world.

But my hunger was huge. It was a heavy, hard thing I carried in my stomach and I knew there was more to be done.

So I made my way. Slowly, reluctantly, to the boat. It was a journey I had watched two people – two figures – make the night before with speed and ease but it took me a long time. Saliva collected in my mouth with every physical exertion. I walked the last few steps to the edge of the rocky platform and peered down.

How now to write what I saw? Alex was lying in the bottom of the boat, his uncovered eye wide and unseeing. His body. If I close my eyes I see it still. I will always see it.

His right arm had been snapped at the elbow and then again at the wrist; a hideous zigzagging of the limb.

Searching for symmetry, I looked to his left and saw the same injuries repeated. Further down, his knees – no longer complex joints but now simply corners.

Why would anyone do this to me? his single eye seemed to ask.

Beneath him lay the notebook, open to the very last thing I'd written before we'd argued about whether Chulainn was in the cave with the other islanders. And beneath that, just poking out, a little blue corner of the folded OS map.

His rucksack was open and on its side, the contents spilling out near his right foot. A bar of chocolate, a packet of biscuits, more crackers, a bag of rice, pasta, some tins of tuna. He had not been starving. He had been eating, nourishing himself in secret, and he planned to accelerate my death by taking what little food remained with him.

Even with this, this final example of his unremitting cruelty and calculation, I still couldn't exalt in it or feel vindicated by the sight of his broken body on the bottom of the boat. I felt, just as I did as we walked up to the stream, that what was happening, what had happened to us, was somehow destined. We were two figures retracing a path, following a rutted track formed on this land many hundreds of years ago. The things we'd done, the stops we'd made, all that we'd witnessed – however horrifying – there was no turning back from any of it. The circuit had to be completed. It is almost complete, I thought, returning all the items to the rucksack.

I sat on the rocky platform, my feet hanging down to catch the incoming wash. I ate some of the biscuits and the chocolate, drank from his water bottle and tried to remember our first meeting in the library. How I found the way he pushed his glasses up his nose with his middle finger amusing. Could it be that he had been drawn into this strange play, this bizarre re-enactment, as surely as I had been?

But then I thought of Daley. Daley who had taught me to fish and told me where to hide. Daley, who had given me Beau.

No. Alex was darkness. He came here to take. Like the raiders from Kisimul, he breached the shores for one thing and while he was here, saw what else he could have. He didn't care what he had to hurt or damage in order to get it.

Daley was the light. You only know one by the other.

What more is there to say? I sat there for a long time, taking small bites and small sips, and when I felt strong enough, I got up and untied Alex's boat. Using all my remaining energy, I pushed it out from under the natural arch. The high tide and north-westerly slope current did the rest, pulling it away, away from the shores of Finish, where people had lived for tens of thousands of years. Where the men fished in the summer and the women salted for the winter; where they spun their wool, kneaded their dough, stacked their peat and lived. Where they did their best to survive in this difficult, often inhospitable, but completely unique place.

And when it came time to deliver a baby, there was one person they trusted above all others. One person who would rather die than let the people she served, down. If it came through her knee it couldn't be helped but it would not come through her mouth.

CRÌOCH: IV

Muirnìn MacKinnon, too lame to climb down to the cave, decided to remain in her cottage. She had been blessed by four moons at Crois an fionnadh. She had the deep blue eyes of the ancient MacKinnon clan. Nobody, she announced, would dare hurt her.

She was right. The sixteen men come from Kisimul who landed in the bay, the men charged with avenging the murder of the chief's firstborn son, who marched up to the village, kicking in the doors and setting fire to every cottage they found, questioned her, threatened her, but they would not kill her. They set fire to her house, dug up her crops but still she wouldn't say a word as to the islanders' whereabouts, taunting them with the same answer: 'If it comes through my knee, it can't be helped but it shall not come through my mouth!'

After three days of searching the island, the men gave up. They walked back to their boat, Muirnìn MacKinnon heaping curses upon their backs.

She kept her silence. She would have died before giving up the innocent souls hiding in the cave.

They set sail from Finish bay in a south-easterly direction, going around the horn of the Ceum a'Mhaide sea steps before heading north, back to Barra. The route afforded one last breathtaking view of the western cliffs of the island. Seven of the sixteen men stood at the stern as the boat made its way past these dramatic escarpments.

Inside the cave, the islanders sat together in families. The walls had been hollowed out to create ledges for people to sit on and this is what they mostly did as they waited for the signal from Muirnīn MacKinnon to say the coast was clear. They waited for days, fearful and desperate. This was not something they had invited or provoked. The raiders had come, slaughtered an animal, raped two daughters of this land. What did they expect? To get away with it?

Catriona and Mairi sat with their families – no longer girls and not quite women either. Catriona had suffered the most at the hands of the raiders and it showed in her eyes. The light had gone. She kept them down at all times, avoiding contact with others. Ruaridh, who sat with his own family – not so far from the MacKinnons – tried not to look at her. Not because his mother had explained she was not to be thought of any more but because he knew it pained her to be stared at. It troubled him, what had happened. How, through no fault of her own or his, their dreams of being husband and wife – games enacted between them often enough among the sandy dunes of the beach – were now just that. Dreams.

In the dark of the cave, as the third day drew to a close, everybody was weary. They were tired of being nervous – the most dangerous time in any crisis. The time when impulses go unchecked, accidents happen and carefully constructed plans fall apart. In the absence of any daylight, people slept at strange hours, stretching out whenever someone got up, laying heads on shoulders, laps, wherever comfort and softness could be found. Babies cried in their mothers' arms; children pushed and kicked at one another before being pulled away and chided so close flecks of spittle flew in their faces. It was dark in that cave; the air fetid, the time unending. Everybody was lost in their own personal hell. And so, nobody noticed Angus MacKinnon get up from his seat beside his sister and move across the floor of the cave, towards the entrance, where thin, spent light penetrated the gaps in the gorse.

With his small fingers he pushed the strands aside, creating a hole big enough to peer through. Except the hole was not big enough. All he could see was the gneiss rock of the cliff-face in front of him and a little of the sea, lapping gently against the rocky platform.

With his foot he widened the hole, dislodging a chunk of gorse and inviting a shaft of light – blinding, unwelcome – into the cave. It made the others squint, put their hands to their eyes, stand up to investigate but Angus was quick. He was nimble. He knew he had to be. If he didn't step through the hole he'd just made, he'd be forced to return to the seat beside the strange woman who looked like his sister but didn't act like her any more.

Angus slipped through and found himself out in the open. The wind was blowing in a south-westerly direction, patting his left cheek like a benevolent uncle, pleased to see him but not quite sure of his name. He crossed the water, climbed the rocky ledge and side-stepped carefully until he was just under the natural arch. From here, with one hand on the wall of the arch, he peered out to sea, craning his neck – as best he could – in a northerly direction.

Of the seven men tasked with watching for anyone, only one remained at the stern. They had almost cleared the island and were pushing out into open water when he saw a head: small with black hair and a very pale face peering out.

The man saw Angus and Angus saw the man. Their eyes locked across the water; a connection so strong and immediate that neither knew, at first, what to do with it. But then the man remembered himself. His job was to look out for any signs of life. It didn't matter that the life he saw was that of an eight-year-old boy, tired of hiding in a cave. He would, many hours later, sit in the feasting hall of Kisimul Castle, his head in his hands, and go over the seconds that elapsed between seeing the boy and saying that word. If he closed his eyes he could still, just about, inhabit that narrow band of time – as narrow as the distance between sea stack and island – and pretend things hadn't turned out the way they had. In that little strip of time where the seconds were still untainted, he could turn away, walk towards the bow of the boat and join his fellow clansmen looking north for Barra.

'Thall!'

It startled Angus, made him lose his balance, almost sent him headlong into the waters below. In a few short hours he'd be wishing it had. But Angus held on; panicked, he made his way back to the cave, to questioning faces in the gloom.

'What have you done?' they asked. 'What was that noise?'

They huddled together as the cracks of light were blocked then cleared. Dark and then light. Left then right, as the bodies of men – many men – crossed and then re-crossed the mouth of the cave. They seemed to say, with their efficient heaping on: you want darkness? Well, here's darkness.

Of course, the adults in the cave knew. Those who had been blessed by the moon at Crois an fionnadh knew that it would give no protection now as the silent, grim, hardworking men beyond the gorse set about suffocating them. They knew their last moments had come. Most held their children close, others kissed in the darkness, some raised their voices in song – the mournful lament a difficulty to some of the men working outside.

But one young man found his way to the girl he had loved since time began. As sure as the mountains rose from the sea and the sand softened their childhood games, she was his. He sat down in the space her little brother had left and, knowing she would not want to be stared at, hooked her little finger with his.

There was some hesitation over who was to light it. The most senior of the sixteen, a nephew of the chief and cousin to the murdered boy should, by rights, have been the one to set it off but he demurred. It was an act of evil to kill so many people. So many women and children. 'Let us wait,' he said, desperately. 'If, when the sun sets, the wind is blowing away from the cave, then we should spare them.'

The men, tired and sore for home, affected by the singing and sound of babies within, sat down on the rocky ledge, their feet in the water and agreed to await the setting of the sun.

But the sun, sickened by the match it had been asked to judge, turned from the earth in disgust and fearful

ELISA LODATO

haste to be gone. The wind blew up in its stead, took over proceedings and sent its breeze towards the land.

It was fated, they all agreed. A sign from God that these people deserved to die. That it was, indeed, a just punishment. The nephew of the chief lit the dry branches at the base of the pile and quickly – aided by the eager wind – the fire took hold.

When it was over, when the screaming and choking and clinging to life had finally stopped, the men – tired from their days on Finish – boarded the boat and resumed their journey north. This time nobody stood at the stern. Nobody looked for any remaining islanders. Nobody saw Muirnīn Chulainn on the headland, her white hair around her shoulders calling to her sons and daughters and grandchildren and every soul she had ever delivered – slick and warm – with her own bare hands. She called and called.

She wanted them to know one thing. She has only ever wanted them to know one thing.

I did not give you up.

# Thirteen

THEY CAME, LIKE CHILD actors awaiting their cue. They walked across the rocky inlets either side of the beach. Ten, maybe twelve of them. She was instantly recognisable to me. Even among so many and after all this time, I saw her, I knew her face, her movements. I recognised her. At her feet, staying close to her now-slender ankles, was a small black dog. She must have felt the weight of my stare because she stopped and stood still even as all the other children continued playing and splashing around her. She stood still and, though I couldn't see the expression on her face from this distance, she seemed to tell me – by her stillness – that she would wait for me. I can do that now, Mum. I can wait on my own.

The great difficulty of today has not been writing such a long account of my time here. Aside from fatigue and a deep ache in my right hand, it has come – for the most part – easily. Some of the events have been painful to revisit, for obvious reasons, but the words themselves, curled up inside me, have come easily, patiently awaiting their turn on the page. No, the biggest difficulty of today has been believing – as the sun set and day turned to night – that Tilly was still there, waiting for me.

The first thing I noticed about the bothy when I got back early this morning was the trail of blood from the stone flags near the door all the way up the stairs to the bedroom. They stopped just beside the bed where, I assume, he must have found the sock he used for a bandage. The three-legged stool was on its side and beneath it the yellow mush turned orange and solid, still splayed around its upended bowl like a child's drawing of a sunrise. The place felt empty, stripped bare by the battle that had been fought between me and Alex.

Downstairs there was enough peat and kindling to light a fire. As I knelt down on the hearth and began sweeping the ash away, I noticed what looked like a small biscuit tin lodged just inside the chimney breast. In it were two hypodermic syringes – both used – and a bottle of some clear liquid, perhaps the sedative he'd used to keep me under after Daley's death. Also, a packet of something called Lorazepam.

I used some of the water in the containers to wash my face and body at the doorstep. It was a cloudy day: the thin wisps I'd seen at sunrise were now thick, like chunky cotton wool wadding that had been rolled out across the sky. But there was no rain. Thank god there was no rain. I don't think I could have done what I did today without a clear view of the children on the beach.

The fire caught nicely in the grate. It spread out its dry, gathering fingers, drawing the peat into its warmth and revealing – as it did – an opening, a fissure through which it was possible to breathe in soil, minerals, strata and substrata, the organic decomposition of birds, animals and people who had lived and died on this land.

As a child I had wanted only to lift up the island and peer beneath it. I had wanted to know its secrets.

I sat down at the desk, before the window. I unfolded the OS map, opened the notebook, still charred from its brief spell in the fire, and began writing this. My ghost story.

This book is for Chulainn but it is also for me. It is her assertion but it is also mine. 'Get on top of internal pain as you respond to the forces without,' Tess said. Neither of us could have foreseen how exactly and precisely I would end up fulfilling her brief.

As I wrote my first few sentences, as I laboured over how to begin this book, I heard the creak of Chulainn lowering herself into the rocking chair behind me. In contrast to last night, her movements in the bothy are slow, quiet and patient. She has had to be so very patient, after all. What's one more day to a woman who has waited five hundred years?

I feel her near me as a presence. I don't want to use the word ghost. To me, she is not a ghost. She is not someone to be feared. I feel about her the way I imagine many a labouring woman on this island felt when she came to the door. Relief. With her quiet, patient presence in the room, I feel I can do what I need to. And I know that through her, because of her, I will have my child returned to me.

It's time to go and tell Tilly we can stay. Together, we can drink the sea.

# Author's Note

Those familiar with the Western Isles of Scotland will recognise Finish Island as a thin fictional veil for the real island of Mingulay, the second largest of the five islands south of Barra in the region now better known as the Outer Hebrides. Though I have used real names when referring to nearby places such as Castlebay, Vatersay and Pabbay, I decided to rename Mingulay for reasons I hope will become clear.

The stone bothy (once the island schoolhouse), burial ground, abandoned village and sea stacks of Mingulay are all real and it was a truly magical experience visiting this exceptional place in the summer of 2023 with my family. My knowledge of the island has been greatly enhanced by Ben Buxton's book, *Mingulay: An Island and its People* (Birlinn Ltd, 2016), which served as a comprehensive, compelling and indispensable account of life on Mingulay through the ages.

But why not just call it Mingulay? Because, in my wider reading, I stumbled across the details of a massacre in a cave (Uamh Fhraing) that occurred – not on Mingulay – but on the island of Eigg, ten miles off the west coast of Scotland in the second half of the sixteenth century. Discovering this horrific event not only altered the course of my story but necessitated a completely fictional setting. For those unfamiliar with this particularly brutal period of Scottish history, I would recommend Camille Dressler's book, *Eigg: The Story of an Island* (Polygon, 1998). I should also point out that the violence depicted in the final chapters of Seren's manuscript for *Ghost Story* was perpetrated not by clan MacNeil of Kisimul but clan MacLeod of Dunvegan.

The MacKinnon coat of arms Seren studies in the bathroom of the Bayview Guesthouse has also been adapted to suit my fictional purpose. There is indeed a boar with a shin bone in its mouth in the first quarter but the baby held in a palm in the third quarter is entirely made up – a genealogical nod to Muirnīn MacKinnon's devotion to the art of midwifery.

There is evidence to suggest a sacred stone circle existed on Mingulay, known as Crois t-Suidheachain ('cross of the seat'), though you would be hard-pressed to find it now. Again, it suited my purpose to bring these stones back into existence, to arrange them in a circle around a font stone that serves as a receptacle for the precious Lixivium and name the whole site Crois an fionnadh.

I owe a debt of gratitude to Margaret Fay Shaw's book, *Folksongs and Folklore of South Uist* (Oxford University Press, 1977) for her vivid and immersive images of island life in the first half of the twentieth century.

The events and places in this novel, both real and imagined, are a curious blend of my historical research, my own wider fictional interests and several glorious hours spent on Mingulay itself. Finish Island is simply the label I have chosen to stick on this particular blend.

# Acknowledgements

First and huge thanks must go to my editor, Arzu Tahsin, for her vision, ideas and perceptive edits.

Alice Lutyens, my agent, for her belief in me and my writing.

Justine Taylor for taking up the torch so brilliantly and to everyone at Bonnier Books UK for believing in and championing this story.

Mary Lodato, Fionnuala Forbes and Teresa Cummins, the Celtic voices in my ear all these years.

Alan Dawson, for sharing his beautiful house in Scotland.

Charlotte Morton and Nick Farnhill, for lending me the *Spes Secunda.*

Angus and Margaret Ann MacNeil and Ranald and Neil MacLean of Hebridean Sea Tours for doing everything they could to get us down to Mingulay.

Jonathan Grant of National Trust Scotland for answering all manner of questions about the bothy on Mingulay.

Ros Sproule, for her unrivalled knowledge of all things wool and for giving of her time so generously.

The Lodatos: my dad Giuseppe, my brother Paul and my sister Emma, my nieces Rhiannon and Genevieve, my nephews Ellis and Luca, my brother-in-law James Orchard and my sister-in-law Lisa Johnson.

The Cowells: my mother and father-in-law, Jennifer and Bill Cowell, my nieces Ella, Lila and Anna, my nephew Charlie, my sisters-in-law, Lucy and Rosie, and my brothers-in-law, Simon Jones and Dave Huber.

My friends, who have listened, supported and counselled over the years: Laura and Alan Ashton, Helen and Jeremy Aves, Janice Azeb, Anna Banicevic, Nisha Bailey, Dahlia Basar, Merrigan Bee, Nicola Cavanagh, Richard and Jules Ellis, Polly Evernden, David and Louise Groves, Francesca Jakobi, Alex Knights, Chloë Mayer, Emma Mercer, Louise Patke, Rachel Pinnock, Sarah Reed, Linda Rothera, Gwen and Mike Sewart, Phil Symes, Alice Thomson, Marisa Vaughan, Jillian and Huw Widgery, Lorraine Wilson-Copp, Blanche Wynn-Jones and Lucy Yarham.

Charlie Haynes of the Urban Writers' Retreat, for looking after me (and so many other writers) so well.

Anne-Marie Randall, for her superb photography.

Maxwell, our lost friend.

Finally, my love and thanks to Jim, Maddie and Tom. I could not do what I do without you.